daisy's adventures in love

Daisy's Adventures - Book 2

nikki sitch

books by nikki sitch

Love, Lust & WTF?!!

Daisy's Dating Adventures Book 1

Daisy's Adventures in Love

Daisy's Adventures Book 2

Daisy's Adventures in Love

"An engrossing rom-com perfect for long summer days..." – The Prairies Book Review

BookView Review rated it ★★★★★

Nikki Sitch

Nikki Sitch

Calgary, AB

https://nikkisitch.ca

nikki@nikkisitch.ca

ISBNS:

Hardcover - 978-1-7780871-5-8

Paperback -978-1-7780871-7-2

eBook - 978-1-7780871-6-5

Audiobook - 978-1-7780871-8-9

Distributed by IngramSpark

Audiobook distributed by Findaway Voices

Printed in Canada by Blitzprint

Cover Illustration by Chad Thompson, chadthompsonillustration.com

Edited by Lauren Diemer with Palisades Writing & Editing. lrdiemer@icloud.com

Interior formatting by Other Worlds Ink

Created with Vellum

praise for daisy's adventures in love

Sitch returns with another witty chick-lit, taking readers on Daisy's journey to true love and happiness. Daisy's Adventures in Love picks up where Love, Lust & WTF left off: David is gone for good, but Brad is back, and Daisy knows he is the one. As the two families come closer, the new complications arise, threatening the couple's dream of getting together. The relationship between Daisy and Brad sizzles (their delicious sexual chemistry is a bonus) while also reflecting the cautionary nature of mature love. Their journey from online dates to lovers and friends is a delight to watch. Both Brad and Daisy's inner dialogue makes for fun monologues that highlight their understandable but frustrating inability to move things along at a quicker pace. Sitch's skills with characterization shine through. Her keen eye for detail as she creates realistic, relatable characters keeps the reader engaged. Through Sara and Brad's story, she beautifully captures the complexities of messy separation and divorce. The secondary characters, particularly Kari's well-wrought emotional struggles complement the main storyline. Sitch hits all the right notes with this smart, witty chick-lit.

— BookView Review

Has all the fun of *Love, Lust & WTF*, but adds a deeper, timely, message about family, diversity, and acceptance.

Daisy seems to have found her man in this new adventure, and with him at her side, she appears to be closing on a new state of domestic bliss, but life is complicated, no two people are the same, and Daisy finds she has a few more lessons to learn. Readers should expect to be constantly thrown for a loop—back to the rollercoaster on the cover of Sitch's first book—as characters come from every angle in an unpredictable succession of challenges and revelations. Daisy's friends from the first book are back, and they are still dating, which supplies the story with new tales of the treacherous, strange, and—very rarely—sublime world of online dating. Lessons and lechers abound in this story, but there is also something more. In this second novel, Sitch chooses her moments to get serious about love and family. Just as her character Daisy must try to embrace a new and larger family, Sitch plumbs what the notion of family really is. And this idea becomes terrifically important as the new, larger, family endures unexpected threats and changes. This deeply personal and arresting story element is skillfully livened by comedic elements from her dating friends, making the whole stronger than either part would have been on its own.

Daisy's Adventures in Love is fun, but it shines a serious light on not just dating and love, but the meaning and value of family."

— Lee Hunt, author of *Last Worst Hopes* and *Bed of Rose and Thorns.*

Witty prose, richly imagined characters, and fast-moving narrative mark Sitch's latest offering, a celebration of family, friendship, and unexpected love. Daisy is finally content; Brad is all she wants in his man: he is caring, sensitive, mature, and shares Daisy's love for the active lifestyle. As their bond becomes stronger, they begin to venture out as a family unit. But with the kids in their teen years, problems seem to be sprouting out of nowhere. The couple must deal with kids' individual problems with utmost precaution or risk losing their trust. The stakes rise when David, Daisy's ex from her online dating world, shows up unexpectedly. Sitch's prose is crisp, her smoothly paced narrative enjoyable, and the storyline intriguing. The story follows Daisy and Brad through dinner dates, passionate sexual encounters, and cozy family gatherings as they march steadily toward building a solid family unit. As they come closer, family conflicts also slowly rise to the surface, such as Kari's struggle with her sexual identity and adolescent drama, Sara's difficult nature. Sitch's expert characterization allows readers to immediately connect with Daisy and Brad's predicaments, and as they grow closer, she aptly shows their often-winding path to oneness and genuine happiness. Laughter is abundant, thanks to Daisy's quirky nature and her constant inner monologue. Sitch also tackles complex, relevant subjects of LGBTQ issues, single parenting, identity, singlehood, acceptance, and understanding while exploring true love, friendship, lust, and passion. Readers who like lighthearted rom-coms will be satisfied by this engrossing novel.

— The Prairies Book Review

notes from the author and acknowledgements

Thank you, fellow readers, for joining Daisy on her continued adventures. Strong and true to herself, she explores new challenges as her kids grow and change.

Writing has become a passion for me over the past few years and I'm happy you've joined me on my literary exploration. Thank you! My hope for the content in my books is to educate and bring certain issues to light that are important. It's quite possible that there could be some discomfort, curiosity, bewilderment, wonder and/or expansion experienced by each book enthusiast. But it will be personal to each of you, which I love. I look forward to hearing your comments and feedback.

To my family and friends, thank you for your support and encouragement through my creative writing experience. What a strange and wonderful ride it's been. Who knew I'd love writing as much as I do, a new passion. You've been nothing short of amazing. Sheri, Liss, Beck & Kirstie, thank you... I never would've picked up my pen without your not-so-gentle nudge to share my thoughts and ideas. Special mention to my kids, you both inspire me on a daily basis. I love you more than words could ever explain.

Thank you to my beta readers Erin Skillen, Gordon Otto and Lee Hunt who were the first to flip through the pages of *Daisy's Adventures in Love*. Your eyes devoured the pages even before I'd settled on the title, ha! Your feedback was outstanding and pushed me to up my game and move to the next level in my writing. Your comments helped me align and reorganize the flow and content, thank you.

To my editor, Lauren Diemer, thank you for your attention to detail and suggestions to make my book better. I nodded often as I reviewed your many edits. Much appreciated.

contents

1
trip to the mountains

WHEN MY DAUGHTERS busted Brad and I mid-thrust — who knows who was on top, I'm not sure, it was a whirlwind of passion, wind ripped from our sails and records were poorly kept — I realized I should've taken him up on his invitation for a romantic weekend away at his cabin the mountains. Damn it, I thought they were at soccer practice, and Brad and I thought we'd be the ones scoring a goal, or goals if we were so lucky, ha! But as we sprang apart, mutually mortified, the shot went wide of the net. And so, Brad and I booked time together at his cabin.

Nestled among the trees, with the exquisite towering Rocky Mountains for a backdrop, sat the most stunningly beautiful rustic cabin, Brad's cabin. A stream meandered languidly through the trees, providing a calming bubble to the perfect scene. A romantic weekend getaway.

Several weeks ago, when we were out for supper, out of the blue, Brad mentioned, "I have a cabin in the woods near Canmore. Would you like to join me for a weekend of skiing and fun? Would you be able to arrange for your parents to take your girls?"

I didn't know you had a cabin.

"Yes, that sounds great! I'll make it happen." And I did. I've been excited ever since!

Life is hectic, what with each of us having two kids and successful careers, finding time to get together is always a challenge, but one that we both embraced. An added challenge is that my girls are with me full time, while Brad's kids are at their mom's every second weekend. My husband, Adam, died in a car accident five years ago and we'd been on our own ever since. Thank goodness my family is close by and are available to help whenever required.

Round two of us dating was going swimmingly. Round one had been quite another story. It had felt magical and then it ended in a crash and a clunk, confusion, disappointment, and a river of tears. He hadn't been ready for a long-term relationship as his divorce had been devastating for him. Thank the stars he worked through his "stuff" and then reached out to me when he was ready. The timing of round two worked for both of us. I had still been stumbling through the disaster of crazy men on the dating circuit when he texted me out of the blue. Our renewed connection and fireworks were through the roof.

We spent the day skiing at Lake Louise. I hadn't been downhill skiing for several years, but it came right back to me, just like riding a bike. I love feeling the wind whipping through my hair as I fly down the slopes. "Woah girl, slow down, I can hardly keep up to you!" Brad joked. He was an excellent skier, very graceful compared to my self-taught fastest-way-down-the-hill technique.

I grinned, "Ha-ha, sure, right!"

We stopped for lunch on the hill: burgers and beer. It felt great to relax, stretch, and chat. Sitting with our knees touching under the table had freed the butterflies in my tummy. *Where did they all come from?* When he placed his hand on mine that familiar warmth spread through my body, right to the tips of my toes and fingers, everywhere. I stared at Brad as he was talking.

Damn it, I'm falling deeper in love.

Falling? Girl, you've fallen.

Yes, I want this man. Forever.

I'd been unsuccessfully trying to protect my heart since we started dating again, but I felt pretty sure that was useless at this point, I had fallen. Hard. I smiled as Brad continued telling me about a project at work.

Yes, I love this man.

The sweet, somewhat simpering voice on my shoulder, Bridget, whispered to me, "He better not get cold feet again. My heart still aches at the thought of it." Princess Pussy, my the louder, hungrier, more carnal, and impulsive voice, shook her head, "He's past that, worry wart. The sex is great. Everything will be fine. He wouldn't have come back if he wasn't."

But was he? Shit! Bridget has a point. What if he pulls away again? I'm not sure my poor heart can handle that again. I inwardly shook my head. *He's changed. He's put in the work. He's ready to be my man. But is he, really? How does anyone know for sure?* I didn't like the answer. *Simple . . . we don't. We love who we love and only we know the reason why. I know my love is true, and deep. And damn it, that's all I can control.*

I snapped out of my trance. *What did he just say? Something about systems and . . . crap, I don't know.*

The afternoon was filled with more swish swishing down the slopes. For our last run, as we were riding up the chairlift, Brad suggested, "How do you feel about moguls? My favourite run is just to the left of here. Shall we try?" *Eek!* I shrugged and nodded, "Sure, why not?"

No problem, I got this.

As we reached the top, my confidence wavered.

Shit, that's why not.

There I stood, at the top of the bloody run, looking down.

How in the fuck am I supposed to get down this?

There were moguls. And not just any moguls, the biggest, most gigantic, steepest moguls I'd ever seen. And for added fun, challenge and benefit, there were numerous large and lovely trees interspersed. *Fuck!*

No room for error here or I'd become one with the bloody trees.

Fuck! Here goes nothing!

I pushed off, and in relative slow motion, I tackled the first mogul, careful to keep my eyes on the prize. Around it I went.

Yeah, success! One down, twenty-some to go. I could hear and feel my heart beating in my ears and my breathing was much too loud for the energy I was exerting. *I'm sweating like there's no tomorrow. Scared and excited as hell!*

I successfully maneuvered number two and then stopped to catch my breath. I looked back toward Brad, smiled, and waved. He nodded and started down the hill. Swish, swish, swish, he flew down the moguls like they were nothing. He stopped halfway and looked expectantly toward me. I could almost hear him say, "Ok, Daisy, your turn, let's go girl! You've got this."

Shit, here I go again.

I made my way down the run methodically. It wasn't elegant, but I did it. And I didn't die. A story to tell my girls.

On our way back from the slopes, Brad surprised me with supper at the Grizzly House, my favorite restaurant in Banff, with a multiple course fondue meal to die for. We enjoyed our evening sipping wine and dining on incredible cheese and bread fondue, veggies, and broth, chicken, beef, shrimp and even alligator cooked on the garlic butter hot rock. We rehashed our skiing adventure while we sipped and nibbled.

As we were sitting enjoying the fullness of our bellies, Brad moved our discussion toward the energy industry.

"Daisy, everybody keeps talking about it, but what exactly is energy transition?" Brad asked. "Is it just a woke buzzword or is it real? Pipedream fantasy," as he moved his hand onto my thigh, "or urgent — necessary — reality?"

Enjoying his touch — instantly wet is more like it — I sighed and explained, "It's all that. Woke buzzword, yeah."

Brad stroked higher and deeper along my thigh. *Mmm, yeah.*

"Fantasy, yeah."

His fingers turned gentle circles on my hot skin.

OMG, yes.

"Real? Yeah."

Keep talking Daisy, so he keeps doing ... what he's doing up under my skirt. Oh, Brad, don't stop!

"Energy transition," I continued, enjoying every second, "is the shift from fossil-based systems of energy production and consumption, including coal, oil, and natural gas, to renewable energy sources like wind, solar, hydro, and batteries."

"Oh, so eventually we'll just be able to survive on solar, wind, and hydro?"

It was taking a lot of effort to focus on the discussion. His fingers were distracting the hell out of me.

"Uh, no, not really. At this point, there isn't anything that can meet all the needs that petroleum and natural gas fill. It's a transition and for the foreseeable future, we need renewables and non-renewables to work together. Kind of a best-of-both-worlds. Cleaner energy."

"Oh, I see," Brad commented, his fingers continuing to work their magic. "A long time?"

The longer the better. It's sooooo nice. Focus Daisy, focus!

"If we ignore the consumer products made from petroleum and just talk power for a sec, the sun doesn't shine, and the wind doesn't blow all the time. If those were our only sources of power then we'd be in blackouts constantly, just think about windless nights. Natural gas is a much more environmentally friendly alternative to coal. It fills the renewable void nicely."

OMG, am I boring him to death? Are his eyes glazing over? Yikes! Almost done. Ha!

"Renewables and non-renewables combined create an opportunity for entrepreneurial innovation. It really is an exciting time for energy."

So exciting.

His fingers turned new circles, and I moaned almost noiselessly.

We're in a restaurant for crying out loud.

"But we can't stop now. We have to keep…keep going."

Brad was nodding enthusiastically as he continued with his discrete movements, listening, staring intently at me as I continued talking.

"It isn't a moral thing," I breathed. "One technique, ahh, source of energy is not 'good' or 'bad', just with different … mmmm … consequences."

"Oh," Brad said, "So it's good we're trying new things and learning what works best?"

"Yes!" I, damn near shouted. "Yes! New things are good."

It IS good.

Brad relented and after a quick trip to the men's room to wash his, uh, face, returning in time for the final course: melted chocolate and fruit fondue. He leaned toward me, "I don't know how I'm going to fit any of that inside my belly, but I'm going to give it my all. It looks and smells scrumptious!" I was way ahead of him. Everything he'd done had worked up my appetite again, after all. My mouth was already filled with chocolate and a strawberry so all I could do was nod and grin.

As Brad swirled his banana — tsk, tsk the one on the end of his fork you with the dirty mind — around in the chocolate, coating it thoroughly, he asked, "What about taking all the power created during the day from solar farms and storing it?"

"Eventually that might be a possibility but currently it isn't on a large scale. Batteries can only store so much."

Brad nodded, "Oh, I didn't realize that. Interesting." We continued to enjoy the luscious dessert. My tummy was rapidly losing any free space it once had.

After Brad settled our bill, I purred, "Thank you sweetie; that was delicious. But …" I paused and laughed, "Now you're going to have to roll me out of my chair, piggyback me out of the restaurant, and down the street back to your truck. I'm so stuffed. Maybe we can borrow a shopping cart?" I giggled, "O-M-G, that chocolate fondue is to die for!"

Grinning, Brad replied, "I know what you mean, Daisy! I'm full to the brim. Let's wander up the main street and give our tummies a chance to settle before rolling back to the truck."

Brad took my hand in his as we walked down the street, staring at the majestic mountains as we reminisced about our day on the slopes. Brad had never experienced a day like ours before. His ex-wife had no interest in going skiing or hiking or doing much activity outside. I'd been lucky with Adam; we'd enjoyed these types of activities together. I felt extremely fortunate that Brad and I shared this as well. It was a must for me. I had zero interest in being with someone who didn't enjoy being active with me. I was beaming thinking about Brad, and us, as our trek took us toward the river.

As we rounded the curve in the river, Brad pulled me off to the side of the path, took my face in his hands and kissed me hard. He smiled, looked deeply into my eyes, and said, "I love you, Daisy Flanigan. You're amazing. Thank you for being patient with me and for loving me. I'm so happy we found each other." Then, he let go of my cheeks and took me in his arms. A muffled, "I love you too, Brad," travelled up from his vest, where my head was buried. I was grinning from ear to ear and so was he.

When we felt our tummies had settled enough, we walked back to the truck, hopped in, and drove straight to the cabin.

2
love in a cabin

WHEN THE TRUCK rumbled to a stop, Brad removed his hand from my knee, where it had resided for the drive. He hopped out, opened my door, took my hand, and led me out of the truck. He wrapped his arms around me, and put his hands on my waist, oh now my back, my ass, his hands were roaming. He kissed me deeply, passionately.

My thighs are on fire. Hell, my whole body is on fire.

I felt that kiss deep within my loins. When we finally came up for air, I let out an extremely satisfied and heavenly sigh as Brad enveloped me in his arms again.

Heaven, this IS heaven!

Moving out of the cold and into the cabin, Brad let go of me long enough to get the fire going. I glanced around. The cabin was Brad. His secret den, his man-cave. But I didn't feel like an intruder. His warmth emanated from the rustic furniture to the log walls, an imperfectly perfect representation. I instantly felt comfortable and welcome within its walls, just like how he makes me feel in his arms.

Ooh, he keeps looking at me with yearning and desire, I love it.

Once the fire was roaring—the other one, the one in the fireplace—Brad turned in my direction, his eyes hungrily devouring me as he strode toward me. I could feel his desire as he tilted my head back and we merged into one as we kissed. He kissed my neck and then slowly removed every article of my clothing, one item at a time, some with his hands and some with his teeth, slowly. Kissing every square inch, surveying my skin and soul with his lips. I was glowing. My body was vibrating. My desire for him was throbbing through my body, everywhere. My erogenous zones were begging for his touch.

Once I was naked, Brad led me to the bed and asked me to lie down on my back. He spread my legs, kissed from my right heel all the way up my legs to my inner thigh and then gently flicked his tongue on my clit before he started to lick and suck. *OMFG!* I moaned, "Oh Brad, that … um … feels … so … good … holy … fuck … I'm …" I didn't even finish the words and cum was gushing into my pussy. As I finished, Brad's tongue hungrily entered my pussy to lap up my cum. Between licks he said, "Mmmm, you taste great." My eyes were rolling into the back of my head in ecstasy, and I wanted more.

Brad ripped off his clothes and flung them to the side. I could only stare, my mouth gaping, at his chiseled body, taught from the hours spent in the pool, on the bike and running. Oooh, triathletes.

I was snapped to attention when Brad commanded, "Get on your hands and knees." *Oooh yes, command me, Brad.* Quickly, I flipped over and got into position. He spread my legs even wider, so I was completely exposed. Vulnerable. I felt a wave of heat as I let go and submitted to his touch. I ached for him. Leaning into me, he spread my lips, and started licking my pussy again. If it was heaven before, this was a whole second level of heaven. Incredible and dirty and sexy and well, fucking AMAZING!

I am so turned on. Am I panting? Yup, I sure am! Oh Brad, I want you inside me.

Next, he tapped my butt gently with his hand, then a mini smack. I jumped. *Ooh, I kinda like that.* Brad grabbed my hips firmly, pulled me to the edge of the bed and he thrust deep inside me. Again. And again. I was cumming instantly. *This is so hot! I love this. We've never even had an inkling of rough play before today. I don't want it to end.*

Brad thrust hard deep inside me several times, grabbing my hips, and pulling me toward him each time, then he took a quick rest after I cummed on him. I was getting dehydrated from cumming so much. *OMG, holy crap this is awesome!* Eventually we both ran out of steam, and he finished strongly inside me, draining every ounce. We collapsed into a deep slumber.

Sunlight streamed in through the windows as the sun rose, signaling the start of a new day. I smiled and snuggled deeper under the covers and into Brad's arms. *It's official, I love this man. He checks—uh licks—every single box for me.* I was daydreaming. I was beaming. I thought of him and our future. I couldn't wait to meet his kids. We'd been dating for four months now, and we were on solid ground. Everything was clicking with the two of us and the next logical step was to meet each other's children. That time was near. Thoughts of the present and future made it damn near impossible for me to put one foot in front of the other some days. *I am so deliciously distracted by this man.*

Brad slowly opened his eyes and pulled me even closer, kissing my forehead and then my nose and my lips. We kissed and enjoyed the feel of each other, and we both felt the pull and desire for more. He kissed me on the forehead and said, "Be right back, gorgeous." As he walked towards the bathroom, I smiled, "Don't be long, handsome."

Soon, but not nearly soon enough, he was back, sliding under the covers and gently rolling me to my back. He had one arm on either side of me and was on his elbows staring down at me. We were lost in each other's eyes for the moment. Alternating between smiling and looking deeply into one another.

He nuzzled and kissed my neck, nibbled on my right ear lobe, then kissed me again as he slid inside me. I took him in and held him there, mine, fit to me. If his dick was his soul and my pussy my own, as I held him there our souls intertwined. Laugh if you want but if you've ever had your soulmate inside you, you'll know exactly how it feels.

We gently rocked together experiencing the depth of intimacy. "Babe, you feel so good inside me. Can we stay like this forever?"

Brad laughed and whispered, "Yes, I intend to, beautiful." After we rocked for a while, we heightened the intensity. He slid in and out faster and was getting deeper inside me. I started to moan and then I was exploding. There was a deep, visceral itch that we both needed to scratch, a connection that went deeper than any level we'd ever reached before. It was touch-the-stars animalistic heaven, a hole-in-one. Something extremely special. A rare experience. We climaxed together and fell into an exhausted and elated heap. We both fell asleep instantaneously.

Brad awoke before me and got the fire roaring while I was still sawing logs. He made a fulsome breakfast for us to enjoy. A delicious bacon scent wafting through the cabin, along with the glorious smells of eggs cooking, coffee and toast, stirred me from my sleep. My stomach rumbled, telling me to jump out of bed and devour the amazing feast. I rolled out of bed, tiptoed across the creaky floorboards, snuck up behind Brad and put my arms around him.

He whispered, "Good morning, sweetie. You looked so peaceful sleeping that I didn't want to wake you. Feeling rested now?"

I snuggled in closer as I yawned, "Oh yes, very much so. Would you still like to go cross-country skiing today?"

Brad turned around, grinned, took me in his arms, kissed me passionately, and said, "Yes, after we have breakfast and make love again." A shiver ran up my spine. *Oh my, yes please.* I kissed him back just as intently, agreeing with his suggestion, with my lips, wholeheartedly.

We enjoyed our breakfast, me wearing his shirt and he in a pair of boxers. I loved that I could inhale his scent from his shirt while eating. It was the most sensual breakfast I'd ever experienced. *Is that even a thing? A sensual breakfast? Sure, why not?!*

Throughout breakfast we maintained physical contact with one another. His hand on my knee, my hand on his, a quick kiss, our knees touching. Our desire for each other drove us to finish breakfast quickly so we could get back to exploring each other again. We made love deeply and passionately, taking time to explore every crack and crevice of one another, connecting on many levels as we made love.

After thoroughly enjoying each other, we bundled up, slipped our skis on and cross-country skied right from Brad's cabin, along the stream. It was a gorgeous day for skiing. After working up a sweat, we returned to the cabin, jumped in the shower and lathered each other up, washing all our body parts. We kissed several times in the shower before the ticking clock reminded us that we needed to get on the road.

As we drove back to Calgary, I looked at Brad and smiled, "Thank you! That was a fantastic weekend. I loved every moment."

Brad took his right hand off the steering wheel, grabbed my hand, kissed it, and said, "It was perfect." The weekend had been out of this world, now, back to reality.

3
measuring boundaries

ON THURSDAY, after work, my girlfriends and I hit our favourite pub to catch up. They knew how much I'd been looking forward to my romantic getaway with Brad so that discussion was first on the agenda. "So, how'd it go, Daisy? What was his cabin like?" Jen asked.

"It was AMAZING!" I gushed over the details of the trip, my horrifying but successful mogul experience, the food, the love making and how we connected. I finished my story as our server brought round two, and we ordered the usual messy and delicious deep-fried, oh so saucy food.

Saucy like my girlfriends. Ha!

I'm such a lucky gal to have such wonderful friends. Friends I can tell everything and anything to without fear of being judged. Well, sometimes there is a little judgment, but we keep negative judgment to a minimum. It felt so great to be free with them. More women need friends like I have!

We are a diverse group, that's for sure. My closest friend is Anne, a fashionista and amazing human. We've helped each other through a boatload of stuff and have both come out relatively unscathed. Jen is our somewhat cautious and easily embarrassed friend. She's certainly come out of her shell a lot more recently. Our wild and sexually in your face gal is Ronnie. Princess Pussy loves her! Bridget remains red-faced and embarrassed almost the entire time that Ronnie speaks. Amy and Ronnie have had a few dust ups as they are polar opposites, although Amy has opened up quite a bit more after starting to do research for her Masters in Gender Studies. I think Ronnie has become a valuable source of information. Twila is always happy to join in for some gal fun.

I asked, "Jen, what's been going on in your world? I feel like we haven't chatted in forever!"

"Well, ladies, I have a new boyfriend," Jen said, blushing. "His name is Chris and we met through a mutual friend. OMG, he is super cute and sweet, we get along amazingly well, we have ton in common, and we have some great flirtatious exchanges." Her shoulders drooped, "Unfortunately, the sex is uh . . . I'm not quite sure how to put it. Hmm … lacking."

"Oh no, how so?" Anne asked.

"It's weird. He's very tentative in bed. Awkward really. Almost like he's scared of something. I think it might be a confidence problem. The best I can guess is that he appears to be very self-conscious about . . . uh . . . the size of his penis, which makes zero sense to me. He's . . . uh . . ." she picked up an average sized banana, studied it carefully and then motioned toward it, "about this size." Her cheeks were flaring fire truck red as she continued, "I just don't get it."

Anne nodded knowingly, "If the banana is an accurate representation, he seems average in size, if not slightly larger, for both girth and length."

"It's crazy how hung up some guys get about the size of their penis. It's just weird," Twila said.

"No kidding," Ronnie blurted out.

"Damn insecure, some of them," Anne weighed in.

Twila shook her head, "So many brag about how large their cock is and then they can't back it up. Either you never see it as they ghost you before you meet, or it's all rather disappointing when they pull out their mini member when you were expecting the big kahuna."

"No shit! Do they think we won't notice the bazooka they promised is a miniature toy gun? Pew, pew!" Ronnie was rolling her eyes as she smirked.

We were laughing our asses off. "So true! Like bringing a knife to a gun party," laughed Anne. Jen tried, unsuccessfully, to muffle a snort.

Twila continued, "Or, on the other side, they're embarrassed about the size of their cock, even when it's average size. I mean, you get what you get but be proud of what you've got man and don't oversell it. Just be real. It's really very strange."

"Have any of you ever measured a cock?" Ronnie asked mischievously.

Jen looked horrified as the rest of us shook our heads, "You mean with a measuring tape? You just measure it?"

Ronnie nodded, "Yup, I've done it with a couple guys, it's kinda fun. Just something a little different."

Interesting. I can't see me pulling out my measuring tape any time soon with Brad. Princess arched an eyebrow, "Why not? Harmless fun." Hmm... good point.

Amy said, "Honestly, I don't enjoy having sex with men whose penises are huge. My vagina's just not big enough to accommodate a large penis. It hurts. It isn't pleasurable for me AT ALL. Average size, so five-ish inches, is about where I'm happy, smaller is fine too. But anything more than six inches makes me cringe and back away. I just can't do it."

"Pass those guys over here," Princess Pussy salivated on my shoulder, "I know just what to do with those guys." Bridget scolded from her perch on my other shoulder, "Princess, shush! Jen's talking." Princess just rolled her eyes, "Whatevs."

Twila nodded, "Honestly, I could give two shits about size. I just want them to have some talent, meaning they know how to tease and play and have some fun between the sheets. If they're talented enough to get me off, I'm happy. Whether that's with their penis, fingers, tongue, or a combo," she added, "I really could care less as long as they can make me cum."

Anne shrugged, "I must admit, I do favor a larger penis. Although, I'm not overly picky so long as they're big enough that they aren't flopping out constantly during sex. Talk about frustrating! That's a major bummer and instantly kills the mood for me. I want to be able to get on top and ride without flop, flop, flop, constant readjustment to slide them back in, or make them harder." Anne giggled, "But most importantly, they need to be able to hit all my sensuous lady bits."

I guess I've been lucky. The guys I've been with have hit where they needed to, well, for the most part, ha-ha! Good to know.

Out of the corner of my eye, I saw Twila starting to laugh, "Ha-ha, I have to share this with you gals. I have the worst luck with guys who are six-three and taller. I'm talking about big, hulking guys, football and rugby players, big manly men. You know the theory that huge hands and feet, means the guy has a big cock? That is utter bullshit. A big, fat, unfair myth. Hand and foot size DOES NOT predict cock size. And this is not a one-or-two-time occurrence for me."

It doesn't? Hmm . . . that's interesting.

"Over the years, I've been with at least half a dozen huge dudes. I seriously felt like I was in the movie "Groundhog Day". Each time, we were getting hot and heavy, kissing, biting, clawing, clothes were flying and down came the boxers. *Fuck! That's it?* And I'm not being dramatic here, we are talking small, maybe three inches fully erect. That's all these big hulking men had. Too small for my vijay-jay. The poor thing got lost in there. I couldn't ride and all they could do was a few pumps and then cum. Talk about disappointing. It became laughable after the third or fourth. Each time, I would pray that the pattern had been broken, but nope. Now I don't date anyone over six-one"

We all laughed, and Twila finished her thought, "I felt so bad for those guys, not like they could do much about it. But jeez! It was seriously bizarre."

"Holy crow, that blows. Wow, have we ever gotten sidetracked. Ok Jen, back to your concern, what are you going to do to resolve it?" Amy asked.

I jumped in, "Before we dive into the solution, I need a bit more info. How long have you been sleeping together?"

"Well, I guess it's been a few weeks now, so we've slept together maybe five or six times. Initially, I thought it might be nerves and getting used to each other, but he honestly doesn't seem nervous or anything like that. I'm at a bit of a loss."

Anne suggested, "The only way to figure this out is to chat with him about it. Tell him the things you enjoy, what he does that turns you on and encourage him along, be supportive. When he's inside you, tell him how good his cock feels. Make sure you're verbal, especially when you're orgasming. Make sure he knows. That'll give him a boost. Probably even turn him on."

Jen blushed, "Um, sure, I can try that. It's not anything I'd normally do but I think I can push my comfort limits if it's going to help our sex life."

"Yes, sweetie, you can do it," nodded Amy.

"Before I met you ladies, I spoke with exactly no one about sex and women things. You've all pushed me to be freer to talk about sex. With you anyway. I know you won't judge me. And that's important."

"Yes, there are lots of judgy people out there, that's for sure," Twila said.

"I've learned so much from you ladies and I've been able to be freer with my partner because of it."

"A very important part of finding a great partner is also finding someone you can have fun with, and connect deeply with, both in and out of the bedroom," Anne commented. "Just look at me. Kyle is awesome. We connected in the bedroom at the beginning of our relationship and then we just didn't. We get along incredibly well, except in the bedroom. There was no ongoing hot steamy bedroom connection, and we weren't on the same plane as far as play in the bedroom was concerned. It was a deal-breaker for me as that connection could only go so far. It was a bedroom fail. I tried really hard to get us back on the same page, but it just wasn't going to happen." Anne grinned, "What with him being into men and all! Square peg, round hole."

I'm so glad she can joke about it now.

Amy nodded, "I need that deep connection with my man. If I don't have it with him in the bedroom, then I best throw in the towel right then and there. Yes, it can grow and change but you need to cut your losses when you figure out there's zero chance of it ever happening."

We all nodded, agreeing that this connection was important to each of us but varied greatly in what it meant to us and how it was derived.

"I agree 100%. For me, the intensity, and passion is super important. But I love smiling and laughing with Brad in the middle of our love making as well. Being free to just enjoy each other. To me it's not all serious. It's fun."

4
meeting my girls

THE SENSUOUS CABIN and skiing bonding adventure in Canmore had cemented my relationship with Brad. We were solid. There was no doubt in either of our minds that we were meant to be together. As the weeks progressed, we became closer and closer, working as a team rather than just dating. We started to support each other behind the scenes relating to our kids and any concerns we had about life in general. As we hit the fifth month of our relationship, we decided it was time to "meet the kids". We needed to bring our kids into the equation so we could continue to build our life together.

This was the week. We felt it would be best to introduce my kids to him Saturday morning. Well shit, the first proper, non-mortifying meeting, that is. At least Brad and I would have our clothes on this time, and we weren't doing the horizontal mambo. *Eek!*

Later that afternoon, I'd meet his kids and we'd enjoy pizza together. If the wheels were still on the bus, we'd bring all four kids together to go bowling that same evening. My 14-year-old girls, Jessica and Angela, loved babysitting so I felt pretty confident they would dote on Kris, Brad's eight-year-old son. It was Kari, Brad's daughter, we were concerned my girls wouldn't gel with. Kari is a year younger than the twins and sometimes, teenaged girls don't play well with others, if you know what I mean.

I was nervous. I hadn't introduced anyone I'd dated to my girls. How would they react? No time like the present. I asked them to join me in the living room. Once they were seated, I cleared my throat and dove in, "As you know, Brad and I have been dating for several months. It's going very well."

Angela interrupted me, "Yes, mom, we know."

"Oh, uh, well, we're at the point where the next step in our relationship is to introduce our families to one another. We were thinking that Brad would join us on Saturday morning for breakfast. How do you both feel about that?"

Jessica started giggling, and said, "Jeez mom, finally!"

Angela was nodding, "We've been dying to meet him. You seriously light up like a Christmas tree when he calls or texts, we know you're into him big time."

I keep forgetting how mature, intuitive, and knowledgeable the girls have become over the past couple of years.

A tear streamed down my cheek as I spoke softly to them, "I had to be sure before introducing you to him."

There sure have been a lot of duds between your dad and Brad. OMG. I can't even.

My girls hopped on the couch with me and smothered me in hugs. Jess said, "Mom, we want you to be happy. You deserve it. And clearly Brad makes you very happy."

Ang ventured, "If you're worried about us because of Dad, DON'T. Dad's been gone for years. He'll always be in our hearts and minds, but time has moved on. I echo what Jess said, you deserve a great guy."

It couldn't have gone better with my girls. Incredible. My heart and soul were overjoyed.

Adam would be supportive of my decision. I just know it.

Brad had a similar discussion with his kids. Kari had been less outwardly enthralled with the idea compared to my girls, but Kris was very excited to meet me. "You can't win 'em all," I commented, "we'll get there with Kari." And I had no doubt that we would.

Saturday arrived and the girls were excited to start preparing the masterpiece menu we'd created for brunch. We'd gone all out with pancakes, crepes, granola, yogurt and fruit, bacon, eggs, and toast. I'm not sure what army we thought we were hosting, and I certainly hoped this wasn't signaling an impending battle.

Yikes! Ha-ha!

Punctual as always, the doorbell sounded at ten o'clock on the nose. My heart leapt.

Yay! Brad's here!

My hands were full, making the pancakes, as the doorbell resonated through the house. Jessica called out, "I got it!" Her sister wasn't far behind, racing to meet my beau.

They're excited. A great sign.

I heard muffled pleasantries as the girls welcomed Brad inside.

Peeking around the corner, I stirred the blueberries into the next batch of batter. The girls were giddy, and Angela had just hugged Brad.

So far so good, phew.

I smiled and said, "Good morning! Why don't you all join me in the kitchen? Many hands make light work, or something like that."

As he took off his shoes, I heard Brad call, "Be right in! Daisy, whatever you're cooking smells marvelous!" I'd just finished pouring the pancakes onto the griddle when I felt Brad's arms slide underneath mine, and close around me. He nuzzled me and kissed my cheek, "Good morning, hun, fabulous to see you, as always."

I placed the batter bowl on the counter and spun around to give him a big hug and kiss, "Good morning yourself, handsome," I smiled and winked. When I peeked over Brad's shoulder, I saw my girls beaming, watching us.

That's also a good sign.

They all rolled up their sleeves and pitched in: turning bacon, flipping pancakes, setting the table, and taking our delicious meal to the table.

"Hey Jess," I called out, "would you mind juicing the oranges, sweetie?"

Jess had just finished setting the table. "Sure thing, mom." She sauntered back into the kitchen and set our juicer in motion. The whirr of the juicer made it difficult to talk, which was just fine as we were all busily working away on our tasks. As soon as the juicer died down, we moved out to the dining room, sat down to dive into our fancy brunch.

Brad smiled at us all, "Thank you for having me over for brunch this morning. I feel honored that you ladies created this fabulous meal for us to enjoy."

He addressed my girls directly, "Jessica and Angela, I was nervous and excited to meet you both today. I played it over and over in my head, but your welcoming words and hugs surpassed anything I could've ever imagined, thank you.

Smiling, Jessica nodded as Angela said, "Brad, we've been looking forward to meeting you for what seems like forever. We gave mom a hard time about waiting so long."

Brad laughed, "It has been a long time coming. I need you to know that I love your mom very much and I'm looking forward to getting to know both of you as we become larger parts of each other's lives. Your mom has told me so much about you but it's great to meet you in person."

Ang nodded, "It's great to meet you too."

Jessica added, "I don't want to sound creepy weird, but we haven't seen mom this happy since before our dad died. Her laugh came back."

Ange nodded her head, "And we think that's cuz of you."

Brad snuck a smile in my direction as a single tear came slid down my cheek. I knew they were right. Brad pushed back his chair, came over to kiss my forehead and leaned over me for a hug. I melted and a huge smile spread across my face as I looked up at Brad.

I am home.

Stuffing ourselves silly, we munched on the incredible array of food in front of us as Brad regaled us with tales of adventures hiking in the mountains. I'd told him my girls both love to hike. He then suggested we do a hiking trip in Canmore, using his cabin as our basecamp.

"We'll bring air mattresses and sleeping bags cause my cabin is basically one big room. It'll be like tenting, without the tent. Would you gals enjoy that?"

Both my daughters nodded enthusiastically, and Angela said, "Absolutely, when can we go? I haven't been hiking since last year."

I was grinning like a crazy hyena. *This is going so much better than I even dared to imagine.*

5
meeting brad's kids

SHIFTING MY MUSTANG INTO FIRST, I parked in front of Brad's place, I shut off my car and heard the unmistakable sound of a ball hitting a glove. As I slid from the seat and headed toward the gate, I heard another, and another ball-glove interaction, resonating from the backyard. Inhaling the sweet scent of lilacs, that grew alongside Brad's fence, I strode around back where my handsome boyfriend and his sweet little boy, Kris, were playing catch.

"Hi, sweetie. Hang on to the ball a sec, bud." Brad stretched his chiseled arm to reach the spare baseball glove from the deck and tossed it to me. "Kris, this is the special lady I've been telling you about. Daisy, meet Kris, Kris this is Daisy."

Kris blushed as he glanced in my direction, whispering a muffled, "Hi," he quickly looked down at his shoes. Tentatively glancing up to better address me he said, "Nice to meet you, Daisy. My dad has talked about you A LOT." I giggled to myself, seeing Brad's reddened cheeks. I noticed that Kris had his dad's strong stature, even at eight years old, his brown hair, and striking blue eyes. It was like looking at Brad as a child.

"Great to meet you, Kris. Wow, do you ever look like your dad!" Kris stared at me intently for a moment, blinked, and said, "Yeah, lots of people say that."

"Buddy, it's your turn, throw me the ball." A long lob from Kris to Brad, which he then threw to me, and, in turn, I threw it back to Kris. We had a three-way game of pass in motion. I could feel Kris relaxing as we passed the ball. After about ten complete triangles, Kris changed the direction and lobbed it back to me. I felt something shift in him. He was noticeably more relaxed and much looser.

We talked about school and Kris told me that his favorite subjects are gym and math. I let him know that those were my favorites in school as well. Kris explained that he'd hit a triple and double at his last ball game. Holding the ball tightly, Kris tentatively looked up at me from under his ball cap, "Daisy, would you come watch my next game with Dad?"

I smiled, and nodded, "Of course, Kris, I'd really enjoy that." Kris beamed, his smile stretching from ear to ear. We continued tossing the ball for another half hour, Kris chattering on about school and sports.

We ventured inside so I could meet Kari, Brad's thirteen-year-old daughter. Brad had talked to me about Kari's struggle with her parents' divorce, but she seemed to have turned a corner recently in her counselling sessions. He squeezed my hand as we wandered down to Kari's room in the basement. Brad knocked three times. No answer.

I looked around as we waited for her response. In the family room, there was a heap of grass-stained clothes, a clean heap, a few pop cans, and partially empty chip bags scattered around the room.

Yup, a teenager lives here.

Why am I so nervous? More than nervous, I'm not sure what to expect.

A grumpy, "Ya?!" came from deep in her room.

"Kari, Daisy is here meet you. Remember, I mentioned she was coming this afternoon? Please come say hello."

I heard paper rustling, objects being moved, and then a loud, "Nah, I'm good Dad." Thud. If that weren't clear enough, deafening music came blaring over the speakers. She may as well have said, "Fuck off, leave me alone. I don't want to meet your stupid girlfriend, Dad. Beat it!" The unspoken message was loud and clear. My shoulders fell. Disappointment hit me hard. Brad put his arm around me, squeezing my shoulder.

Obviously still clinging to the fantasy that her mom and dad would get back together, she clearly wanted nothing to do with me. To her, I was the wedge keeping her parents apart. Brad turned toward me, "I'm so sorry, Daisy, I thought she'd come around and was ready to meet you."

I stepped forward and leaned into Brad. He raised his sparkling blue eyes to meet mine, "We knew this might be her reaction. I'm not concerned, just a bit disappointed. I'm sure she'll let me in when she's ready. No sense forcing her, it'll just set her against me more strongly. Let's leave her be and go for a wander with Kris."

Brad reached out and pulled me close in a giant bear hug. He laid a wet, juicy kiss on my lips and sighed, "Yes, let's go."

He knocked on Kari's door again and received the crankier than cranky response only a teenager gives, "What?" Brad took a deep breath, "Daisy, Kris, and I are going for a walk in Fish Creek. You're welcome to join us."

Silence.

How long does one wait for a grumpy teenager to respond? "Ok, sweetie, we're going. See you soon. I love you." More silence apart from the increased volume of music as we walked away.

As Kris amused us with his theatrics scooting back and forth while we walked along the river path, I exhaled, "I forgot how gorgeous it is in Fish Creek Park. The river is so calming. The nature is so, uh, mystical and peaceful. We're so lucky in Calgary to have so many gorgeous parks and so much space to enjoy."

I must make time to do this more often . . . or perhaps we? Hmm . . .

I looked down at Brad's fingers intertwined with mine. My heart glowed and seemed to want to jump right out of my body with excitement.

I hope I never lose this feeling. The pins and needles, the fulfilment when we're together like this.

The sun was glowing, the trees danced with their array of greens and the river seemed to be singing to us as we explored. It was a lovely afternoon filled with the sounds of nature and bonding with my man and his son.

I am happy. My heart is full.

When we got back to Brad's, Kari was in the kitchen sipping an iced tea. I smiled warmly at her as we walked in. Kris ran up to her, gave her in a giant hug, and breathlessly said, "Did you meet Daisy, Kari, did you? She's the most awesomest. She plays catch, she asked all about my school and my friends and baseball. She likes going for walks and she's coming to my next ball game. Isn't that great?"

Kari looked down at her little brother and gave him a squeeze, "Not yet buddy. But no time like the present." Kari confidently strode across the room in three steps, stuck her hand out formally, and said, "Hi Daisy, sorry about earlier, my hormones are wigging out. I'm on my rag. Pleased to meet you." She even managed a small, possibly even genuine, smile. Then she curtseyed awkwardly. Yes, she actually curtseyed. Ha! With a flicker of a mischievous grin on her face while doing it.

This girl has a sense of humor! Thank the stars!

Shockingly, I was able to keep a straight face not sure how I did, but I did. Reaching out, I shook her hand heartily, "It's great to meet you, Kari." She looked at me stoically.

While still holding her hand, I curtseyed back. No longer able to hold back my laughter, I let it fly. Kari started to laugh. I used the opportunity to build on the moment, "Your dad's told me so much about you. He says you're an incredible water polo player."

Kari blushed, "I love it."

Ice broken, we continued to talk about her passion for playing water polo.

She's starting to warm to me. This feels great.

Laughing and chatting away, Kari and I started making the pizza crust, spreading pizza sauce, and laying out our toppings. Next, we called in Brad and Kris to pick and add their toppings, and then the cheese.

"There's no such thing as too much cheese, keeping piling it on there, Kris," I laughed. There was a mountain of cheese exploding everywhere.

"Ok buddy, I think that's enough," Brad laughed. Kris crinkled his forehead as he turned to look at his dad, squinching his eyes and lips while cocking his head, "Ok, Dad! If you say so."

While the pizzas cooked, I texted my girls and let them know I'd pick them up for bowling after their volleyball practice. They both texted back, rapid fire:

How'd it go?

What are they like?

I can't wait to meet them!

Me too!

Are we five or ten-pin bowling.

My phone screen was lit by the group text!

I laughed heartily as I read and responded to their barrage of questions,

It went well, not surprisingly, they're great kids. Brad, Kris, and I tossed a ball around for a bit and then wandered in Fish Creek. Kari came out of her shell after a bit of time. We talked lots about her water polo. You'll meet them in a couple hours. Pick you up at seven.

Oh, and ten pin. Now get going to volleyball or you'll be late. See you soon girls. I love you both very much! xoxo.

I was still smiling as I turned back to Brad, Kari, and Kris. Kari looked inquisitively at me. "I just let my girls know that we'd pick them up at seven to go bowling. They're both very excited to meet you." My smile broadened as I focused on Kari and Kris. Kris jumped up and down, exclaiming, "Bowling, bowling, bowling, yay! Bowling and I get to meet your daughters? I love meeting new people. Your daughters sound great, woohoo!" Kari hesitantly nodded in what appeared to be somewhat reluctant agreement.

Well, at least she's coming bowling and appears open to it.

6
bowling for six

BALLS THUNDERED down the alley as we entered the bowling alley and wandered over to get our fancy? . . . erm . . . cheesy '70s bowling shoes. Angela squinted sideways in my direction, "Uh, mom, isn't it kinda gross to use shoes that tons of other people have used?"

Smiling, I nodded, "Normally, yes, yes it would be. However, they use some kind of a very strong alcohol spray solution to disinfect the shoes. See, they're spraying that pair that was just returned."

Angela squinted, "Hmm, ok." She grabbed the shoes that the shoe attendant handed to her and nodded, "Thank you!"

We bowled to our hearts content on side-by-side lanes, three versus three. I couldn't remember laughing so much for a long, long time. My twins took Kari under their wings and insisted they challenge the parents and Kris to a showdown.

"You are so on!" *Prepare for a smack down girls!*

The first game was very close, but the parents and Kris won by a couple points. It was down to the wire, but we stole it in the last frame. The girls blew us away in the second game, like we were standing still.

Shit! I hate losing.

They found their groove and there was lots of fun, competitive chatter back and forth. We're all sports nuts, so this came naturally to us, the joking and teasing.

As we continued to bowl, I suddenly felt a gnawing feeling in my tummy and then it spoke loudly, "Grrrrrrrr!" . . . hunger. The pizza we ate hours ago was but a distant memory. We ordered nachos, pop for the kids, and Brad & I both had a beer.

As we nibbled away on the nachos, I couldn't believe how great it felt to be out bowling with Brad and our kids. I imagined the future and saw very clearly how we could be a successful and cohesive family of six.

Hmm, now that IS something to ponder. Don't get ahead of yourself, Daisy!

But we were heading in that direction. The future seemed so certain and comfortable that I didn't even think much about it. It just felt right. From the look of it, our kids seemed to be bonding big time.

The all-girl team, appropriately named "Girlz Rule", had snuck ahead of us again in the fifth frame. "Come on, mom, pick up your game," Jessica teased, as I went up to grab my ball.

Yes dear, on it!

Boom! A strike. I laughed. I'm only slightly competitive. I nodded over to my girls, a smile plastered across my face, "How'd that work for you?"

The girls were equally competitive, and it was Angela's turn. Her throw looked great, the ball was rolling straight for the head pin, and then it slightly deviated just before it hit the pins. All but one fell. Another shot and she knocked out the final pin for a spare. Team "Parents and Kris" pulled ahead by two points. Back and forth we went. We were down to the final frame with two points separating us. In the end, the girls smoked us. We just ran out of steam. A great game and a fun time were had by all and there were high-fives all around.

The three girls had hatched a plan during bowling and out it came as we were finishing our drinks. Jessica and Angela exchanged a couple looks, that I couldn't quite read, and then I saw a little nudge by Jess. Angela spoke hesitantly, "So, uh, mom, we were talking about having Kari over to watch a couple old classic movies she hasn't seen—*The Princess Bride* and *Sixteen Candles.*"

Old classic movies? WTF? Those are '80s movies! My jam! Am I getting old? Damn, I guess being the girls were born in the twenty-first century . . . Ugh!

Ang continued, despite my confused look, "We thought it would be fun to do tonight, get some popcorn, and chill. She could sleep over. What do you think?"

Glancing at Brad, I was pleased to see that beautiful smile spread across his face. He gave me an almost imperceptible nod and squeezed my hand. I looked at the three girls, "That sounds like a great idea, as long as Brad is good with it as well."

Kari looked at her dad with imploring eyes, laughing, Brad reached out and squeezed her shoulder, "Yes, that's fine by me."

Brad, Kari, and Kris made a quick pit stop at their place so Kari could pack her bag. Brad told me a bit later that Kari had flapped around their house like a crazy person throwing seemingly random items into her bag, running upstairs and downstairs, and then finally she announced she was ready. Once we were all gathered at my place, the girls immediately took over the basement with pillows and sleeping bags. The smell of freshly popped popcorn wafted through the house. I snuck a handful or two as they walked by.

The girls were having a riot watching the '80s flicks downstairs, while Brad and I hung out on the main floor. Brad gave my ass a little squeeze and planted a delicious kiss on my lips, "I have to get Kris home to bed. It's way past his bedtime. I wish I could stay." I reached up, linking my arms under his and pulled him closer. Lost in Brad's eyes, I sighed, "I know. I want you to stay so badly. Today was just perfect, I don't want it to end."

Brad smiled down at me, "Soon sweetheart, soon." Then he planted a kiss on my forehead and then my lips one last time. "Ok hun, I've gotta go and get my little man to sleep. I love you. I'll give you a call after Kris is sawing logs."

We talked for hours on the phone that night, rehashing the events from the day and what a big step it was for us as a couple. As a family. I filled Brad in on the girls' movie fest events and how well they were bonding. Occasionally, I heard a wave of laughter coming up from the basement. They were enjoying each other's company immensely.

*And the CLASSIC movies. *eyeroll**

I could feel Brad smiling through the phone, "Kris talked non-stop all the way home about bowling and your daughters. I think he may have a little crush on Jessica. He made it crystal clear that his day was amazing. He was asleep as soon as his head hit the pillow."

We both said, "Good night! Sweet dreams, love you!" I snuggled deeper under the covers, my heart exploding with warmth as I thought about the day.

7
are you open?

THE FOLLOWING WEEKEND, A LONG OVERDUE GIRLS' night out with Anne, Jennifer, and Twila emerged. We had a BBQ at Anne's place and lounged on her deck, chatting, and sipping wine into the wee hours of the morning, catching up. Always gorgeous, I observed that Anne's to-die-for long blonde hair was particularly amazing tonight. Anne had a bee in her bonnet about something, which revealed itself almost immediately, "Freddie and I have been together for almost a year and suddenly, last week, he drops a bombshell in my lap. He suggested that we should have an open relationship."

An open relationship? Wow, this isn't something I've heard Anne ponder before.

"Ladies, I'm struggling. I'm confused. I don't understand why he wants to sleep with other women. This hurts me, right to the core. Does he not love me? Why be together as a couple if he wants to fuck someone else? What's the point? Has he grown bored of me already? I really don't get it."

Anne started to cry. I walked over and gave her a big hug. She was sobbing. Suddenly, she pulled away, and looked up at us from beneath her eyelashes, tears still streaming down her mascara-stained face. "He wants me to decide this weekend. I have this crushing feeling that if I decide not to engage an open relationship that he will leave me. I'm so lost and hurt. What do I do?"

Twila, Jennifer, and I were shocked, what a terrible position to be put into. It really did sound like there were only two choices on the table: an open relationship or to break up. I shuddered.

The single life, when actively looking for a partner, is for the birds. Cruel and unusual punishment. But when the choice is sharing your man? No thanks!

Bridget was fretting, wringing her hands. Princess just yawned.

Jen spoke up, "That's a tough one, Anne. I don't think I could have an open relationship. The thought of my boyfriend sleeping with other women isn't something I'd be interested in entertaining, not even remotely. It would still feel like cheating to me. Yeah, I'm a HARD NO on that."

Twila flashed a flirty grin. "On the other hand, it might be kind of fun being able to sleep with other men with your boyfriend's consent. Hmm … I wonder? The only way it would work is if you both felt completely secure in your relationship. It would require respect and some strict rules. Although, even with that, I've heard several stories of people leaving their spouse for the person they're fucking on the side, but that can happen whether it's an open relationship or someone's cheating. The more I think about it, the idea's fun but when it comes down to it, I don't think I'd have the desire to do that. I wouldn't want to sleep with other men, and I wouldn't want my boyfriend sleeping with other women. That just feels wrong to me. It would crush me thinking about him with someone else. No, there's no way I could do it."

I nodded, "I definitely couldn't do it. Maybe I'm old fashioned, but I truly believe in marriage and one man and one woman sleeping together within that relationship. The idea of watching Brad fuck another woman is my worst nightmare. It would be torture to me. Something I'm not sure I'd get over, EVER! Have you chatted with Ronnie about this? Remember she had that one friend with benefits ("FWB") where the guy was in an open relationship? I think she exited stage left when he mentioned that his wife wanted to meet her and make her their play toy. Yikes!"

Shaking her head and smiling, Anne said, "Oh yeah, I'd forgotten about that. Ronnie sure gets herself into some interesting and complicated situations. I'll reach out for sure. Knowing her, she'll have a pretty good sense of the husband's perspective. Where is she tonight, by the way?"

Twila laughed, "That girl is always on an adventure of some sort. I think she's in Jasper for the weekend with one of her FWB flings. If memory serves, I believe his wife is away on business, so they decided to take advantage and enjoy a weekend away. Oh wait, maybe that's next weekend. Oh, and maybe that one is single. Crap, I can't keep all her men straight, you need a frigging spreadsheet to keep track. Oh, right, right, I remember now, this weekend she's at her niece's wedding in Waterton."

We all shook our heads as we laughed.

Boy oh boy, did Ronnie ever get into some thought-provoking and fascinating situationships.

When the laughter subsided, Anne looked each of us in the eye, one-by-one, and said, "Thank you for your words tonight, ladies. You've set my head straight. I've made my decision. I'm not going to be bullied into having an open relationship. I don't want that. If he doesn't want to be with just me, then he's free to go. Come to think of it, I may show him the door regardless. He put tremendous pressure on me to have an open relationship. In fact, he manipulated the situation to the point where I felt that I was being selfish if I chose not to have an open relationship. That didn't occur to me until just now. That kind of manipulation and pressure isn't something I'm interested in. No thanks! This gives me something more to ponder this weekend, but I think we're done. Next topic, please."

"We haven't chatted in what seems like forever. Daisy, what's going on with you? How's Brad? Have you heard from super-stud David since you and Brad got back together?" Jennifer queried.

I knew this was going to come up. David, well frig, where do I start? I giggled to myself, not there!

"It's unbelievably fabulous with Brad and me. In fact, we just introduced our kids to each other. I honestly wouldn't be surprised if we're living together and on the road to marriage within the next year. He is seriously amazing! I'm so in love!" I gushed. "How about you Jennifer, what's going on with you and Chris?"

Jen shook her head, "Not so fast missy. You conveniently failed to tell us about David."

Damn, I'd hoped they wouldn't notice.

It still hurt thinking about it. David had broken my heart. Up until now, I'd only confided in Anne and now I unloaded the full story on my other gals. "Shortly before Brad popped back up in my life, David asked me to go for a drink. We'd been communicating more often, and we were becoming solid friends. As we scarfed back wings and beer, he told me that he'd been dating a woman for the past six months. He said that he'd asked her to move in so felt compelled to break off our FWB relationship."

No shit.

Jen and Twila's jaws dropped.

"He wanted to fully concentrate on his new relationship. As you can imagine, I was rocked to the core."

"What in the actual fuck?" Twila exclaimed.

I tilted then shook my head as I continued, "As he spoke, I stared intently at him, and my chin dropped so far that I thought it may have actually detached from my face as it hit the table."

"As he continued to talk, I flashed back through the past six months. We had fucked at least ten times, including the super fun dom session. My mouth continued to gape open as I stared at him. He was silent, looking at me expectantly. Then I thought, "Shit, did he ask me something? What'd I miss?" My eyes widened as I looked back at him. He was waiting for a response of some sort from me. "Oh, uh, congratulations," I mumbled. It must have been what he'd been looking for as he continued talking about his girlfriend, going on about their future. I wasn't listening so I have no clue what he said."

Glancing quickly around the room, I saw looks of shock on my friends' faces. I continued, "My mouth slammed shut as I realized it wasn't that he didn't want a relationship, it was that he didn't want it with me. I teared up instantly and told him I had to go. He grabbed me by the hand and asked me to stay, he said he wanted to talk more about it and that he was sorry. I shook my head and walked out of the restaurant. I cried my eyes out that night as it hit me. Why didn't he want to be with me? What was wrong with me? That night, he messaged me, apologizing again, and asked if we could still touch base occasionally, just to talk. I said that would be fine if it was only occasionally. Commence the crying again."

"Shortly after that night, Brad reached out to me and several simple texts grew into phone conversations, one date then another, and then, boom, the rest is history! Onward and upward! I get a message from David here and there, but I've distanced myself as I want to be respectful of his girlfriend and of Brad. And yes, I know nothing is wrong with me, we just weren't right for each other."

I looked up at Jennifer and Twila, their eyes had gone bug eyed, "Wow, just wow!" Twila blinked rapidly as she spoke. "He had a girlfriend?"

I nodded, "Yup. That he did. The jerk lied to me. And yet, I've forgiven him already. Why, I don't know. But I have. No sense hanging onto that crap, I guess. Or maybe it's because he was such an amazing lover, and I just couldn't bear to cloud all those memories up. Or something like that. At the heart of it all, he is a good guy."

Jennifer shook her head and said, "I'm sorry, sweetie. It sounds like the timing was right though. If he hadn't ended it, you would've had to when you and Brad got together anyway. It's just too bad David hadn't been up front and honest with you when he met his girlfriend. You're truly better off without him in your life."

I nodded.

I know that, but it still hurts, even to this day.

Brad is 100% right for me, but I had fallen hard for David and there were lingering feelings of love and hurt relating to him, they may always be there. Both David and Brad had hurt me. David had been clear that he didn't want a long-term relationship ("LTR"), but my heart had other plans. Then David dated another woman. This had stung me deeply. Hopefully those feelings would lessen with time. Brad, on the other hand, had disappeared. We had just been starting up and my heart felt hope, but not love, not that early. Probably it was a mess of lust and hope. But he came back to me when he was ready. And now . . . I was gushing at the thought of it.

I wasn't interested in talking about David anymore, "How about you, Jen? Last we heard you and Chris were having some issues in the sack, anything new on that? You're still together, right?"

Jen glanced at all of us and smiled broadly, "Yes, we're still together. I chatted with him as you all suggested, and lo and behold we were able to talk it through. He WAS concerned about his size. It stemmed from a relationship he had years ago where she made fun of his penis, telling him he couldn't satisfy her because of his size. It sounds like she was extremely cruel. I explained to him that he wasn't on the small end of the spectrum and that woman was clearly very rude."

"Very rude? She was a C-U-Next-Tuesday," Twila exclaimed. "Unbelievable; these crazy sorts messing up other people."

"Yeah, it's unfortunate. A crazy person for sure. That was at least a decade ago, so he's been the walking wounded for that long. But you know, opening the door to sex talk has made an enormous difference for us. We're both more vocal about what we like, and as a result, it's become absolutely amazing, very intimate and fun! Our connection is through the roof."

"That's awesome Jen!" we all cooed at once. It had been a long time coming for Jen to find someone who was a fit for her. Amazing!

We all looked towards Twila, "And you, young lady, what's the latest and greatest for you?" I queried.

"Well, I most certainly haven't found Mr. Right. Ha-ha! . . . a whole lot of Mr. Wrongs are banging on my door these days. The good news is that I've become more efficient and effective at spotting the yellow and red flags now. My detective hat is always on trying to read these guys. As you know, you can't seem to take anything they say at face value. Which reminds me, this one guy, Jordan, seemed like the perfect fit: intelligent, communicative, the cutest dimples and a sexy smile, supposedly honest, and looking for a relationship. We had several long conversations and we connected intellectually, which was very cool. I started to get my hopes up, but I should've known better. I've had so many disappointments on first dates; either they don't look like their picture, they're completely off their rocker, their mannerisms are bothersome, or I'm just not drawn to them at all."

Jen and I nodded in agreement, understanding exactly what she was talking about. I giggled as I remembered the weird scent guy, just bizarre. "Remember that metallic scented guy I dated? OMG!"

Twila continued, "I know, right?! Jordan asked me to join him for a walk one Saturday, so we met at Nose Hill. It was obvious that we were attracted to one another physically, so I was happy to hold his hand as we walked along the paths, marveling at the array of green colours. He seemed very excited and at times was acting like a total goofball, super immature and just weird, then he would be all normal again. I started to wonder if he was on drugs or what was going on. It got all hot and heavy behind some trees and he grabbed my breasts and pussy at one point, was kissing my neck and grabbing my ass. A bit handsy for a first date, I thought. I was into him though, and it'd been a long time since I'd been touched. I was craving that touch, so it felt good to have his hands on my body. When we chatted that night, everything seemed normal."

Jen said, "Well, that sounds promising. Nothing wrong with a little hot and bothered touching in the bushes, ha-ha!"

Twila laughed, "Just wait, the next night he was completely MIA and the next day it was obvious something had changed for him. He was more distant and less interested, not playful at all. To be honest, he may have been feeling some of that from me too, as I was still thinking about the weirdness of our date."

"The next day, he texted me "Twila, I really like you, but I need to take it slow. I need time to digest everything that's happening between us. I want to be with you, but it needs to be at my pace.""

"I was taken aback by his comment, especially after his MIA thing. I hadn't asked for any sort of commitment. We'd had one date and I wasn't ready to commit to him either, but his message confused me. I wasn't sure where it was coming from. "Ok, sure, no problem, we can go at your pace, but I need to understand your motivation. If it's truly to process and just take it slow, that's just fine but if you're dating multiple people and playing the field then that's another matter. I just want to understand what I'm dealing with." He said, "Twila, I'm only interested in you. I DO NOT date multiple women at a time." Ok, fair enough, I thought."

Twila continued, "The next day, he invited me over to his place and then backpedaled and changed his mind part way through the day, saying he was too busy with work. Ok, fine, except . . . that night he was completely MIA again. I'm no detective, but this was suspicious to me. The flashing yellow flag had been upgraded to flashing red flag."

"The next morning, he was MIA again until after noon, which was out of character. I was relatively certain that he wasn't at home. The GPS from the dating site had him somewhere roughly twelve kilometers closer to me than he normally was. I cut it off at this point. His bullshit was starting to leak through heavy in his stories. How disappointing."

Twila shook her head along with the rest of us, "So many of these dipshits like to play games. Play with women. Not sure what the purpose is but boy, is it ever irritating. It makes me want to delete all my dating apps and pick up cat minding or knitting. Much safer than dealing with these jackasses."

We all shook our heads in disbelief and Jen said, "I ran into a few of those game players too, rude assholes. Honestly, I think that most of those ones are married and just looking to cop a feel, flirt a bit and then move along. It's just entertainment for them. Jerks!"

8
carson's birth

OUR FAMILIES SPENT ALMOST every waking hour together over the summer when Brad and I weren't working. Even when we were working, often our kids hung out together. Kris never starved for attention with three big sisters looking out for him. Brad had his kids the lion's share of the time; his ex-wife had them every second weekend. Reflecting on it, I was shocked how well our two little families were melding together. It was quite unbelievable.

I met Brad's ex-wife, Sara, shortly after I met their kids. She was polite but cold and that was just fine. We didn't have to be friends, just respectful towards one another. Brad and Sara had a reasonably cordial relationship. They clearly understood that it wasn't about them anymore, that chapter closed a long time ago. It's about the kids now, so whether they like each other or not, they suck it up and work together to ensure the kids are supported. At least they did up until this point.

It shocks me when people are petty with one another. It's only the kids who suffer. And honestly, who has that much time and energy to carry that garbage around and be angry all the time? Yeah, everyone's situation is different and I'm sure it's tough to remain the mature adult when the ex is acting like a spoiled brat, but one of the roles of a parent to rise above, be the bigger person, when you can. Some exes are ridiculously infuriating so I get it why sometimes people lose their shit and get sucked into the vortex of all-out war, but the key is to yank yourself out as fast as possible. Don't play their game. Don't stoop to their level.

One weekend, Brad went on a guys' fishing trip, and I was happy to chill at home: just me and the girls. That gorgeous Sunday summer afternoon while snuggled into my favorite lawn chair, indulging in my latest book club novel and sipping on a delicious lemonade, when I heard footsteps. It was Jess. She was standing and staring at me rather seriously, "Um, mom, do you have a minute? I need to tell you something." Those words yanked me from my book. "Of course sweetie, what's up? Is everything ok?"

Jess sat down, took a deep breath, rearranging her legs beneath her, "Well, I'm not really sure where to begin."

This wasn't my first rodeo as mom, and with a precision borne of instinct, love and too many fuck-ups from not seeing it sooner, I knew something was up. Something real. She was holding tension in those broad shoulders of hers.

I did what I had learned.

I dropped some of my own tension and put a smile on.

Time to be patient.

Time to listen.

Mama bear is here.

"Go ahead, sweetie," I coaxed. Another big exhale. "It's about Kari, mom. She called me last night and told me a few things that are life changing and it affects all of us. She's scared to tell her mom. I think she's going to talk with her dad tonight when he's back from his trip. At least that's what I encouraged her to do." She shrugged and looked around the backyard, clearly very uncomfortable with this conversation.

I'm in the dark sweetie. I have no clue what you're talking about.

But in another very real way, I'd been here before.

I'm listening.

And I waited a few pregnant seconds before asking, "Yes, what is it, Jess?"

"Well, I should get to the point," she said, sounding so adult and composed, despite the stress she was clearly struggling with.

"Kari feels that she has felt very *off* for a long time," Jess said in an even ton. "She didn't know how to express what she was feeling or even what she truly felt, just that something wasn't right. She's been struggling for years with her gender and sexual identity. At first, she thought she was gay but that didn't feel quite right. She felt it was deeper and different than that but couldn't put her finger on it."

There was an organization to Jess's words that told me she had taken some time to arrange her thoughts. My daughter was no pedant—I knew that was her, and likely Kari—sorting out their words, their language. Working to find an expression to relate a deep and important realization, something difficult to explain and so it needed its own words.

I was so proud of her.

"Then after a lot of research and talking to people," Jess continued, "Kari figured it out. She's a transboy. There, now you know."

A giant relieved exhale left Jess's lips and her shoulders visibly relaxed. Clearly, she felt that weight had been lifted from her shoulders.

I had so many questions.

Transboy? What does that mean, really? I know the term but what are the realities? What does she need from us? How do we support her? I don't know how this works. How is she feeling? Who can we talk to? How does she know? Is it a phase? When did she first feel this way? How is Brad going to feel about this?

But besides the questions, I knew two things: this was important, and I needed to listen to her. I needed to still my heart and control my stomach, which had dropped, because while I was no expert on transgender issues, I knew that Kari was probably suffering. She needed mama bear to be there for her.

And so did Jess.

And so, when I asked my questions, I asked them like a child *and* like a mother, "Okay, honey. I know. Thank you."

I smiled. "I know—you've told me—but I'm ignorant about how all of this works for Kari and what she wants. What she needs."

I paused and looked into my daughter's eyes. "How is she feeling about all of this? What does she need? Of course, we'll support her."

Jess said that she didn't know most of the answers. "Did you let Kari know that you'd be talking to me about this?"

Jess nodded. "Ok, so how best do we support her?" Jess looked towards me and said, "Well, one thing she asked is if we can start calling her Carson, rather than Kari, and start using 'him' and 'his' pronouns instead of 'she' and 'her'."

I was taken aback, oh yeah, I guess that's right.

Shit, I have a lot to learn about this and I have no clue who to talk to.

My stomach was roiling. But I also knew—I KNEW—these kids needed my reaction to not be about me, or my ignorance, or my damned stomach.

"Does Angela know?" I asked, my brain finding its gear again.

Jess shook her head, "No, not yet but I told Carson that I'd be talking to both of you today." I nodded.

Ok that's good.

Jess had been 100% respectful of Kari . . . er . . . Carson's wishes. This was going to require some effort and focus.

As I was mulling over the news Jess had relayed, she said, "Oh yeah, one more thing. Carson is pansexual." My brow furrowed.

Pan-what? What on earth is that?

Jess laughed, "Mom, I see you're confused. I can help you understand this one. Just a sec, let me just google the definition: "Pansexual - of, relating to, or characterized by sexual or romantic attraction that is not limited to people of a particular sexual identity or sexual orientation.""

I nodded but my mind went to bisexuality immediately as that was a term more familiar to me, "So, similar to bisexual but different? What's the difference?"

Jess smiled and said, "Well I'm definitely not an expert but I think bisexuality is limited to people who identify as female or male, whereas pansexuality isn't. Pansexuality doesn't limit a person in sexual choice by biological sex, gender identity or gender. It says here that pansexuality is a category of bisexuality, though it's not limited by the traditional genders, like traditional bisexuality."

Hmm, ok, this is a whole other curve ball for my brain, something else that I need to wrap my mind around. Clearly, I don't understand it. But shouldn't it be the other way around? Shouldn't bisexuality be a category of pansexuality? Pansexuality was more all-encompassing and broader. Hmm.

Language.

Somewhere deep inside a connection was made. A bell dinged. I saw again what I'd seen from the start.

This is important, and people need to own their own words for it.

Okay. Pansexual.

Before Jess went inside to tell Angela, she made me promise to not tell Brad. Naturally, Carson wanted to tell his dad himself. Jess waved me off when I asked if she wanted me to join her. I felt a bit strange knowing something about Kari . . . er . . . Carson that her, shoot, HIS dad didn't know about yet. No one I knew had experienced anything like this. As I was mulling over how best to support Carson, I started to google.

While I was searching for transgender youth counsellors, I was horrified to stumble on a religious counsellor whose tag line was that he would "lead your child to the light" and the description sounded damn near an exorcism, for crying out loud. "Remove the demon from within your child that was poisoning them to dare mess with what God had given them."

Whoa dude, yeah, we'll pass. Go back under whatever rock you crawled out from under.

Suddenly, it occurred to me that people might actually go to see him, which scared the crap out of me. Those poor kids had been so brave to come out to their parents and now they were subjected to this looney toon. Insanity!

Mama bear growled.

More searching led me to a few counsellors and psychologists who specialized in transgender counselling, but I soon discovered that they only worked with adults. Suddenly, a light bulb went off in my head. I don't know why it hadn't occurred to me earlier, I remembered Anne's ex-husband, Kyle, was a counselor specializing in LGBTQ+ youth. Surely, he'd be able to help or at least be able to point us in the right direction for more information.

Reaching out to Anne, I picked us up some coffee and went over to her place. First, I swore her to secrecy. Then, I relayed what Jess had told me about Carson. Anne said, "Oh wow, that's some big news! I'd have no clue what to do either. How are you feeling about it?"

I nodded, "Well, one thing that's certain is that I'm here to support him. But I'm a bit lost about how to. I have so many questions. I did some googling and stumbled onto some crackpot religious dude performing gay and transgender exorcisms, seriously, what the fuck?"

Anne laughed, "Crackpot is right, that dude must be smoking something alright. What a jackass. Those poor kids. Did you find anything else?"

"I found a few counsellors, but they all specialize in transgender adults, not youth. Do you think Kyle might be able to help or have some resources or know of someone he could refer us to?"

"I have no doubt that Kyle will be a huge help. Hopefully he can help answer your questions and support Carson directly, but if not, he'll be able to put you in touch with the right people. Aside from reaching out to Kyle, let me know if there's anything that I can do to help support you and Carson."

"Thanks Anne! I love you! Thank you for being you!"

"I love you too, sweetie! And, you're already an amazing step-mom!"

"Aww . . . thanks, Anne!"

I'm so lucky to have such awesome and supportive friends.

9
carson's emergence

Brad

MY FISHING TRIP WAS GREAT. Much-needed time away, just me and my buddies at the lake. On my way home, I picked up Kari and Kris from their mom's. I was exhausted from the trip but could tell immediately that something was up with Kari. And it was big. She had a look about her. Tight. Scared. Held in.

When she asked if we could chat one-on-one tonight, I said, "Sure thing, sweetie, happy to chat with you about anything."

But I wondered what it was I'd been missing. And for how long.

For some reason, my mind went to a video I'd watched of some daredevil hippie-type dude on a tightrope—no, a slackline—strung between two towering rock pillars.

Well, that's a weird image. Why would that come to mind?

After supper, Kris asked to watch a movie. I got him all set up in the bonus room so Kari and I could chat in relative privacy. "Dad, I'm nervous talking to you about this, but I need to do it NOW. I've waited long enough. I'm just going to blurt it out. You can ask questions after."

I nodded. I hadn't always been good at, well, just listening. But funny how important it can be. Something told me it was one of those times to close my mouth and open my ears. My baby girl had something important to share with me.

Just listen.

Kari took a deep breath and exhaled, "Here goes nothing. I'm a pansexual transboy."

Silence. I waited. Shocked, but desperately trying not to show it.

Kari blew out another huge breath and added, "There I said it."

A what?

I sat very still. Attempting to process what I'd just heard. A feather could have knocked me over. Nothing could have prepared me for this. My brain was trying to process but I didn't even know where to start. I limited knowledge about either word Kari had muttered.

Kari continued, "I know this is coming at you fast. I've researched and soul-searched and internalized this over the past few years. I've never felt right as a girl. It always felt wrong. I felt awkward. It just took me a while to figure out what felt right. And before you ask, no, this isn't a phase. The reality is: I am a transboy."

I nodded, playing for time.

The video came back to me then, an overpowering image and feeling. The slackline, only it was me that was on the tightrope. I was balancing precariously over a steep faced gorge, with nothing but air and sharp rocks below.

I had so many questions. I felt so much love for my oldest child right now, lots of confusion, and I just wanted to hold on to my not-so-little girl.

I struggled for balance.

I'd heard the terms before, I guess, but I didn't really know what they meant.

But I could feel the breeze. The air flowing over me, high on that slackline. I couldn't panic there. I couldn't lose my cool or pretend what was happening to my daughter was an affront to me. An affront at all. It wasn't about me—it was about her, and if I reacted wrong and lost my balance, maybe it wouldn't be me that fell—it would be her dropping so far, end over end, flailing onto the sharp and unsympathetic rocks so far below.

What do I do?

But some instinctive part of me knew what to do. I folded her into my arms, next to my heart, where she belonged. Always. I felt her try to pull away, but I wasn't ready to let her go, and I pulled her in closer for another minute before releasing her.

"Dad, you haven't said anything. What are you feeling?" Kari whispered.

Holding her, I felt my balance coming back. I was scared, still. Scared for her. But I knew something at that moment.

"We aren't on a tightrope," I said.

"What?" she asked.

Oops, that was my outside voice. That must've sounded extremely weird to her.

"Sorry sweetie, I'm a bit shell shocked. But we're going to be fine."

I didn't know that. Some part of me knew that peril surrounded us—surrounded *her*, who I would've gladly fallen off any cliff to save, but I also knew that it wouldn't be an act of physical bravery on my part that would help. It would be something else.

Summoning that something else, I said, "I want to be respectful in my response. It's a lot to take in all at once. But I want you to know that I love you and I'm here to support you through anything and everything, always." I exhaled, clearly understanding that things had changed in a big way. Not knowing quite what to do. I stared at my girl sitting on the couch. I heard the birds chirping outside. Nothing had changed for them. "How do I support you, Kari? What do you need from me?"

Kari released the air she'd been holding in, and a small smile touched the corners of her lips. "Ok, there are a few things I need from you right now: I would like you to start calling me Carson, not Kari. Also, use the pronouns 'him' and 'he'. I know this will take some getting used to, but I'd appreciate it if you'd start trying immediately. I've closed the door on Kari; she's gone."

Gone? What do you mean gone? You're sitting right here. You're Kari, but you're not. My brain was scrambling, trying to find some semblance of logic and organization. I was grasping at straws and failing miserably.

I felt the air again. The high cliffs and the endless fall below. I was back on the slackline. I knew I shouldn't say anything until the swirling stopped.

I'm not on a tightrope. We're not on a tightrope.

If Kari was gone, I now had Carson.

I nodded, "Yes, sure thing, honey. I'll do my best. Please be patient with me. Would you like to tell Kris together? What about your mom?"

Carson nodded, "Yeah, let's tell Kris tomorrow after school." I agreed, wholeheartedly.

"Oh, and Dad, I told Jess. I think she was planning to tell Daisy and Angela today. I don't know how I'm going to tell mom though. I'm pretty sure she's going to . . . excuse my French . . . lose her shit. I'll need to get up the nerve to tell her." Carson smirked, "Do I have to tell her?"

I grimaced, thinking how ugly that was likely to go. If anything, that thought steadied me. Carson needed me. And damn it, she's—no, he's right, Sara won't take this news well.

The chances of her being supportive is about the same as a ballerina hockey player tap dancing on top of the Calgary Tower.

"Yes, you do, sweetie. We'll figure out a way to do it together. Would you like me to help you share your news with her?"

Carson exhaled, "Yes, please. Thank you, Dad. I think that'd help me to be strong. Ok, I'm exhausted and need to go to sleep. We can talk more tomorrow. Thank you, Dad. I love you."

I gave Kari, *damn it,* Carson another hug and kissed her, *holy hell,* HIS forehead. "Good night, sweetie. I love you."

I got Kris moving to brush his teeth and get his pjs on.

This name change is going to take some serious concentration to get it right.

There was never even a nanosecond when I had any doubt about supporting my child through his journey. There was no question about it. I became a parent unconditionally, to love and support my children unconditionally. Yes, I said it twice, and now a third time . . . unconditionally. That is what a parent does. However, I had no idea how to in this instance.

Yikes! Dad's got some learning to do!

With the kids asleep, I called Daisy. I was 99% sure that she'd be aligned with me as far as support was concerned. She'd have some ideas where we could seek help.

"Hi Daisy, I missed you! How are you?"

"Hi Brad! I'm great. How are you? How was your trip? Your kids?"

Ah, she's playing it smart, not wanting to spill the beans about Carson. Or maybe Jess hasn't told her yet. Hmmm I wonder.

I told her about my trip and then I shared Carson's news. As anticipated, she was completely understanding and supportive. Maybe too supportive if that were a thing.

Daisy told me she'd reached out to Anne. I felt a twinge of irritation. I was taken aback. This was my news, my family, not hers. I grumpily asked, "You told Anne?"

Daisy nodded, "All I could think about was getting help for Carson."

It was my turn to nod, "Yes, I understand that you meant well, but you overstepped. It wasn't your place to seek help, Daisy, not your problem to solve."

Daisy's face fell as I uttered those words. She had a tear in her eye and her voice waivered as spoke, "I'm sorry, Brad. I didn't mean to take over. I really was just trying to help, to be supportive."

My brain did a reshuffle and I chided myself. I felt embarrassed for thinking it, never mind saying it aloud. Daisy did what Daisy does, one of many things I love about her. She went above and beyond to support us in the best way she knows how. She had already taken my kids under her mama bear protection, which spoke volumes for our big interlacing family. I took her in my arms, kissed her on the forehead and whispered in her ear, "I know, baby. And thank you. I guess I'm used to being the lone wolf with my kids. On top of that, it feels weird because we're at that awkward stage moving toward one family, but not quite there."

Daisy grinned up at me, "We're getting there. You're right though, I should've asked you before reaching out to Anne. The timing was just all weird. But still." We came up with a game plan to reach out to Kyle to find an appropriate counsellor for not only Carson, but us.

I reached out first thing Monday morning. "Hi Kyle, my name is Brad MacDonald. I'm Daisy's boyfriend and well, to get to the point, my son came out to me last night as being transgender and pansexual, and quite honestly, I'm lost. Anne told Daisy that you might be able to help us out with some counselling and resources to set us in the right direction. I really want to be able to support my kid through this."

Kyle responded, "Yes, Anne let me know you'd be in touch this week. Rest assured, I can answer all your questions, get you and your son set up with counselling and provide you with as much literature as you can handle. I imagine you work Monday to Friday, would a Saturday work best? This Saturday?"

I felt relieved already, "Yes, this Saturday works for us. Thank you so much. Is there anything we can do to prepare?"

"No, but if you'd like, I can send you a few links to check out that may answer some of your questions. How does ten work for you both?"

I nodded, even though I knew he couldn't see me. "Yes, that would be great, thank you. See you on Saturday at ten."

I sent Daisy and Carson separate but identical texts, using good ole copy and paste. "We're booked in to meet Kyle on Saturday at 10:00 a.m. He's going to email some information for us to read and then, on Saturday he'll answer any questions we have."

A very heavy weight was lifted from my shoulders as it all sunk in. We were getting help.

I was leaning back in my office chair when I recalled that we still had the problem of Carson's mom. We knew she wasn't all that supportive of the LGBTQ+ community in general.

How will she handle our oldest child coming out as being transgender? I hope that Kyle will have some ideas relating to that conversation. I'm very concerned about the backlash landing on Carson. How can I shield him from that?

Somewhere in my mind, I felt the slackline under my toes again.

I'm not concerned about myself falling, but Carson. Carson needed to be ok.

10
catfishing meow

ARRIVING SOMEWHAT LATE to our gals get together, I could see, and hear, that Amy was seething the moment I sat down, "Mark bailed on me again this past weekend. My freaking boyfriend was MIA. AGAIN!"

As I took off my coat, I said, "Aww shit, Amy! What now?"

"Some bullshit excuse about work and his kids. He didn't even have his kids last weekend. We were supposed to Canmore for a little romantic getaway. And on top of that, something felt off. I'll get into more of that in a bit."

I nodded at Amy, "Believe your gut. And go with it. Always."

Amy nodded, "Yup. I am. Last-minute cancelling jerk. But you know what, the weekend actually turned out good in the end."

Atta girl! Pull yourself up by the bootstraps. Fuck him. You do you!

"I was bored out of my tree, so I decided to do some work on my Gender Studies Masters project. It's been fascinating studying the way men and women behave while dating."

We all nodded. Anne smiled, "Yes, I can't wait to hear your findings! I mean, we've all been living and experience the bizarre male dating behavior!" I laughed, remembering what a mess it had been for me, what it still was for my single girlfriends. I'm relieved I'm not in the dating pool anymore.

"It'll be a bit yet. I still have a lot of research to do," Amy said.

Grinning, Anne commented, "It'll be fascinating, I'm sure."

"With some unexpected time on my hands, I decided it was time for me to dive into some field work, get my hands dirty, take it to the next level. To the dating sites, I went. When I completed research previously, I'd set up a regular type of profile, looking for a long-term relationship, yada yada, kind of like what we've all put on there, so I had that research already. This time I decided to go for the gold, try a different angle to see what motivates guys on dating sites."

"Uh, sex?!" Ronnie laughed.

"No shit!" I shook my head, giggling.

"Just wait!" Amy laughed, "I created a fake profile using the name Tara. I searched for, and found, a stock photo of an attractive, but not unbelievably so, woman in her mid-forties. Blonde with blue eyes, sweet smile, a likeable type."

We were nodding, wondering where this was going.

Anne asked, "You catfished them?"

"Well, yeah, but it was for research purposes. And only for the weekend. No harm, no foul."

"Hmm . . . I guess," Anne reluctantly nodded.

"It's not like I catfished them for a scam or to trick them into meeting with me. It really was necessary for my research. I couldn't very well go on as myself."

"Makes sense," Ronnie nodded.

Amy continued, "I carefully chose the wording on Tara's profile. I wanted it to be simple. Somewhat direct, but not to the point of bluntness. Tara had to know what she wanted but needed some softness and femininity about her. I wanted maximum attract-ability. This is what I came up with for her profile:

Tara
Looking for ongoing, amazingly mind-blowing fun with a dominant man.
Those interested in one-night stands need not apply. Must be clean.

Separated
Wants to date but nothing serious
Looking for a man for hang out
Occupation: Accountant
Height: 5'3"

Conversation starter: What are you going to do with me to make me wiggle and squirm?"

"Oh wow, I can guess WHAT you attracted with that profile," Ronnie smirked.

"It was nuts! I had over 350 messages, yes messages, in twenty-four hours and another 150-200 in the next twenty-four hours. That doesn't even include the likes and winks. I couldn't keep up. My phone was going off every few seconds . . . ding, ding, ding . . . it was over-the-top crazy.

"Wow, that sounds overwhelming! Five hundred messages in forty-eight hours? Holy fuck! I think the most I got when going onto a new site was 100, maybe," I was stunned.

"I know, me too. Even in my first experiment, it was the same."

"So, all those guys looking for no strings sex, eh?!" I shook my head.

"Yup!"

"Hmm . . . I can't say I'm surprised," Anne laughed, "that certainly aligns with what I've stumbled onto while looking for something more committed and longer term. So many looking for FWB, a dirty diva, or a sex kitten on the side."

"Amy, what did the guys say? I'm curious!" I nudged.

Shaking her head, Amy said, "There certainly were some interesting ones."

"I received a solid forty that simply said, Hi or Hey."

I was giggling, "I hated those guys. Uh, dude, don't waste my time. You're gonna have to bring your "A" game when Tara has 500 messages. Pull up your socks, sweet cheeks. A hard swipe left for you, sir."

CarlSwings74
Tara. Hello, is it me you're looking for?

Chances are, no. But thanks Lionel Richie.

FreddyPrince
I'm sure that every guy and their uncle's and brothers have probably hit on you and sent you a million messages with indecent marriage proposals (lol), but . . . I gotta tell you, you are FANTASTICALLY BEAUTIFUL. I wanna find out if your personality is as sweet as your picture. Let's grab a cup of

something delicious, share some laughs, and stimulating (*sexually?*) conversation (*physical? Let our bodies do the talking?*). If nothing else, we can be awesome friends. I have a man cave full of cars, classic muscle and high-end new. By the way, I come with a 30-day return policy. No questions asked.

But do I get a refund?

HardnHung1973
I got a hard cock for ya. Wanna meet halfway and fuck in my truck?

Oh, how coy. Such a turn on. NOT! Right to it then? Let me just jump in my car. Be right there. WTF dude?

CunnilingusExpert
Multiple rounds and I can do tongue push-ups.

"What in the fuck are tongue push-ups?" Ronnie giggled.
"No clue. I asked and he said I had to meet him to find out."
Well played, dude, well played!

Gushalicious4U
Squirm or squirt? Clearly squirting is much more orgasmic than just plain ole squirming. But ya, I can make ya squirm. Hell of a lot more than that.

He understood the assignment.
Amy was shaking her head, "Holy man, and this one guy, I can hardly believe it. We were chatting a bit, but he was rather boring, blah, blah, blah, so I said, "Thanks for your interest but I'm not interested. Best of luck with your search." His response was telling . . . "Well thanks . . . good thing I'm not into chubby chicks . . . have a chocolate covered bonbon for me, too.""
Sorry to hear your poor little ego can't handle rejection. Poor thing. Fuck you dude. I shook my head, "What a dick. What did you say to him?"
Amy snorted, "I said, "Wow, you're a bit of an ass, aren't you? Enjoy your hand.""
Ronnie roared, "YOU said that? OMG Amy, I must be rubbing off on you,

girl." They high-fived. Anne laughed, "You're coming out of your shell in the dating world, Amy. What did the douche bucket say? Or did you just block him?"

"No, I wanted to see what his response would be. He said, "Enjoy your fingers." To which I replied "Hey asshat, I have messages from 450 guys on here. I'm pretty sure I'll find what I'm looking for. You on the other hand . . .""

"He responded, "No offense, I had a chubby last night and they're just not my thing.""

Way to show your true colors dude.

""You got it up last night? All by yourself? Good for you." Then I blocked him."

Ronnie, Anne, Amy and I were absolutely dying we were laughing so hard. Ronnie was wheezing, "A chubby! Bahaha!" I was shaking, in fact I thought I might actually pee myself. I nonchalantly crossed my right leg over my left, just in case.

Eek! I'm too young for depends.

Amy wasn't done . . .

BornRomantic1234

Hello Tara, I'm on one knee. Will you marry me, my beautiful princess?

But sir, we've just met. Not even. You sent one message. People are crazy. ~~Ha!~~

I shook my head, "Seriously, a marriage proposal?"

"Yup, I received three, if you can believe it."

"Three? Really?"

"Yeppers!"

"They weren't serious?" Anne queried.

"I imagine not. But who knows with some of these cracker jacks? I swiped left on two of them and asked the third for his VISA so I could order the cake and book the hall. He disappeared," Amy was giggling.

"I bet! Certainly, it was meant to be some backasswards compliment," I suggested.

Bridget was shaking her head in disbelief. Princess was rolling her eyes wondering when the good stuff was going to start.

Amy just shrugged.

TheDominator

Under my dominance you'll do a hell of a lot more than squirm. I'll tie you to the bed spread eagle with a gag ball in your mouth, nipple clips on your titties, while I alternate between whipping you and fucking you until you beg for mercy or use the safe word "jollyrancher".

So many things wrong with that. WTF? Jollyrancher? Whipping? Gag ball? Did we somehow fall into a scene from Pulp Fiction? Uh, swipe left. Next.

BabyBlues4U

Does your idea of fun include being thrown down on the bed, tied down by the wrists and fucked relentlessly by a big dicked, hard bodied, aggressive man?

Princess Pussy perked up, "Pick me, pick me!"
Ronnie's eyebrows arched, "Yup. Where do I sign up?"
Princess gave her a dirty look, "Dibs, I called him first."
"The second message gets much more, shall we say, interesting?!"

You have a sweet and cute face that makes me want to see how sexy it looks while you've got a thick, throbbing porn-sized cock going in and out of your pussy. Your hair looks like the perfect length to grab and use as a handle to maneuver you around with, especially when I bend you over the side of my bed. Would you like to know more?

On high alert, Princess was bouncing around and squealing something fierce from my shoulder. Bridget was shaking her head, "Princess, stop devaluing yourself. All he wants is sex."
Princess turned toward Bridget, "Your point? I'm not devaluing myself; I'm having fun. You should try it sometime." Bridge whined, "I do have fun." Princess raised her eyebrows.
I caught the tail end of Ronnie commenting, ". . . keep talking to him?"
"Yes, he told me some fantasy he had about having a train of women that he fucked back- to-back. Tara wasn't into that as she was looking for one man, so she quickly exited the conversation."
We all laughed. Ronnie commented, "Good luck finding that train, dude. A

train of guys? Yeah, maybe, it's possible. A train of women? A tad more difficult, me thinks."

"Now for the big reveal," Amy said mysteriously.

"The big reveal?" Anne was confused. We all were.

"This was the last one before I called it quits and deleted Tara's account:"

TreatURight1975

Squirm? Hmm . . . let's see . . . I walk in. The lights are off. I push you against the wall, pinning your hands above your head, slapping your ass, gripping your hips, cock pushing against you, and tugging your hair. I can hear you getting more turned on. My left hand holds wrists in place, while my right hand slides under your dress, my finger hooking your panties, pulling them down, past your knees to your ankles. You want more?

Amy continued "I replied, "Don't tease me. That's so hot. Keep going, dreamboat.""

Sure baby, I'll keep going. I whisper in your ear that you're mine as my fingers are massaging your clit, teasing your pussy lips, only to the point where I feel how wet you are. I push you to your hands and knees, your ankles tied with your panties, I grab your hips and thrust deep inside. That'll make you squirm.

Princess Pussy was doing handsprings in excitement.

I had to admit, hearing about Amy's tales was quite the turn on, or more accurately, Tara's tales.

"Why'd you delete Tara's account after that one?"

"Well, it wasn't related to that one, the timing just coincided. As I was chatting with Mr. TreatURight1975, hearing his plans for Tara, a picture popped up on my screen. It caught by breath, I heard my heartbeat in my ears, and I felt like I wanted to throw up."

A tear ran down Amy's cheek as she inhaled deeply, regrouping to finish her story. She had our undivided attention. I knew where this was going.

That fucker!

Amy's voice was shaky, "It was a picture of Mark, my now EX-boyfriend. It was a picture I'd taken of him, too."

"What an asshole!" Anne bellowed.

"What did you do?" Ronnie asked.

"Being that I was undercover, I felt really weird about it. After shaking off the heebie-jeebies, I figured I had two options: I could catfish him and arrange to meet with him for drinks and bust him in the flesh or just take a screenshot and get the hell off the site. I wasn't really sure what to do so I messaged him. He told me some pretty erotic stuff he'd do to Tara, then Tara got his phone number. Same phone number that I call him on. Fuckhead! I didn't need any more proof than that. I deleted my profile, then sent him a text with a couple screenshots."

"How'd he react?" Anne asked.

"You didn't do it in person? You know, to see him squirm," Ronnie asked mischievously.

"I didn't feel he deserved the respect of me doing it in person. No desire to see him squirm. I just wanted to be rid of the asshole. He tried to deny it and then I sent him the message where he included his phone number."

Hook, line, and sinker.

"What'd he say then? Did he continue to deny it?" I asked.

"No. He said he had a problem, that he was a sex addict."

Did he steal that one from David Duchovny?

Chiding myself at that low blow, I shook my head.

Sarcastically mocking him, Amy said, "Mark said "Oh Amy, you're so great. I don't deserve you. I really didn't mean to hurt you. You know, I thought if you didn't know, everything would be just fine.""

Anne was shaking her head, "If you didn't know? So, it's ok if it's behind your back, as long as you don't find out? Wow! What a selfish jerk!"

"You know what's funny? Our sex life was a bit dull. Had he done something similar to what he described, I would've been jumping for joy. The spicy fun would've been amazing."

Princess Pussy was nodding and rubbing her hands together. Bridget shrugged and then reluctantly nodded.

"That's unfortunate," said Ronnie, "So few couples are open with each other about what they want in the bedroom, and in life really. Who knows what would've happened had you been keyed into one another?"

Amy nodded, "Yes, that's something for me to examine for sure. But what the fuck? Why do I keep attracting and dating guys who cheat on me? I seriously don't get it. I don't have the energy to get into that whole discussion right now, but fuck."

"Ok, Amy, we can chat about that whenever you're ready," Anne commented.

"Did your abrupt departure from the dating site allow you to get enough material? Were you on for long enough?" I wondered aloud.

"I sure did. Lots of repetitive comments and ideas so I don't think I would've learned much more if I had extended the time, never mind it being bloody exhausting! All those freaking messages! The non-technical moral of the story? Conclusion of my research? Hmm . . .

- Blonde's do have more fun. Ha!
- In general, on that site, men clamber over each other for no-strings-attached sex.
- Dating sites should be called sex sites, that being the goal of the majority of the men on them. Us poor gals looking for LTR don't stand a chance to find a guy who's truly after the same. Even the ones saying they're looking for LTR get sucked into the sex only gals."

"I've got a lot of material to sift through before I'm able to incorporate it into my thesis but those are some initial thoughts, somewhat tongue-in-cheek."

We all giggled.

No kidding.

We'd all been on the dating sites recently, some more recently than others, and we were all very familiar with this story. I was looking forward to seeing how Amy would work all these crazy experiences into her thesis.

11
busted cheater boyfriend

AMY LOOKED EXHAUSTED as she excused herself and headed home. Ronnie launched into a rehash of the Tara online dating stories and then landed squarely on the Mark finale, "You know what I would've done if I were Amy, and I caught my boyfriend online?"

Buckle up ladies, this is going to be entertaining AF.

Anne laughed, "I can only imagine, Ronnie. Let's hear it!"

"I would've catfished that fucker all the way, dragging it out for weeks. As he's begging for it, I'd arrange a meet at a hotel. But with a twist. TreatYou-Right1975 aka Mr. Stud would meet me there first and we'd play out the fantasy he described as my freaking pussy is soaked just thinking about it. Then, Mark aka Fuckstick would arrive just after me and Mr. Stud finished round one. I'd have Mr. Stud go in the bathroom when Fuckstick arrived. I'd answer the door in my sexiest lingerie and tell him to sit the fuck down. It's my show. Handcuff him to the dresser. No talking. No touching. Himself or me. Make him think that it's some kind of kinky thing that I've arranged for him and me, his loving girlfriend. Keep him in the dark. Then I'd bring Mr. Stud out and fuck the living daylights out of him, do some super kinky stuff, have him slam me against the wall, fuck my ass and pussy, and cum all over his cock. Then I'd casually get up, walk over to Fuckstick and whisper in his ear, "You're dismissed. Out. And by the way, we're done you piece of shit." Then

I'd walk him to the door, lock it behind him and then go back to ravaging Mr. Stud."

Laughing and then frowning, as I thought more about it, "You wouldn't!? That would be some kind of punishment., him knowing he's been busted and not sure what the hell is going on. Watching his girlfriend fuck some dude and all he can do is sit there and watch or ask for the handcuffs to be unlocked so he can leave."

Anne was laughing, "Yeah, unless he's into watching."

A lightbulb went off in my head, "Oh yeah, I hadn't thought of that. Hmm . . . Wait, isn't forcing him to watch considered abusive, or even against the law, forcing him to watch against his will? That's not consent."

Ronnie was nodding, "Yeah, I wouldn't really do it, but the thought is awesome. And, whether he likes it or not doesn't really matter. He got busted in the best way possible. Perfect."

I nodded, "Yup, fair enough. That would be some sweet revenge. If I were in that situation, I'd handle it a little differently, I think. Busting him in person would be necessary for me. Asshole! I'd want to see Fuckstick's face as I busted him. I'd keep talking to him and push for a quick meeting. Dragging it out would kill me because I'd be too disgusted with him to face him, and it would be hard to hide that."

Knowing me better than I know myself some days, Anne laughed, "No, Daisy, you wouldn't. You'd call him on it the first chance you got."

Nodding and smiling, I continued, "I'd arrange to meet him in a pub or something, arrive early so I could get a good vantage point of the door, but a place where he couldn't see me as he walked in. My instructions would direct him to the table behind me, so he was looking beyond. As he walked by, I'd casually say hello. He'd stop, unsure, thinking it was a coincidence and maybe I'm meeting someone from work. His mind would be scrambling, he'd think he narrowly escaped, feeling badly for the woman in the next booth that he wouldn't be meeting today. I'd ask him to sit down. He'd sit across from me. I'd be pleasant for a minute, asking about his day and then I'd casually ask him who he's meeting. I'd want to see him to squirm. Watch him tell another lie. After he mumbles some bullshit about who he's meeting, I'd look steely-eyed at him and just say, "No." He'd look at me quizzically and I'd continue, "Tara isn't coming today." I'd watch the redness creep up from his collar and spread through his face, his mind spinning, trying to figure out his escape. There won't be one. I'd shake my head and say, "We're done, you cheating piece of shit." I wouldn't listen to a word he had to say, and I'd walk out."

"That sounds like a chapter out of my playbook, Daisy. You wouldn't be so cold, you'd ask for an explanation."

Nodding, I said, "Yup, you're so right, Anne. But I like the story."

We all laughed.

How much would that suck though? Finding your boyfriend on a dating site. Gross!

Ronnie brought the chatter back around to the fantasy dudes. "What about that BabyBlues4U guy? What I wouldn't do to have a couple hours with that man in a bedroom. Dominate the hell out of me. Swing me around by my hair and bend me over anything that stands still. Use that porn cock on me again and again until I beg for mercy. YES! YES! YES!"

Princess Pussy was pirouetting on my left shoulder, whistling catcalls. Bridget was cowering in the corner.

Nodding her head, Anne said, "Yes, BabyBlues4U, hell ya, pin me down by the wrists and take me on the bed. Kiss me hard and make me cum. Absolutely. Leave my hair out of it though."

Ronnie shot a sideways glance at Anne.

"What? Do you know how long it takes me to do my hair?"

I giggled, "We sure do!"

Gotta protect that hair! I thought, as my giggling slowly trailed off. Then, a new thought occurred to me.

"What if you just set it up so that BabyBlues4U is waiting in the dark hotel room for some sexy hair mopping and instead of you, Ronnie, it's Mark who heads there with instructions to leave the lights off and find you."

Ronnie had a hand over her mouth. Shoulders shaking.

Anne exclaimed, "And they find each other, in the dark."

"And we'd find out," said Ronnie between fingers still over her mouth, "who makes who into a mop."

12
making sense of it all

Brad

SATURDAY ARRIVED AT LAST. Counselling day. Finally, an opportunity to get some answers to my many questions. It'd only been six days since Carson had come out to me, but it felt like an eternity. I'd read until the cows came home trying to understand and educate myself. Daisy and I had discussed and researched together, but still, there were so many lingering questions.

It was raining cats and dogs. Carson and I were on our way to meet with Kyle for the first time. As we were driving, Carson muttered, "Uh, Dad. I'm nervous. There's only a handful of people that I've told. It feels pretty freaking weird to be going to talk to a stranger about something so personal."

I glanced at Carson and then quickly looked back at the wet, slippery road. "I know, buddy. We need some expert and qualified support and Kyle comes highly recommended. He'll help us navigate through the muddy waters we have ahead." I could see Carson out of the corner of my eye. He was nodding, so I continued, "I mentioned your mom to him when we chatted briefly on Monday. I thought maybe he could help us put together a plan; a strategy on how you come out to her." I quickly added, "But only if you're comfortable with that, and with him."

Carson nodded and said, "Sounds good, Dad. I hope he has some good ideas. I'm seriously dreading that." A few more minutes of driving with classic rock playing on the radio until we arrived.

The six-story brick building loomed ahead through the gushing rain. We walked, heck, we ran, towards the building in a feeble attempt to avoid getting soaked. At the door, Carson rang the buzzer, Kyle buzzed us up straight away. As the elevator took us up to the fourth floor, I shook off my jacket.

Rounding the corner and entering the office, we caught our first glance of Kyle. He was a jolly looking fellow, complete with a pasta belly and a big welcoming smile, spreading from ear to ear, as we stepped off the elevator.

He had been married to Anne?

I was having a hard time visualizing the two of them together.

His large hand extended towards me and we shook heartily. "Pleasure to meet you, Brad, and you must be Carson. Great to meet you, son." Carson's hand was lost inside Kyle's bear of a grip, momentarily. "Come, my office is this way."

Once we were settled in his office, with Carson and I on one side of the large, rectangular table. Directly across from us, Kyle said, "Well first things first, thank you both for coming today. To begin each session, we'll introduce ourselves, mention something interesting about our day or week, and identify our pronouns. I'll go first so you get the gist of it. My name is Kyle and I've been looking forward to our chat all week. My pronouns are 'his' and 'him'. Would you like to go next, Carson?"

Carson nodded, "My name is Carson. I just told my dad, on Sunday, that I'm a pansexual transboy. Going public with it scares the hell out of me, especially telling my mom. My pronouns are 'his' and 'him'." Carson shot a look at me the moment he swore and then quickly looked back at Kyle.

Kyle smiled, "Yes, I'm sure you're nervous. I'll help provide you with some tools to assist you with coming out to others. You're very brave, Carson. I'm proud of you and I feel honored that you've both reached out to me to help you with your journey. Brad, it's your turn now."

I introduced myself, "Yes, I'm Brad and I'm feeling quite confused and not quite sure how to support Carson. I guess that's why we're here."

Kyle said, "And your pronouns?"

"Oh right, uh, 'him' and 'his'," I mumbled.

This is going to take some getting used to.

Kyle very patiently and informatively answered every single one of Carson and my questions. It seemed like we had about eight billion of them. I, tentatively, and almost embarrassedly, asked, "Carson mentioned that this isn't a phase, but how do we know it isn't? How does he know?" I didn't want to be disrespectful toward Carson, but I also didn't want that elephant in the room to remain.

Kyle explained, "This isn't something that's the flavor of the month. It's very serious and isn't taken lightly. There are a lot of obstacles that one comes up against when coming out as being transgender. Society isn't all that accepting of people transitioning, although it's much better than it was a decade ago, thank goodness."

"I struggle with how a child comes to the conclusion that they are transgender. And how they get to the point of choosing that."

"It's not a choice, Brad. It just is. It's what feels right and is right and what is. I'll give you an example that might be a bit easier to understand. There are some similarities to when someone who's gay comes out, speaking from experience. A number of folks asked me about how I chose to be gay. I didn't choose it; it's how I was built. Do you think anyone would actively CHOOSE to be gay in the current state of our society? There are societal obstacles and hurdles to being gay, and even more to being transgender. Our society is set up and, for the most part, assumes that everyone is straight and cisgender."

Cisgender? What in the fuck is that?

I must've had a weird look on my face, Kyle knew right away that I had no clue what cisgender meant. "Cisgender relates to a person whose gender identity corresponds with the sex the person had, or was identified as having, at birth. Whereas transgender relates to a person whose gender identity differs from the sex the person had, or was identified as having, at birth."

I nodded, "Ok, so . . . I'm cisgender. I've never heard that word before."

Kyle nodded.

Duh!

The hour flew by with Kyle responding to all our questions. We rebooked for the following weeks. Kyle suggested regularly scheduled counselling sessions: some with Carson only, some with us together, but most would be a hybrid to start.

On the drive home, I asked Carson how he felt about Kyle and the counselling session. Carson said that it felt like a perfect fit. I heartily agreed. It was clear to me now how Kyle and Anne had been together. Great guy!

Daisy

That evening, Brad and I were in Fish Creek, walking hand-in-hand, enjoying the beautiful and peaceful evening. We were chatting about the counselling session. Brad was explaining how everything went with Kyle, how impressed he was by Kyle's sensitive yet straight on approach with both he and Carson, and how favorably Carson responded to Kyle. I was intrigued hearing the explanations that Kyle had provided.

It was the first that I'd heard the term "cisgender" as well.

"Isn't it interesting that there's a name for us but that we didn't have a clue?"

Brad nodded and continued, "Kyle really is an incredible person. The difference he is making for both Carson and me, well, for all of us really, it's over the top!"

I nodded, "Yeah, he's amazing. Him and Anne were such an incredible couple."

As we continued to walk, our conversation wandered, and Brad suggested that we organize a trip out to his cabin soon.

"That's a great idea! Work has been pretty busy for us both lately, not to mention everything that Carson's going through. I think we would all appreciate a week at your cabin."

As we continued our wander by the river, a strange thought jumped into my head. "Have you ever thought about those 'Baby on Board' signs that so many people have in the backs of their vehicles?"

Brad looked at me. I'm sure he was wondering where in the hell I was going with this, and to be fair, you never really can tell, the way my mind works.

A spiderweb of random and complex thoughts and ideas! Ha!

Brad, his head cocked slightly, "Uh, no, I've never really thought about them."

"What do you think the purpose of them is? I mean, when I'm screeching to a halt, trying to avoid an accident, am I supposed to see the 'Baby On Board' sign and make an extra special effort to miss hitting that car? 'Oh, avoid that one, there's a baby on board.' Ha-ha! If I could miss hitting any car, I'd choose to miss them all! I don't want to end up in any kind of car accident."

"Or maybe it's the happy family announcing the arrival of a new baby. 'Yay, we have a baby and we're out taking our baby for a drive.'"

"Ohh, perhaps it's meant as a warning to all of us. 'We have a new baby. We are sleep deprived. Watch out for us, we might be a danger behind the wheel.' Or something like that."

Brad started laughing, "You know, that's one of the things I love about you, Daisy. Your mind! You come up with the most fascinating thoughts. I've never thought about that before, but now I'm wondering. I think maybe a combination of one and three might be true. I doubt anyone intentionally drives sleep deprived, but it happens with little ones."

He pulled me in close for a quick kiss and a pat on the bum, a love tap.

Mmm . . . don't ever let me go, baby.

13
ronnie's fab fun

ONE SUNNY SATURDAY AFTERNOON, Ronnie, Twila, and I were in Twila's backyard chatting about life and dating. Twila shared, "Recently, I've received a string of bizarre messages from strange places. When I checked, I noticed that my search area had been strangely expanded. Thank you very much online dating site. What's that all about? A change in algorithm?"

Ronnie confirmed, "Ya, I've experienced the same crap. It's like crazy has gone rabid overnight. I can't find one normal guy to talk to. Even the regular 'all-I-want-is-sex' dudes have gone loopy or have disappeared like a rabbit in a magic hat. It's like something's in the water for crying out loud." Twila shared some of her more bizarre dating tales including the recent onslaught of scammers and just plain strange people she'd come across.

Laughing, Ronnie asked, "Do you want to hear about my crazy adventure last night?"

Ronnie always has the most interesting dating stories and they're typically pretty graphic as she's currently in a "hey let's fuck" phase. Ha-ha, it's been a pretty long phase.

"Shoot, sexy girl!" exclaimed Twila.

Ronnie didn't need any more encouragement than that. "I met this super-hot guy at the grocery store, his name is Marc. He's hefty, just how I like my men, with a little meat on their bones and bounce-ability for extra fun. Mmm . . . yummy." She licked her lips.

Crinkling my nose a bit, I thought, *not my type, but there's a lid for every pot.*

Still licking her lips, Ronnie continued, "Anyway, he invited me over for supper. He made a mean rack of ribs on the BBQ. That boy can cook! By the time we finished clearing the dishes and loading the dishwasher, I was chomping at the bit, horny and wanting him. He hadn't even kissed me yet."

WTF? She didn't jump him when she walked in the door? Was she sick?

"You know me, I threw myself at him as soon as I heard that dishwasher hum. We started making out big time. Hands exploring everywhere. He was kissing me hard. Suddenly he broke away, wheezing he said, 'I need a break. Need to breathe.' Ok big boy. I'll wait. His kissing was a bit sloppy and all over the place, kind of like what I imagine kissing a fish would be like." *Eek!* "But I was undeterred. There was something about this guy that I wanted to explore."

"Once he recovered, I tried to coach him a bit. I gently, yet firmly, guided his lips and tongue while we kissed. After a bit of tongue wrestling and once I had his tongue in the sleeper hold, he finally relented, ha, there much better! I thought, 'Hooray, he's coachable.' As I leaned toward him for another kiss, I felt how hard he was beneath his pants."

"He felt my hand brush against him, and he gloated while he shoved it all in my direction, 'That's all for you baby.'"

"I smiled, and said, 'Oh, I want all of it, take me to your room and show me big boy.' I didn't have to ask him twice."

"He led me to his room. 'Give me a little strip tease, babe.' While he took his clothes off, I gave him a strip tease, of course. I flirtatiously flung my bra at him while he was slipping off his shorts. Wiggling my ass in his direction, I then turned around and grasped my boobs with my hands, simulating where I wanted his hands to go, tweaking my nipples to make them erect."

She's not missing a single detail. I love that we can be so open with each other and talk about this. Princess Pussy is tuned in to every detail. Bridge is reading a book.

Ronnie continued, unaware of the thoughts running through my head, "He said, 'Ooh, you have awesome tits.' Starting to masturbate, his eyes were glued to my breasts. Things were heating up alright."

"Then I looked down, he'd left his bloody socks on. So hot!" She rolled her eyes. We all laughed, a little.

Been there, experienced that.

"Then he said, 'Bring those jugs over here, I'm gonna milk you dry.'"

Jugs? Milk her dry, eh? Is she a cow? Moo! "Come milk me big boy, my udders are getting heavy and full. Time for a good milking." *WTF? Talk about turn off. Not even dirty, just plain weird, creepy maybe. Even Princess scrunched her nose at that. Bridget pretended she didn't hear.*

"I shook my head and laughed. He was a goofball. For as weird as it sounds, it was very hot in the moment. Once he was done 'milking me', whatever the hell that is, he laid on his back and asked me to ride him."

"'Sure thing, boss,' I complied. As I was bouncing and sliding up and down on him, he started flopping my breasts up and down like they were silly putty. Odd! Next, he started flicking my nipples, but in a weird way. I thought to myself, *Dude is this your first time?* It was a complete turn off for me. I asked him to kiss or suck my nipples but not randomly flick them like they were the pink end of an eraser that had pissed him off somehow."

"He took my nipple in his mouth and started to nibble, which I thought was a bit hot as he sucked, and then he started to bite and twist. 'Ouch!', I said, 'I'm not a big fan of pain during sex.' The biting, pinching scene was not my thing, at all. Then he flipped me over and started biting the inside of my thighs. He chomped down on my right thigh." Ronnie's eyes were round like saucers while she was explaining the scene.

What the fuck? I mean I've heard of nipple pinching and clamps before, but biting the inside of thighs and biting and twisting nipples? What kind of sideways shit is this guy into?

Ronnie shook her head and continued, "I jumped and yelled, 'Ouch!' There was blood running down my thigh for fuck sakes! He was evidently surprised by my reaction, 'Oh, you don't like that?'"

"Blood running down my leg? Uh, nope. I looked at him like he had two heads, and said, 'Nope, not one bit. A touch of pain mixed in with the pleasure only, please.'"

"He said, 'Oh, sorry, do you want me to stop?'"

"Yes, Marc, I want you to bloody well stop biting me until I bleed, that's a total turn off, but I would like you to continue fucking me.'"

I laughed to myself. Ronnie was bound and determined to enjoy a good fuck with this guy. A little pain was easily forgotten and focus quickly returned to the subject at hand . . . sex.

"He nodded and said he'd kill the biting and then slid back into me but this time he was on top. If I thought the biting was a turn off, you won't guess what happened next. He started pounding away at me with his cock but rather than it turning me on, I was disgusted. He was drooling, sweating, wheezing, and squishing me to the point when I couldn't breathe. He labored on and I started to feel like I might actually cum in spite of the drooling and the rest of his lovely display. My pussy was wet in anticipation."

Ronnie had Princess's full attention now.

"Then his phone dinged. A text message. The fucker actually pulled out of me to reach across the bed to read it."

Is nothing sacred these days?

"He went soft. As he read and started typing his response, I saw the name on the phone 'Hot Swim Chick – Decent Bang'. Great, I wonder what my tag line is. He clumsily typed with his fat, sausage fingers, 'Can't wait to fuck you on Friday! Just banging one out now.' I was stunned. After he put his phone back on the nightstand, he rolled back over on top of me, folded his limp cock, and shoved it inside me. Not sure if you've ever experienced the folded cock shove, but a hard pass on that from me."

What the hell?!!

"Believe me, there's nothing remotely hot or enjoyable about that sensation. He may as well have been shoving his elbow up my pussy. Rock on dude, rock on. He grew hard inside me, but it was too late. Any moistness dried instantly. Complete and utter disrespect."

"Scratching his ass, he prepared to pump again. Thrusting deeper inside me, as I was reeling, evaluating the situation, and seriously leaning toward aborting the mission. As he thrust inside me for the third time, he let out a gigantic wet fart. Holy fuck, it was actually wet. I felt a giant squirt of it slosh onto my leg. He launched wet shit all over my calf! I was so grossed out, I heaved."

What the fuck?

"He shit on you?!"

Twila and I were staring at Ronnie, clearly mortified.

"I was in shock. That fucker dumped a big blob of shit on my leg."

What in the ever-living fuck?

Ronnie was still talking, "I was so unbelievably grossed out that I burst out laughing. Enough! I shoved him off me and as he was rolling over, I said,

'Yeah, I don't think this is going to work. I'm out. That was disgusting.' He stared at me blankly. Really dude?"

"I wiped the turd off my leg with his sock, which had come off at some point in the commotion and tossed it on his sweaty belly as I left the room, still pulling my clothes on."

"As I walked out the door he wailed, 'Where are you going Ronnie? I'm not done yet."

You're more than done man. You drained your bowels on my friend, dude! Bridget and Princess were both gagging.

"I giggled a bit before I sternly called over my shoulder, 'Oh ya, you definitely are dude.' I was stifling uncontrollable laugher. I couldn't get out of there fast enough. I damn near tripped as I ran down the stairs and up the walkway. As I was closing my car door, I burst out laughing, like a rolling-on-the-floor-full-belly laugh. What in the actual fuck was that?"

I was giggling, "Holy shit, Ronnie. Pun intended! That's fucking disgusting. He was texting some chick and then shat on your leg? How the hell did he actually hit your leg? Never mind, I don't want to know. Ha-ha! What's wrong with people? And he seriously had no clue why you exited the scene? What a complete and utter clueless douche."

Ronnie was laughing hysterically, "Seriously, he had no idea. The absolute best part, and why I can say for certain he had no clue, is that he texted me later in the evening and asked when he could see me again. Try never, dude."

No shit! Ewwww!

She smiled deviously at me and said, "Guess what?" I laughed, I knew this story was far from being over. "Spill it, Chica."

Ronnie explained, "Once I finally gained an ounce of control and stopped laughing like a crazy hyena, I called one of my regular FWBs. I suggested we have a quick rendezvous in my car. He was in like slim. I picked him up and we went parking."

"Super-hot, just like the teenagers do!" grinned Twila.

"At least you saved the night!" I smiled.

"We popped into the backseat, he laid me on my back and licked me until I was nice and wet and then he slid inside me. We were kissing and he was pounding me something fierce, it was so good. Then he flipped me over and took me doggie style until we both cummed. Just what the doctor ordered. The memories of 'Shit Stain Henry', er, 'Shit Stain Marc', were long forgotten."

14
dead name

Brad

WHILE DAISY and her girlfriends were visiting, Carson and I had our second appointment with Kyle. After we'd gone through our introductory discussion, I dove into something I needed some help with, "Carson asked me not to use his birth name anymore. I'm trying hard to respect his wishes but I'm struggling with that, along with switching over pronouns."

Kyle nodded, "Yes, it'll be tough for a bit, but it's imperative that you don't use Carson's dead name again, ever."

Kari? That's his dead name? Oh.

"It's hard. We've been using that name and those pronouns with him for thirteen years. To switch, all of a sudden, is a big adjustment. The . . . uh . . . dead name comes so naturally. I know it's a habit I need to break but I'm struggling."

"I understand how difficult it is but try to understand it from Carson's perspective. It's extremely disrespectful and hurtful to Carson to use his dead name. It shouldn't be uttered and those who use it should be corrected immediately. Carson, jump in here if you would like to add anything."

Carson nodded, clearly satisfied with Kyle's explanation.

"I'm not trying to be obtuse, just trying to understand. Why is it so important NOT to use the . . . uh . . . dead name?"

"Carson's dead name is from a time when he was mistakenly thought to be female, which he's since come to understand is false. That name and the words 'she' and 'her' bring up all kinds of memories for him, and most are negative. It reminds him of a time when he wasn't living as his true gender, when things weren't right in the world for him and life felt false. Many of my clients will say they felt like they were living a lie."

I sat up straighter in my chair.

I nodded, ready to agree, but then stopped myself. Something wasn't right, I could feel it in my gut.

The breeze came up, cool on my face. I was high up on the slackline, feeling for my balance, but something was pushing me backwards. I could feel my arms pinwheel as I fought for balance, and I looked back, trying to place my front foot behind to keep from falling.

Something wasn't right. It was …

"Morbid," I said aloud, opening my eyes.

"What, Dad?" asked Carson, concerned.

Kyle leaned forward and asked, "What's morbid?"

I turned away from Kyle, towards Carson. My eyes were blurry for some reason. "The thought process, it's morbid. Do you really want to forget everything from before? Your life, who *you* were, who *we* were?"

I was sobbing, I hadn't cried that hard since I was a child. The cold air curled around me, and I flailed, losing my connection to the slackline.

"Does it have to be dead? Why dead? Why a dead name?" I said, my voice cracking. "Can't it be good, too, but the new name is better? Kari was a good name, a good name for a beautiful person. Your mom and I spent months carefully choosing a name for our beautiful girl."

I stopped. An epiphany. *Girl. But you don't identify as a girl. Shit.*

I started to nod, finally realizing, understanding a small piece on my own terms "Carson is your new name. It's better, but the old name wasn't the name of a bad person. Just a different person. A female person."

I stood up. I didn't remember standing. Transported back to the slackline, I was wheeling, about to fall through infinite space. One of my feet came off the line.

I was about to fall … but a hand reached out and took mine.

I opened my eyes again. *When had they closed?*

Carson had my hand. Kyle was up out of his seat, eyes wide.

"It's okay, Daddy," Carson said. "It's okay."

"I'm so sorry, son," I cried.

"Why? What are you sorry for?" Carson's voice, scared, but his hand held mine, and I now had his.

I steadied on the line.

Took a deep breath.

"I'm sorry there is so much pain, son," I said, finding myself, finding the father in me, matching my concern with what was needed, my own pain with what needed to be done.

"You are Carson," I said firmly, "I will continue to try my very best. Know that if I mess up and call you the wrong name or use the wrong pronoun, I'm not doing it to hurt you, it's an honest mistake."

Carson nodded, "Yeah Dad, I know. I appreciate it. Just try your best. That's all I ask."

I smiled at him, remaining strong, through eyes full of tears. "And I'm starting to understand how painful all of this must be."

I turned to Kyle, "There is a danger of morbidity and negativity in this mindset. You must know that. I'm not calling 'Kari' a dead name, but I'll stop using it."

I turned back to Carson. "You *were* Kari. A beautiful soul. You *are* Carson. A beautiful soul. Whatever you need from me, you'll have, but no memory of you will ever die. Not in my heart. They're all beautiful to me."

And I squeezed the hand that had saved me.

No one said anything.

Did a minute pass?

Kyle sat down. "That was beautiful," he said. "How do you feel about it, Carson?"

My son shook his head ruefully. "I think my dad is trying to translate this into something he can understand positively." He paused for a moment. "It's fine."

"Okay, said Kyle. "Listen, Brad, I need to speak to Carson one on one about some other aspects of this."

"Oh, sure thing, of course," I pushed back my chair and headed for the bright and cheerful waiting lounge.

I have a lot of learning to do.

I knew that tightrope wasn't going away anytime soon. For either of us. All of us would be up there. I shook my head, wondering if the politically correct words used, like 'dead names', would later be found to be harmful. Or perhaps upheld. Perhaps I was wrong or thinking too much of myself and not enough about my son.

What do I know anyway? Maybe it's personal? Different for everyone? So many ways to think about this stuff.

It was obvious that I had a lot more to learn more about all this, but it was more than that, it was opportunity to learn more about myself and how I reacted to it.

I kinda lost my shit in there.

A new thought hit me.

If this is so hard for me—never mind Carson, who it's so much harder for—what will others be like? I love him and know him.

I'll not only be supporting Carson but also advocating for him. We'll need to help educate our family and friends, so they understand and teach them how to support Carson as well. Thank my lucky stars I have Daisy and that she's so supportive of Carson. What a gem that woman is. I'm so lucky I found her. I can't believe how badly I screwed things up the first time. I can't believe she gave me a second chance.

I texted Daisy as soon as I was seated in the waiting room.

Hi sweetie, the counselling session is going great. My head is swimming. I'm learning so much. It's a bit overwhelming. Kyle has been wonderful. Are you still coming over tonight or would you like us to come to you?

Daisy responded immediately,

I'm glad Kyle's been helpful and informative. Do you think Carson will feel like company? I'm sure this is a lot for him to digest.

I think so.

Either way, I have to bring Kris back over, so I'll bring the girls too. We just won't stay if Carson needs some time. The kids are in the midst of a water gun fight. Text me when you get home and we'll come over. I was thinking we could BBQ some burgers, what do you think?

That sounded like the perfect meal to me. "Yes, we can heat up some soup and noodles for lunch and then burgers for supper. Sounds great.

Daisy and I continued to text for twenty minutes before Kyle called me back in. Kyle explained that he and Carson had been discussing how to tell Carson's mom.

Bloody hell!

Kyle relayed the plan the two of them had come up with. "Carson would like to invite his mom over to your house and then he'd come out to her, explaining that he's a pansexual transboy. He's anticipating that she'll take it poorly."

That's an understatement. She's going to blow her top, pop a blood vessel in her forehead. I can imagine the blood gushing everywhere.

"He wants to have you there for support when he shares the news with her. It's clear that he needs to be in a safe place."

I nodded, "Yes, I think that's a good plan. He's right, I don't think she'll be accepting at all. We need to be prepared for that. I'm hoping I'm wrong, but I think that's unlikely. I'm happy to put that plan into action whenever Carson's ready."

"Thanks, Dad!"

Kyle nodded and smiled, "Great! Carson, if your mom has any questions when you come out to her, she's more than welcome to come for a session or give me a call. I'm happy to answer her questions and help her work through her concerns."

As we drove home, Carson hit me with another one from out of left field, "Hey Dad, can you order me some binders?"

"Don't we have some in the office?" Of course, my assumption was that he was talking about three-ring binders.

Carson stifled a laugh, "No, Dad. I mean binders."

Huh?

A look of confusion must've spread across my face. I looked over at Carson and shrugged my shoulders, "Uh, I'm not sure what you mean. We have lots of spare binders. Do you need a different size?"

Carson shot me a sidelong glance, "Chest binders."

What? What in the hell is a chest binder?

I kept my mouth shut for a minute and googled as I parked the car. *Oh.* "Yeah, we can do that, Carson. Is it safe?"

"It's not a great long-term solution but it helps a bit with gender dysphoria, or so I'm told. I've read some stuff about rib damage, or even broken ribs, and breathing issues if you wear it too long."

Clearly uncomfortable and concerned, I nodded, "Uh, broken ribs? That doesn't sound good. We should talk to the doctor about this, I think. If he clears it, then yes, we can order some."

Carson looked devastated, "I guess. I was hoping to get some within the week."

"Maybe we can text Kyle about it and order one for you to try in the meantime."

Carson brightened considerably, "That works. Thanks, Dad!"

Kyle confirmed for us that a number of his clients use chest binders regularly with reasonably effective results. He cautioned against wearing the binder 24/7 and suggested that we follow up with Carson's doctor.

15
open love

THE COFFEE WAS PERCOLATING as I carefully measured a shot of Bailey's into each go cup. Who am I kidding? I free poured. Ha! There's no such thing as too much Bailey's on a beautiful Saturday morning. *Is there? Nope.* Once our fun drinks were prepared, I strolled over to Anne's place to pick her up for a walk and Irish cream coffee. I was thoroughly enjoying the short jaunt, smiling, and feeling fantastic, excited to be alive. I had a noticeable skip in my step. You know those days? The ones where your outlook is nothing but positive, everything feels like it's going your way.

As I turned to walk up her front sidewalk, she came flying out of her house. She damn near knocked me over, coffee sloshing, with her embrace.

"Woah!" I laughed. "Great to see you, Anne." I said as I hugged her tightly with my free arm. We were both raring to dive into some much-needed girl chat, with the added benefit of stretching our legs.

Picking up where we left off weeks ago with our open relationship discussion, Anne jumped right into her latest news. "After we chatted about Freddie's request to have an open relationship, I decided that wasn't for me. I'm pretty sure you figured that out when we were talking about it. To be completely honest, I firmed up my decision while we were chatting."

"How'd Freddie take it? What happened?"

"Well, he said he understood and that he'd be fine with continuing as we were, a monogamous couple."

"Oh? I thought it was a requirement, a need for him?"

"Apparently not. He said he wanted to keep dating and he expressed how much he loves me. But I have to admit, I was thrown by the whole open relationship conversation. I don't understand how one minute he insisted that in order to be happy he needed an open relationship with me and then the next he just wants me. That I'm enough."

That you're enough? No shit! You're more than enough. What a fucked-up situation.

"Hmm . . . yeah, that seems a bit strange. A huge swing in needs and desires. But you ARE awesome."

Clearly more than "enough". Whatever the fuck that means.

"Maybe he finally realized how incredible you are. Not sure what took him so bloody long, but it sounds like he made a choice to just be with you."

"Perhaps. We kept dating, but it started to feel off to me. The open relationship discussion fundamentally changed our relationship for me. Doubt started to creep in, and I wondered whether he was pining for other women, wishing he were sleeping with them. I'd never worried or thought about him cheating on me before he dropped the open relationship bomb. But since, I'd been shaken, and I hated that feeling. I'm not a jealous person but my trust was blown. Nothing had happened physically, to my knowledge, but now I questioned things more deeply. And quite honestly, Daisy, my heart broke when he suggested an open relationship. I felt crushed."

"I'd feel exactly the same way. Heart-broken and downright destroyed. If Brad was bound and determined for us to have an open relationship, I'd be crying in my room for weeks, utterly devastated."

Anne nodded, "After a week or so, I couldn't handle it anymore. We went for a walk and chatted. During our conversation, it became clear to me that he still longed for an open relationship. So, I broke it off with him."

"Oh, Anne!" I reached over and gave her shoulders a squeeze. "How are you doing?"

"I'm ok, now. My heart still aches but I'm ok, I really am."

Is she trying to convince me? Or is she really doing fine? A different approach is required perhaps, "How'd he take it?"

"Extremely well, which in itself is a sign that we shouldn't be together. He didn't fight to be with me, to stay with me and keep our relationship alive, he just walked away. He may as well have shrugged, 'Oh well.' We're on different paths so it's all for the best. I'm remarkably fine. No regrets at all."

She sounds positive. "That must feel good. It does sound like you made the right decision."

"There's no doubt in my mind!"

"I'm proud of you, Anne!"

Anne gave me a huge hug and whispered in my ear, "I love you, Daisy. You're an incredible friend."

"Love you too, Anne! I'm always here for you, girlfriend!"

As we continued to walk and sip our coffees, I was reminded of some recurring thoughts I'd had over the past few months. It felt like it'd been eons since my gfs and I'd enjoyed a weekend girls trip away. We were overdue. "Hey, Anne, thoughts about heading to BC to do a girls' golf trip, soon?"

"Absolutely! I'm completely in 100%! Radium Hot Springs? Golf during the day and enjoy the hot springs at night." We excitedly started making the arrangements.

My parents, sister, and Brad offered to look after the girls while we were away. I'm pretty sure my parents would've strung me up by my toes if I'd said no to their request for a special weekend with their granddaughters. Besides, Brad and I were still figuring out our go forward plan, and I wasn't quite ready to enter into that discussion with my parents. At least, not until a concrete plan was in place.

We reached out to Ronnie and Twila to see if they were interested in joining us. Both were eager for a girls' trip, and they happily jumped into our adventure with both feet.

Anne booked the hotel, golf for two of the days, and spa appointments for the third. Spas are rather foreign to me, so I poured over the pamphlet Anne circulated for a ludicrous amount of time, before booking a hot rock massage, a facial, and then extra time on a foot rub, my favorite. I was pumped for a wonderful weekend away with three of my best girlfriends.

I can't wait!

That night, I was feeling horny. Brad was at his parents' place for supper so we couldn't get together. I was missing him, longing for his touch.

As usual, Princess Pussy was primed and ready to go, "Hey Daisy, why don't you sext Brad?" Huh? Sexting? Oh, you mean what I did with that one guy years ago? Lot of good that did me. That was Mr. Stinky. And besides, he's the one who led that convo. I'd have no clue what to say.

Princess tapped her foot, shaking her head, "And? Brad's your boyfriend. I'm sure he'd love it. Take some sexy, flirty pictures, talk dirty to him, and then work the pictures into the convo." That feels weird. Is that sexy? Do couples do that? Bridget was shaking her head, "Nope. Not a thing." Princess was smiling, "Of course, they do."

Hmm . . . I need some advice and not from the two gals inside my head.

I asked Anne about sexting. She sided with Princess, "Yup, it's definitely a thing. Think of it this way, wouldn't you like it if Brad talked all sexy, dirty with you? Wouldn't that get your juices flowing?"

Hell ya it would!

So, I decided, fuck it, I'm gonna do it.

What to wear?

Anne suggested that I do some teasing and sexy shots, not too revealing, with my laciest lingerie. I dug through my drawers and found a sexy little outfit. I slipped into that "something less comfortable", then I maneuvered my camera around, trying to take sexy shots.

Holy hell, this is harder than I thought! What will Brad find sexy? Hmm . . . a nice picture of my lacy torso, accentuating the curve of my hip. Sure, that looks pretty good. Ok, after about 73 shots I'll have one that I like. Frig. The constant clicking was becoming monotonous.

A few more slightly more risqué shots, a little tease of my breasts and the shape of my ass underneath my black lingerie.

Hmm . . . I don't love those. Click. Click. Click. *Oh, ok, now I have three or four that I'm happy with. Let the sexting begin.*

Hey there hot stud. How's my stallion tonight? Ha-ha, that'll set him off kilter a bit! Get him in the mood.

Uh, hi, Daisy. I'm good. You?

I'm great, baby. I'm all hot and bothered. Wanting my sexy man.

Hey, I didn't say I was good at this!

I sent my first sexy picture. I waited for a couple minutes. No response.

How did you like my picture? Does it turn you on?

No response.

What the hell?

I sent another one with a note, Hey baby, I wish we were naked together right now.

Have you gotten into the wine?

That's it? He must see what I'm trying to do here. Or maybe not. What the fuck? Does he know how long it took me to get that picture just right?

No, I'm not drinking, I'm sexting you.

Oh.

Three or four minutes went by. Nothing further came from him. I felt tears welling up. I felt rejected. Humiliated really. I went out on a limb, out of my comfort zone to do something I thought would be super sexy and fun to do together. He was completely disinterested. I crawled into bed. Turned off my phone. Closed my eyes. I lay in my bed trying to sleep. Thoughts running through my head. Tears prickling.

Well, that sure backfired. I feel like we're on shaky ground now. Shit, why did I do that? Wait a minute, I did nothing wrong. Damn.

I turned my phone back on. There was a message from Brad. All it said was, good night, sweetie. As if I hadn't sexted at all. I felt crushed. Completely distanced from him. I debated what to write in response. I decided to simply send, Good night, Brad, and leave it at that.

The next morning, I woke up feeling cruddy. My heart plummeted as I remembered the exchange the day before. When I looked at my phone, there were three text messages and one missed call. All from Brad. My heart started to rise and feel hope. Maybe it was just a goofy misunderstanding.

The first was sent right after I said good night. Are you ok, Daisy?

Then came the 2:00 a.m. texts, Daisy, is everything ok? Your pictures are cool. Call me, please.

Cool? Well, I guess that's a hell of a lot better than no response. Fuck though. Would it kill you to say I look great, or sexy, or something more descriptive than "cool"?

Why am I reacting so strongly to this? My two shoulder buddies were taking it as hard as me. Bridget was sulking and picking at her fingernails, clearly hurt from the comments. Princess was pouting in the other corner. She too had felt his withdrawal. *Bridget looked over at Princess and said, "Do you think he'll disappear again? That's what happened last time he withdrew." Princess shook her head, "He sure the fuck better not be going down that path again. Your heart and my libido can't handle that shit again."*

I messaged Brad and got straight to the point, Hi. **How am I? Confused. Hurt. Scared. I think we should meet in person and talk today.**

Brad showed up at my door within the hour. His face was white. Mine was tear stained. Bridget had bent my ear and I'd spun out of control as she repetitively reminded me about the last time Brad had pulled away. And it scared the shit out of me. He grabbed my hand as we walked out my door and then pulled me in close for a giant bear hug. I let out a sob. A release. He didn't need to say anything. His actions spoke loudly to me. It had been a misalignment.

We walked for hours as I explained my disappointment in how the whole sexting thing had gone. "I was trying to do something fun for both of us. I thought you'd get a kick out of it, if nothing else. I thought my pictures would turn you on."

We stopped walking. Brad turned to face me, took my head in his hands, and planted a large smooch on my lips, "Oh, Daisy. Your pictures were amazing. You are so sexy."

"Why didn't you say that to me last night? Instead, I thought you were disinterested. I felt hurt and rejected. It took me for a spin. Brought me back to our first round of dating when you completely pulled away. I was scared the pattern was repeating, Brad."

"Oh, Daisy, yesterday was a brutal day for me. Sara has been a super bitch lately and I was struggling with that, and the weight of everything Carson has been going through. Damn tightrope was back. It was all too much. I just zoned out. Last night I couldn't handle anything, even my fabulous girlfriend sending me super-hot pictures. And I'm sorry about that sweetheart, I should've said something."

Brad hugged me close and told me he loved me and that he'd never leave me again, "I'm here Daisy, for you and your girls. And let's try sexting again. This time I won't be such a dufus."

I giggled as I brought my mouth to his again, kissing him deeply.

He's not going anywhere. He's here to stay. Bridget and Pussy were worried for nothing!

16
family cabin adventures

THE FOLLOWING WEEKEND, Brad and I surprised all of the kids with a trip to Canmore, a fun camping cabin adventure. Thursday night we told them to pack for an adventure that included hiking and sleeping bags. But it turns out, we weren't all that sneaky. They all guessed within a matter of minutes when we suggested what was required to be packed for our surprise trip.

Damn! They're getting too smart to be fooled by the likes of us!

Jess exclaimed, "Finally! Since you guys talked about your last trip in the winter, I've been looking forward to exploring the wilderness and seeing your cabin, Brad."

After the kids were done school on Friday, we beelined it straight to the cabin. The hour-long drive flew by as we excitedly chatted about our plans for the weekend. Upon arrival, we threw our gear in the cabin, enjoyed a quick snack, and headed out for a hike while the sun was still high in the sky. Brad led the way as we trudged through the meandering creek, sloshing in the mud and water. We walked up a path that brought us to the main trailhead for Grassy Lakes. We hiked up the path and around a corner we were in awe. The lake was gorgeous. Tourists surrounded the lake on the one side, snapping pictures to their hearts content. We could hear German being spoken, Australian accents, and a number of accents and languages that we couldn't quite place.

Are we ever lucky to be so close to this heavenly sight! We really are spoiled to live here.

Thinking back, I realized that Jess and Ang hadn't been on this path since they were around four years old. No wonder they were in such awe. Kris and Carson were old hat at this hiking trail and the scenery. They didn't even bat an eye at the beauty. We wandered back to the cabin and set up our giant cabin camping area, complete with sleeping bags and mats. Brad and I planned to sleep in his bed, of course.

After we'd gone to bed, I heard Kris stage-whisper to Jess, "Are you awake?"

Jess mumbled, "If I wasn't awake, I sure am now. Could you whisper any louder? I think the bears heard you!"

"Sorry, I'm excited. All of us camping in the cabin is cool."

"Me too. It's ok, buddy. Go to sleep so we can have a fun-filled day tomorrow."

Soon snoring was heard from Kris's sleeping bag. I snuggled into Brad as his arm draped around me. He whispered, "Are you awake, Daisy?" I nodded, knowing he couldn't see me but that he could feel my head moving.

"Do you think everyone's asleep?"

I nodded.

Brad whispered in my ear, "I'm having a hard time with what I'm supposed to do with all the old pictures of Carson. They look pretty girly, and Carson is uncomfortable with keeping them and especially having them on the walls. I've taken them down, but I don't quite know what to do with them."

My head was on Brad's chest and it was so quiet in the cabin, I could hear his heart beating. I squeezed Brad's hand and kissed him on the cheek as he continued, "I feel torn. I want to, change that, I need to respect Carson and I understand those pictures are a reminder of experiences and times that are bad memories for him. But, for me, those memories are all I have of him as a child, and I struggle with just erasing those memories. They happened. What do you think? I value your opinion, Daisy."

"Well," I said archly, "good choice. My opinion IS valuable." And I laughed before continuing, "Yes, I understand completely how that would be a struggle."

I did understand. Brad had told me a short version of the dead-name-is-morbid conversation at Kyle's office, but I'd gotten a much more colorful description of the whole thing from the girls. Carson's reaction to it had been complicated, part of him proud of his dad and part of him apprehensive—though, somehow, not about his dad.

Brad shifted to his side and flipped me with him. We were now spooning. I was little spoon, and he was big.

"Definitely take any of them down that you haven't already," I said carefully. "If it were me, I'd put them in a box and store them out of sight but keep the pictures. It's a delicate balance as you said, but you need to honor both you and Carson."

I could feel Brad nodding behind me, and as he spoke, I heard a slight snuffle as he started to cry. "You know, Daisy, I really feel like I've lost a daughter. There's not just a dead name, but a dead child or . . . no that's not right, not a dead child, thank God. But a loss, nonetheless. I don't know how to describe it. All my hopes and dreams for her have been obliterated, they're dead. Yes, she's been replaced by a son. Carson is the same person, but I still feel a loss."

Turning to face Brad, I took him in my arms, "Yes, it's a loss, and also a gain. Have you talked to Kyle about how you grieve the loss of your daughter and celebrate the birth of your oldest son?"

Brad hugged me back, hard, "I hadn't even thought about grief—just been affected by it. I'll talk more to Kyle about that. I'm caught between supporting Carson and the theory Kyle puts forward and some of my own feelings. You know, I've never wholly accepted anyone's advice without critical review before, and here I am in a situation so fragile that I'm afraid to be myself and do that—ask those questions, raise those objections—because I fear it might come out as unsupportive. So, I support and agree, and everything is fine. Until suddenly, I blow up in Kyle's office."

I shook my head, "No, Brad, your feelings are completely valid. I'm sure most parents of transgender children feel that same way. After speaking with Kyle, I think you should also talk to Carson about that. He needs to understand how you feel as well."

I didn't think it was possible, but Brad hugged me even tighter. "You're right, Daisy. You're so right. Man-oh-man, do I ever love you, sweetheart. You, my dear, are my rock. I don't know how I'd get through this without you."

"I love you too, Brad. Is it possible to be each other's rocks? 'Cuz that's exactly how I feel too—you're my homing beacon, sounding board, and you ground me, too."

Sweet dreams.

Late the next morning, Brad led the way as we hiked upstream deeper through the vibrant trees and into the mountains. Shortly after noon, we stopped for a picnic beside the stream we had slogged through yesterday, laughing at Kris' tales. I was relieved to finally be able to put the raft down, that I'd been packing, jeez I felt like a sherpa. Ha! Looking at the raft sitting there, I was reminded that we would need to blow it up before floating downstream. Our lunch consisted of wine for the adults and juice boxes for the kids, sandwiches, veggies, and fruit. We threw a couple lines into the stream to see if the fish were biting. After about 45 minutes we gave up, it was likely too late in the day.

After we gathered the remnants of our lunch and rolled up the picnic blanket, we stripped down to our swimsuits. Carson looked around cautiously and then down at his feet, as he kicked the dirt.

Oh shit, this must be so uncomfortable for him.

He left his shirt and shorts on but packed his shoes and socks in his backpack. Nudging Brad gently, I tilted my head towards Carson. Brad glanced over at his son and moved in his direction. Grabbing the air pump, I walked over to the raft, called over my girls and showed them how to work the pump. In no time, the started to take shape.

Carson

Swimming pools and water and swimsuits in general are not my friend these days. I feel plain awkward when people start putting their swimsuits on. I want to wear swim shorts with no top, like my dad and Kris. But I can't.

Damn breasts. I want to hack them off. They are foreign and unwanted.

My dad came over to talk with me. He, or more likely Ms. Amazingly

Perceptive Daisy, picked up my sense of discomfort. I nodded as my dad asked if I were ok.

I am, really.

"Yeah Dad, I'm ok, I've got it sorted." Dad patted me on the back and gave me a wink as he whispered, "I love you, buddy. You're awesome. So strong."

Back to me

Packing everything into waterproof and floatable bags, we were almost ready. Kris jumped in the raft with a paddle. Jess started giggling as Kris pretended he was paddling down wild rapids, bumping and jumping, and making all of the sound effects. Throwing all the gear into the raft, we were ready. Kris manned the raft and the rest of us floated beside it, enjoying the pull of the current, all the way back to the cabin. *Thank goodness we didn't encounter any of those rapids that Kris had imagined!* My mind drifted from a big project at work I knew I needed to tackle first thing on Monday, Carson's bravery and strength, and my sweet Brad.

I'm falling deeper in love with Brad and his two boys.

I also thought about my girls.

Life is great. The future is so bright for us all.

Driving home, the kids chattered incessantly about the amazing weekend we'd shared, reminiscing about their favorite experiences. As their chatter continued, Brad put his hand on mine, our fingers interlocking, he squeezed briefly, as I drove. Taking my eyes from the road for a brief moment, I quickly glanced at my beau, smiling and winking. With my eyes back on the road, I exhaled a satisfied breath, feeling fulfilled.

17
the big "t"

Brad

CARSON WAS ANTSY TODAY, he wants to move forward with testosterone injections, to look more like a man to both himself and the outside world. Deeper voice, broader shoulders, facial hair, more hair everywhere, maybe a boost in height, if he got access to testosterone early enough. He wanted the benefits of testosterone. And now.

"Kyle, how do I get on testosterone? I'd like to do that as soon as possible."

Kyle cocked his head slightly, "I'll refer you to a transgender-supportive doctor and clinic. Unfortunately, there are long waitlists for everything and anything transgender, but I think I can get you into a doctor in relative short order, while you're on the waitlist for the Metta Clinic. Most doctors won't prescribe testosterone to you at thirteen. Instead, they'll put you on hormone blockers until you're sixteen. There's no legal age requirement for testosterone to be prescribed but that seems to be the accepted and recommended practice."

"Why?" I asked.

"It's my understanding that the guidance circulated to doctors is based on a study that was done in...possibly Sweden...where the age of consent is sixteen. Unfortunately, it has no physiological or physical ties."

This was the first time I'd heard this, but Carson was very aware. "Let me get this straight: doctors, for the most part, won't put kids under sixteen on testosterone if they're transboys because of some study in another country where the factors were limited? I imagine the hormone blockers just stop puberty in its tracks. Assuming this is true, they're just going to put puberty on hold for the next three years until he reaches sixteen? That sounds wrong, maybe even dangerous to a growing boy. I don't understand the logic. Won't that cause damage to him relating to growth and hinder the transition to male gender?"

Kyle and Carson both nodded. Kyle spoke, "You're correct, it doesn't make a whole lot of sense but that's the current state-of-affairs in our fair province. We're trying to work through issues like this with the government through various avenues, including a group called Skipping Stone, but we're hitting a bit of a roadblock at the moment. There are very few doctors who will deviate from this guidance, but I'll find one of them for you, Carson, to see if we can't speed up the introduction of testosterone."

Carson nodded happily, "Great, thanks!"

Daisy

After Brad and Carson got home from meeting with Kyle, Brad said, "As you know Daisy, Kris has been asking, no, begging, to see the new Spider-Man ever since seeing the trailers. I asked him if he wanted the full experience with the seats that shake and move. He was a 'hard no' on that."

"Dad, he looked at you like you were nuts," Carson laughed.

Booming with laughter, Brad said, "I know! Like I had grown an alien head and a big freaky lizard tail."

Kris was nodding and smiling, "Yup, I don't want to get seasick while trying to watch Spider-Man! Gross!"

I shook my head and giggled. "Right on, buddy! You know, I think this is the first movie all of us have gone to together. Brad, did you have any issues finding six seats together?"

"None what-so-ever! We got our poop in a group far enough in advance that I was able to book the seats exactly where Mr. Kris wanted them."

"Excellent! We aren't right at the front, are we?"

Kris shook his head, "No way! I don't like staring up their nose holes and seeing their nose hair. Ick! What if there was snot?"

"Good call Kris! That would take away from the movie for sure," Carson shivered with an "Ick!" and scrunched up nose.

Jess chimed in, "I think I'm almost as excited as Kris to see it. Mom, do you remember how much I enjoyed the Spider-Man TV series when I was a kid? I swear, I never missed an episode."

Nodding, I smiled, "I sure do! Angela was always trying to get you to watch Dora the Explorer and My Little Pony. And you were having nothing to do with those shows until Spider-Man was finished. That was really the only time the two of you fought."

Angela giggled, "Yeah, Spider-Man has stood the test of time though!"

For their fourteenth birthday, both my girls asked me to take them to the registry agency so they could take their learners test so they could start driving. They had been studying up a storm over the past 3-4 months, quizzing each other and competing on the practice tests. I mentioned that they're competitive, right? Ha-ha! They both grumbled about some of the questions on the online test but they both passed. In the car on the drive home they asked to take driver's training. I registered them right away, classes started the following week.

After a few weeks of lessons, Jess asked if she could drive with me. It was an eyeopener to say the least. Sitting in the passenger seat with no steering wheel and no brakes while your fourteen-year-old drives for the fifth or sixth time is rather disconcerting. Driving up our block, we kept inching closer and closer to the parked cars and I started to get concerned about the side mirrors. The last one I damn near thought we were going to crash into, "Uh, Jess, you're too far right, too close to the parked cars. Move slightly left." I forced the calmest voice I could muster in the situation. It didn't matter.

Jess exclaimed, "What? Left?" She wrenched the steering wheel to the left. We shot clear across the road, thank goodness there was a break in oncoming traffic, we accelerated up and over a bump, spun around, and landed on the shoulder, facing the wrong direction. Angela had been lifted up out of her seatbelt, which had failed, and was thrown across the car. Her nails then digging into the seat back trying to hang on.

FUCK! Looks like we're both alright.

I turned back to look at Angela.

We're all alright. Shit, I damn near forgot Angela snuck into the car with us at the last minute.

"Is everyone ok?"

"Physically," Jess said. Angela just sat there, staring.

There was then a silence that must've lasted a full minute, which is a very long time with me and my two daughters.

Abruptly, from zero to a hundred decibels, Jess screamed, "Mom! What happened?"

There was indecipherable mumbling from the back seat.

"Sweetie, you may have turned the steering wheel a touch too hard and too fast. It's ok though. We're all safe and sound. No harm, no foul."

"I don't want to drive ever again," Jess exclaimed.

Reaching over, I gave Jess a hug, "It's alright, sweetie. Don't give up. This is an opportunity to learn. An important lesson about the power of the vehicles we drive."

"I can't drive now, Mom."

I nodded, "Completely understood, sweetheart. Let's switch spots." As I turned to open my door, I glanced into the back seat. Angela's eyes were the size of saucers. She was looking back and forth between Jess and me, muttering, "We could've died. I saw my life flash in front of my eyes. I'm not ready to die. I'm too young to die. I haven't even been kissed."

"Yes, you have!" exclaimed Jess.

"I haven't been kissed twice."

"Angela, we're all ok," I said, ignoring the kiss talk, for the moment. "There were no oncoming cars, nothing to hit, hun."

We are very lucky there weren't.

"Ang, Are you ok? Did you injure yourself?"

Angela spoke more clearly now, "Yeah, I'm ok, Mom."

"Ok, good. How'd you fly from the passenger side to the driver side?"

Did you not have your seatbelt on?

Angela held up the broken seatbelt. "The seatbelt. It broke!" She had half of it in one hand, the other half was still firmly attached to the seat. A complete and utter seatbelt fail.

Scary. WTF happened there?

Thank goodness Angela wasn't ejected from the car or got injured.

I made a mental note to contact the car company.

Not cool. At all.

The next morning over breakfast, Jess suggested, "Ang and I were talking, we think we need to get back out there. Now. Before we get too scared to go back out driving again. Can we go as soon as we clean up after breakfast? Maybe we can go grab a tea at Starbucks? I haven't been through a drive-thru with your car yet."

I nodded.

Good idea girls.

I'd been concerned they might be too scared to get behind the wheel again. I wanted them to be independent, self-confident, and strong girls, and eventually women. I didn't want them to have to be dependent on others, or on public transportation, to get around. I let out a giant exhale internally.

I nodded, "Sure thing girls. I'm proud of you. We don't have much on the go today. And I sure could use a chai tea latte."

My girls took turns driving. Naturally, they were cautious to begin with, but the further we drove, the more confident they became. *Phew!* No more loose steering wheel action or jerky or clunky movements. They had learned a lesson from our near collision. While there hadn't been any cars coming, there were so many unforgiving and unmovable objects to avoid.

18

girls trip unwanted visitor

FINALLY, our girls weekend arrived. In reality, it'd only been two weeks since we booked it, but time had a funny way of behaving these days. On one hand the time had flown, I'd been busy with work, life, my girls, and Brad, and on the other, it'd seemed to take forever.

It took some delicate arranging, and a few choice words grumbled under my breath, to fit four sets of clubs and luggage into the back of my vehicle. I must've reloaded the damn thing at least half a dozen times. But in the end, we rocked it! Loading ourselves into my new SUV, the Mustang wasn't built for a party of four, never mind six, so I'd sold it. We began our trek through the Rocky Mountains. All of us chatting a mile a minute as we travelled along, listening to classic '80s pop: Madonna, Cyndi Lauper, Michael Jackson, The Police, you get the idea. Great driving tunes to bop and sing to!

It's like a freaking '80s karaoke bar. I'm in heaven.

Each of us knew every single lyric to these songs from our youth.

How is it that I can remember every single bloody word from a song I haven't heard since I was ten years old, but I can't recall what I went downstairs for?

The scene brought me back to my childhood, roller-skating in my friend's cement floor garage belting out tunes, telling stories, and pretending that Sting was our boyfriend. I smiled at the thought of it. *Good memories.*

Our karaoke session was just ending as we pulled up to the hotel and all piled out, lugging our bags up to our fancy, shmancy suite. Anne was the vacation booking queen, so it came as no surprise that she'd picked out a spectacular hotel and suite, with three bedrooms and bathrooms. I thought I might get lost in one of the bathrooms, never to be heard from again. It had a fancy steam shower and a humungous soaker tub, amazing!

Ok ladies, you can go. I'll just hang out in the tub all weekend!

The towering Rocky Mountains filled the picture-perfect view from our room. Throwing our bags in our respective bedrooms, we quickly freshened up and headed down to the pub. Well, Ronnie and I did. Anne and Twila were busy primping, curling, fluffing, make-upping, and doing who knows what else. Ronnie and I grabbed a table and ordered drinks. Ronnie grabbed a paralyzer (Danger, Will Robinson! Danger!) and I ordered a beer, my favorite, Kokanee.

We're in BC after all!

Ronnie and I don't get one-on-one time all that often, so it was great to connect deeper with her. Her crazy sex stories were legendary but today was something a bit different. "What's the latest with your adventures, Ronnie?"

"My regular boys are still on speed dial, for when I'm in the mood, of course. But recently I stumbled onto an intriguing new guy. Jamie does things to me that make me hit notes I've never hit before. To say he's talented in the sack is doing the man a disservice!"

Princess and Bridget were all ears. Ronnie and one man? Ooh!

"It's more than just sex for us, so that's new for me. We've been seeing each other for a month or so, although it feels like way longer than that. He's spoiled me rotten. I'm not used to that. At all! He's taken me out for numerous meals and refuses to let me pay, sends me flowers, and yesterday he booked a trip to Las Vegas for us in two weeks. Woohoo! The best thing is that he wants an open relationship."

Hmm, another open relationship. Interesting.

"Oh? What do you like about that?"

It isn't really difficult to imagine what Ronnie likes about that. Ha! That girl has sex on the brain 24-7!

"Well, you know I love sex and I don't want to be tied to just one guy. I like variety. It's awesome that he does too. It's not about ego. It's perfect for me. We totally agree."

"It doesn't bother you that he's sleeping with other women?"

"Not really. It's so new and we're starting to be really connected to each other. We're completely honest about everything. We check-in with each other before we sleep with others and make sure we're both safe and good with what's about to go down. Then after, we talk about it. So far, we fuck immediately after and reconnect. It's amazing as hell! Mind blowing really!"

"Wow! Sounds like it's right up your alley. No jealousy?"

I'd be jealous as fuck. Not to mention uncomfortable and just plain broken up. Not my thing.

"So far, it's been great. We both have longstanding FWBs that we aren't interested in dating, so that makes it easier as far as feelings are concerned. Even in the short amount of time, we've built trust because of the absolute honesty we've shared. It's pretty cool. We really seem to be the missing puzzle piece for one another."

"Wow! Ronnie, it sounds like it's a perfect solution for the two of you."

"It is for sure. We respect each other and we . . ." Ronnie stopped mid-sentence, turned around and looked behind her, where my gaze was firmly planted.

"What's up, Daisy? Who is that?"

Before I could respond, he turned around, fuck, it was exactly who I thought it was . . . JACK! And behind him, was an extremely irritated looking woman with long, stringy blonde hair, a tiny waist with curvy hips, and huge breasts, glaring at him. Trinity. The woman Jack had left me for.

Fuck! Where did I leave my damn invisibility cloak? That'd really come in handy about now. I quickly looked around. *Nowhere to hide. Damn it! Hmm, could I inconspicuously fit under the table?*

Jack looked at me.

Fuck!

He lit up, rushed across the room, swept me up in his arms, hugging me long and hard. "Hi Daisy! How are you? It's been so long."

Well, if she'd been glaring at him before, Trinity now sent a death laser into his soul. *Zap!* I couldn't really blame her with the way he was acting toward me.

This is so uncomfortable.

I hadn't seen him since he broke up with me and quite frankly, I wasn't interested in seeing him now. Never mind that Trinity had turned her evil glare on me.

Hey sweetheart, you can have him. Zero competition from me over here. He's all yours.

Jack and I had met in a dance class, and we'd fallen head-over-heels in love with one another. Three months into our relationship, Trinity, his ex-girlfriend, had informed him she was pregnant. After they broke up, they continued to sleep together occasionally. He'd slept with her the weekend before we met.

"Hi Jack. I'm good." I nodded toward Trinity, "I'm guessing that's your wife?"

Jack looked over toward Trinity, apparently he only just remembered she was there, and he beckoned her over. She sauntered, begrudgingly, over to the table, looking at me haughtily as Jack said, "Trinity, this is Daisy."

"Yeah, I figured, asshole," she snarled.

I swallowed my pride, smiled, ignoring the dripping hatred she had spewed, and said, "Hi Trinity, nice to meet you. This is my friend, Ronnie. Ronnie, meet Trinity and Jack."

"Hi Jack, Trinity," Ronnie smiled as she shook Jack's hand.

Trinity rolled her eyes.

Wow! How old are you? Twelve?

I leerily peeked over at Ronnie and saw her mouth at me "Jack? Oh fuck!" She knew how crushed I'd been when Jack broke up with me.

Trinity ignored Ronnie and me. Her eyes were squarely on her husband. "We're going upstairs NOW!" It wasn't a question or even a suggestion. It was a command. Get your ass upstairs!

Jack shook her off, "I'll be up in a bit."

Oh shit. Wrong answer, Jack! Quick, everyone, run for your lives! A death bomb is going to detonate, and her name is Trinity. It (she?) will annihilate us all in an apocalypse worth of revelations. Trinity is here. Duck for cover. Shelter people, shelter!

Throwing a retort over her shoulder, Trinity stormed off, "Fuck you, Jack."

Huh. That was it? I expected something more biblical.

Jack pretended like he hadn't heard her, and asked, "May I join you ladies for a drink? I can't stay long but I'd like to catch up with you, Daisy."

Holy hell man, are you dense?

I didn't offer him a seat. "Uh, are you sure you want to do that Jack? Your wife is mighty pissed."

Never mind the fact that I sure as fuck don't want to play nicey, nice catch up with you.

He lowered his voice speaking directly to me, "Yes, I'm sure. She's always mad at me. Daisy, it's been awful. I miss you terribly."

I stared at him. Not saying a word.

"I made a huge mistake. A horrible decision. And it's led to this."

A little late, Jack.

I exhaled deeply as I uttered, "Jack, you broke my heart and gave me no choice. I moved on long ago. I'm in a serious relationship with a wonderful man. We're happy. I think you should follow your wife."

But even if I were single, no thank you!

Ronnie gave my hand a little squeeze of encouragement and support, under the table. Jack was still standing there, staring at me, obviously yearning to sit down and catch up. I hadn't even asked about his kid, boy or girl, and quite frankly, I didn't care. I was fine with being polite, but I wasn't interested in being friends. I felt uncharacteristically cold toward him.

Noisily, Anne and Twila entered the pub and beelined it for our table. *Perfect timing!* I was so happy to see them, perhaps this would give Jack the push to leave.

At least there's nowhere for him to sit at our table now.

Jack ignored my approaching friends, and said, "Daisy, I love you."

"Sorry, Jack, but that ship sailed a long time ago. I wish you luck with your life." It took every bone in my body to be strong and dismiss him. But it had to be done. He made his bed when he made his choice. Onwards and upwards for me.

Anne and Twila got to our table just as Jack looked down at his feet and muttered, "Ok, I'm really sorry, Daisy." Focusing on my approaching friends for the first time, Jack said, "Hi Anne."

"It's been a while, Jack. Have a good night," smiled Anne.

She read the situation bang on. Man, I love my friends.

I nodded, "Goodbye, Jack." He stood there staring, like a lost puppy, a little boy. But he wasn't a boy, he was a man and he had to live with the choices he had made. Snapping out of his trance, he slunk out of the pub, tail between his legs.

Yikes! He's going to get one hell of an ass chewing from his wife tonight. Choices, dude, choices.

Even in my somewhat crumpled state, I was concerned about him.

Shit. Why do I care? Sometimes I think damn the empathy I feel for others. But that's part of what makes me, me. I loved him. I forgave him. But I wasn't gonna let him back inside to hurt me again.

Anne and Twila pulled out their chairs and sat down, both looking at me with concerned expressions. A single tear slid down my cheek. Anne put her arm around me and gave me a hug, "Damn, honey. Are you ok?"

I nodded, "Yeah, it was tough to see him and his wife together and unhappy. It's weird. I was right and I feel absolutely no satisfaction in it. The situation is sad, I feel for their child. I'm ok though."

"Trinity is here, Daisy? Oh, man!"

"Yeah! She shot daggers at both Jack and me. I tell ya, if looks could kill I'd be six feet under right now."

Anne shook her head, "What an absolute mess!"

"Definitely! But when I think of it, that mess had to get cleared away to make room for Brad. Everything that was meant to happen, did. I really do love Brad. We've been talking about moving in together, you know." I couldn't help but grin as I told my gfs about our plans.

My heart is full. I'm on the right path.

After I called my girls to wish them good night, I then called Brad and told him about my run in with Jack. "Oh, sweetie, I'm sorry. I bet that was tough. Close your eyes and imagine me there with you, wrapping my arms around you, holding you tight."

"Thanks, sweetie! You're the best. I need to close my eyes and sleep. We have a 7:00 a.m. tee time. I love you, Brad!"

"I love you too, Daisy. Sleep well, honey."

"You too!"

19
freaky dreams & golf

I DRIFTED into a deep sleep after Brad, and I said goodnight. I woke up at two a.m. with a start. I had woken from a strange dream, at a beach resort.

The sailboat was dipping up and down, along with each wave, while Anne, Ronnie, and I chatted and enjoyed the sun. Suddenly the outline of a man appeared. It was very light at first, became bolder and then poof . . . it was David. WTF? He took me in his arms and kissed me on the cheek, then his girlfriend appeared and embraced me as well. The sailboat faded out.

Floating in the pool on an air mattress, I maneuvered my way to the swim-up bar to order a piña colada. I popped off my mattress and almost immediately felt a man's arm encircle me. It felt all wrong. I swung my head around to see Jack. He pulled me in closer and tried to kiss me. I pulled away and said, "What do you think you're doing? I told you, I'm with Brad." He faded into the surroundings. I shrugged and accepted my fancy piña colada, served in a pineapple.

That was all I could remember. What an odd dream. Seeing Jack had definitely stirred up some stuff deep inside. Wondering what that dream was supposed to mean, I drifted into a fitful sleep.

On the beach, I was running for my life, trying to escape the wrath of a very angry lion. Muscles tensing and straining with each step, running as fast as I could manage, but slipping and sliding in the sand I wasn't making much progress. With every step, he was gaining on me. Then, the lion pounced. He knocked me hard to the ground, my face pounded deep into the sand as his paws weighed heavily on the middle of my back. Is this it? I felt his weight shift as his paw quickly and effortlessly flipped me over onto my back. I was done for. Spitting out sand and wiping it from my tear-stained face. The lion was circling me. Stalking me. He roared so loudly the ground shook. I squeezed my eyes tight, closed in fear. The lion roared again and pawed the sand. My eyes snapped open as I shook with fear.

I heard howls in the distance. Wolves. Suddenly, I felt a shift, a realization. The lion wasn't there to harm me, he was protecting me, keeping me safe. The wolves wanted to harm me. Staring at the lion, I saw a flicker, something weird in the air. Right before my eyes, the lion shifted into the shape of a man. My eyes were glued to this changing thing, this lion turned man. As the evolution continued, the man's features became clearer. It was Brad. He walked over, kneeled beside me, took my hand, pulled me to my feet and embraced me. He kissed me deeply, our souls connecting and becoming one for a fleeting moment . . .

Flashing back to the pool, I was basking in the sun next to Anne and Jen, alternating between napping and reading. A gentle snoring coming from Anne's chair, I giggled.

On the beach again, Brad's arms encircled me, he was staring intently into my eyes. I was wearing a blue flowery dress, the breeze tousling my hair, my dress flowing at the whim of the wind. I could feel myself melting into him. He kissed me sensually, hungrily. Suddenly, he knelt down on one knee. I was drowning in his gaze as he reached for my hand, kissed it, and said, "Daisy will . . ."

Beep ... beep ... beep ... beep.

Damn it. Fucking alarm. Mmm . . . yes Brad, I will. A million times, yes. Oh Brad, I love you so much. I sure hope this is foreshadowing.

Anne and I rolled out of our beds, I had a quick shower and threw my hair into a ponytail, put my hat on, and pulled my hair through the hole in the hat. I went downstairs and met Ronnie for breakie. A repeat of the night before, Anne and Twila were finishing their impossibly complex getting-ready-routine. I enjoyed a great spread of berries, yogurt and granola with coffee and orange juice, *yum*.

The morning was perfect, golfing and spending time with three of my best friends. I couldn't ask for anything more. Our laughter echoed through the course as we enjoyed our round of eighteen holes, making shots from crazy places, living in the beach (*pesky sand traps*), water balls (*they place water hazards at the darndest places*) and those amazing trick shots out of nowhere, off trees and down cart paths. We all had a great game, although Ronnie refused to keep score.

After golfing, we went to a local brewery where we enjoyed beer and lunch, experiencing some local flavors. We spent our afternoon on the patio chilling and chatting.

Ronnie updated us all with stories about her new boyfriend, Jamie. Anne was surprised, "You've found someone to settle down with Ronnie? Wow, that's incredible. I'm so happy for you."

Ronnie laughed, "It's only been a couple weeks. It's looking good but we aren't moving in together quite yet nor picking out china patterns," she snorted.

We all giggled at the thought. Ronnie has been so footloose and fancy free, it was great to hear she'd found someone she clicked with.

She cooed, "He's amazing. I never thought it'd happen to me, ladies but yes, I'm smitten. It feels pretty good. Between us girls, I'm feeling pretty vulnerable though. I haven't allowed myself to catch feelings for a guy in a long time. I don't love feeling vulnerable, but I think it's good for me. He's definitely worth the effort, I think. All the signs, and my gut, are pointing me in that direction anyway. And it's perfect because he wants an open relationship."

"That's so awesome Ronnie. And you're good with the open relationship?" queried Twila.

"Hell ya! I love it."

"Excellent. I'm glad you found what you want."

We had a late night, chatting about anything and everything. As a result, we had a slow start the next day. But we made it to the spa in time for our array of appointments by eleven. It was heavenly to relax and be pampered with no stressors in sight.

Bloody Jack and Trinity better not show up here. Can you imagine? Ugh!

When your foot is encased in bag of hot wax, you know that you are in fact, at a spa. Either that or you've had a rather unfortunate incident at a candle factory. *Yikes!* No, spa it was for us gals and man did my feet ever feel great.

That wax sure did the trick. My whole body felt amazing. Hot stones carefully laid on my back had a calming effect on me, just want I needed.

While we relaxed in the pools after our treatments, Twila was telling us that Marc had been acting strangely recently. "He went internal for a while. He seemed like a different guy, really moody, which is very out of character for him. I asked him about it several times and he wasn't forthcoming. Naturally, I kept reading into it and quite honestly, I was starting to take it personally. I thought something was wrong with us, that maybe I'd done something wrong. He denied that anything was wrong, until last Saturday when he finally opened up. His mom was diagnosed with breast cancer, his sister-in-law miscarried, and his doctor asked him to come back in because they found a lump in his testicle, all in the same week."

The three of us were clearly shocked. Twila continued, "Clearly, he was in overload. I wish he would've shared with me earlier."

"That's a whole lot to deal with, Twila, holy shit," commented Anne, "Is his mom ok? What about his lump?"

"It sounds like they caught his mom's breast cancer early, thank goodness. Her doctor has high hopes that she'll be just fine once she has a lumpectomy, then goes through a round of chemotherapy. Oh, and she's been prioritized for a lumpectomy, so that's good news. And the lump in his testicle was nothing, phew."

"Oh, thank goodness, on both counts. Hopefully all goes well with his mom's surgery," said Anne.

"It sounds like his mom should be just fine. Apparently, the lump is quite small."

"And his brother and sister-in-law, how are they doing?"

"Naturally, they are devastated, it'd taken them a long time to get pregnant, but it sounds like they're handling it well. As well as can be expected, I guess. His doctor did a biopsy, and it came back negative, just yesterday. Thank you to the heavens. Phew!"

The rest of the weekend was great. We played Texas Scramble on the last day while we golfed. This meant that we would move our balls to the best shot ball each time. It was a lot more fun for Ronnie, less pressure. We laughed a ton as we enjoyed the final hours of our girl's trip.

Brad texted me just before we left the resort, inviting Jessica, Angela, and I, over for supper, which I readily accepted. The winding drive home through the mountains was beautiful and luckily there were no major delays. As we got closer to home, my brain did a shift from the gal's weekend to family. The thought of seeing the girls, Brad, and his kids made me smile.

I dropped off my friends and their gear at their respective homes, threw my suitcase and clubs in my garage and went to Brad's. Jessica and Angela flew out the door, nearly bowling me over as I was came up the steps. Brad had offered to pick them up while I was driving back.

"Did you miss me? Great to see you," I smiled warmly as I embraced them both. They were talking a mile-a-minute about their weekend. As we moved inside, Carson and Kris came upstairs and joined the group hug. Finally, the kids stepped away and Brad swept me up in his arms and laid a big juicy kiss on my lips.

Mmmm, home sweet home.

20
telling my mom

Carson

WHILE KRIS and I were at our mom's place, I asked her to come into Dad's house when she dropped us off on Sunday. Ugh, of course she asked why. So, I told her Dad had something to talk to her about. Not true but I didn't want to get into it before I was ready. I needed Dad's support. Dad arranged for Jess and Angela to be there to distract Kris so my dad, mom, and I could talk in peace. The butterflies and knots in my stomach reminded me how nervous I was to tell my mom. I felt like I could throw up. It reminded me of that song, I used to listen to as a kid, by Fred Penner, "A peanut sitting on a railroad track, his heart was all a-flutter, a train came roaring down the track, toot-toot, peanut butter!" I felt like I was about to get steam rolled.

No point beating around the bush. Let's get this crap over with!

"Mom, it's actually me who wanted to talk to you today."

She looked irritated already, great. "Why didn't you just tell me this weekend?"

'Cuz I'm pretty sure you're gonna freak out.

I held my breath.

This is the moment I've been dreading. The moment of truth. How's she gonna take it? Fuckety fuck fuck!

"Mom, there's no easy way to break this news to you so I'll just say it. I'm transgender. I'm a transboy. And I'm pansexual."

"Hmph! Ya, I don't think so. No daughter of mine is hopping on the fucking trendy trans bandwagon. No Kari, it's not happening."

My face reddened. I could see my dad make a move to talk and I waved him off, "Mom, I'm not asking for your permission. It's not a trend. I'm a pansexual transboy and my name is Carson. I . . ."

"No, your name is Kari, and you are a girl. I will not support this bullshit, these shenanigans. I will NOT support the daughter that I birthed behaving like a trans-freak. What, are you bored? Craving attention? Is this the latest cool thing going around school? The flavor of the month?"

Her words took the breath from my lungs, squeezing it out in the most painful way possible. I was devastated, but not entirely surprised. It still hurt like hell. I sat there staring at her, not believing the sheer lack of understanding and the cruel words, words spoken by my own mother.

My dad was speaking but I only half heard what he said. Something like, "Sara, your accusations are horrendous, hurtful, and transphobic. And definitely not ok. DO NOT call our child names. If you can't be respectful, you can leave, NOW."

I looked at Dad, tears running down my face, and ran straight to my room where I knew Jess, Ang, and Kris would be waiting with open arms.

Brad

"You're just fine with this, Brad? That our daughter is choosing this . . . uh . . . ridiculous lifestyle? Parading around like a fool?!" exclaimed Sara.

I remembered the tightrope but this time, my balance was firm. I was strong for my boy. I had to be, Sara sure as hell wasn't.

Ignoring her slags, I addressed what I felt was the core of it. "Sara, yes, of course I'm supporting our child. He has a long and possibly treacherous road ahead. I'm here for him, whatever he needs. Oh, and to be clear, it's not a choice. This is him."

"SHE. Whatever SHE needs."

She doesn't get it.

"No, Sara, whatever HE needs. He's going by the name Carson now. Kari is his dead . . . er . . . old name. It's hurtful to Carson to use that name."

"Have you lost your mind, Brad? Dead name? Carson? Him? What the fuck? What kind of water are you guys drinking over here that's poisoning everyone's brains? Making them soft?"

I pushed on, "Carson is in counselling sessions to help him navigate the process and work through his thoughts and feelings. I've spoken with the counsellor as well. He's helped me to understand the terms and the process. You may want to reach out to Kyle."

"Pass. I'm not accepting this mumbo jumbo witchcraft crap. Kari, Kris, I'm leaving come and say goodbye."

Kris walked into the living room to say goodbye and give his mom a hug. He uttered, "It's Carson, Mom."

"No, Kris, it's Kari."

Kris shook his head, turned around and walked straight out of the living room, muttering to himself, "Oh, Mom."

"Kris, get back here!" Sara yelled.

As he was walking down the stairs, I heard Kris whisper, "Mom, you don't get it. Kari is gone."

Those words broke my heart. How could my little guy get it, but their mom was so obstinate that she couldn't even begin to see it from Carson's perspective. She had zero empathy, and seemed so overcome by her own cognitive dissonance that only the anger and frustration came out. I was disappointed in her, "Ok Sara, that's enough. It's time for you to go. Carson's not coming up. You've handled today horribly with him. I'm disappointed in your response and lack of support. I hope you can dive deeper and figure out if you want to have a relationship with your oldest child. Right now, it's not looking good."

Carson

I heard some muttering and then the front door slammed. My mother was gone. I exhaled.

Kris walked into the basement, shaking his head. He tilted his chin up to look into my eyes. I could see tears bubbling there. I hugged him hard, "Buddy, I'm the same person. My name and pronouns are just different now."

Kris wiped his eyes, "I know. I'm not happy with mommy. She's hurting you. I don't like that. She's rude."

"I know, buddy." I ruffled his hair, "I love you, Kris. And buddy, you don't have to worry about me. I'll be fine. I have some choices to make but I don't want you to feel like you need to do anything except just be you, ok buddy?"

Kris nodded.

'The disagreement I'm having with Mom isn't because of you. It's between her and me. Ok, buddy?"

Kris hugged me tight and buried his head in my chest, "Yes. And I love you too, Carson."

Dad's familiar footfalls echoed down the stairs, heading our way. He swept me up into a gigantic bear hug. "I'm so sorry, buddy. I'm extremely disappointed how your mom reacted."

I nodded, "Yeah, Dad, I heard."

Dad continued, "The rest of us are here for you, whatever you need." Jess, Angela and Kris morphed into the hug and said, "We're here for you, Carson. We love you."

"Dad, I don't want to go Mom's anymore."

My dad nodded, "I know, buddy. I'm not going to force you to go. It's your decision."

"Good! I can't stand to be around her."

"Understood. I'm sorry for how she acted today. I'm so disappointed in her. Hopefully she feels terribly about how she treated you and one day she'll come around."

"I'm not holding my breath. It went about as well as I thought it would. At least I told her."

"Yes, you did. And Carson, I'm so very proud of you, son. You've been so brave. And Kris, you've been my brave little guy too, backing up your brother and understanding what's happening. My two boys. I couldn't be more proud."

21
gals out yacking again

THE FOLLOWING THURSDAY NIGHT, I met my gals for drinks at Dixons, a long-standing local bar in Midnapore. It was a fun place to hang out, there were lobster cages, ropes, lanterns, miniature ships, funky underwater gear that looks like a Martian wore it to go scuba diving, lots of ship memorabilia there. I was a bit late arriving and as I sat down, I heard Twila giving us the latest about Marc. I gathered quickly that something bad had happened.

That damn meeting running overtime made me late and now I'm out of the loop.

"Sorry I'm late, ladies. Twila, what's happened?"

"Do you remember me telling you that Marc's sister-in-law miscarried a while back?"

I nodded, *hmm . . . where is this going?*

"It sounds like the problem is how Marc's brother's sperm interacts with his wife's eggs. That's why they've had so many miscarriages."

"Oh? I didn't know they could tell those kinds of things."

Twila shrugged, "Apparently, they can. The doctor gave them several options and one was to use different sperm or a different egg. They elected to use different sperm and they asked Marc to provide it."

"Oh, shit. That complicates things. Wow, that's a big ask. Talk about a whole bunch of layers and complications with invitro and extracting sperm from Marc, never mind how that affects your relationship."

Twila nodded, "Yeah, no kidding! How our relationship will be affected is what I'm struggling with."

"There's no 'should' in how you feel. YOU just feel it," suggested Ronnie, "no expectations, just your gut and your heart."

"The worst part is that they've decided not to do invitro. They want to do it the old-fashioned way, so Marc would have to sleep with his brother's wife."

"What?!" Anne exclaimed.

What in the ever-living fuck?! That's hugely messed up. Who does that?

Twila teared up, "Yeah, and Marc's family has been very clear that I have no say in it, that it doesn't affect me. In fact, his mom told him last night that she thought I was being selfish telling him my concerns. She said it's none of my business. It's family business."

"Holy Dinah!" Amy said, clearly bewildered. "What a cruel and hurtful thing to say. You're his girlfriend, of course you need to be a consideration for him when he's thinking about sleeping with another woman. Whether it's purely for procreation or not. I'm stunned."

"You and me both!" Twila shook her head.

"Family business?" I questioned. "What kind of fucked up family business is that? Sorry but that feels twisted to me and that they're minimizing the impacts on you and your relationship with Marc, that's just plain fucked up. If they were just using sperm and doing it by invitro, that would be a whole different thing, but sleeping with your brother's wife, that's some messed up stuff."

Twila nodded, "I'm glad you said that, Daisy. I was wondering if my normalcy meter was off. They made me feel like I was the one acting bizarrely. You're right, it IS fucked up. I'm super hurt by his family's comments, and his as well. I'm not sure we can recover from something like this when it's been made clear that my opinion and feelings mean nothing to him or his family."

"Aww, I'm so sorry Twila," Ronnie said bear-hugging Twila from behind.

Twila wiped a tear from her eye and said, "Can someone change the topic? I don't want to talk about this mess. I'll deal with it tomorrow but tonight, I wanna have some fun with you gals."

Anne picked up the gauntlet and made a huge shift, "It's a shame about Betty White's passing. Such a ground-breaking woman, an incredible comedian, absolutely amazing."

I nodded, "And just shy of her 100th birthday too. That would've been quite the celebration."

We discussed different scenes from our youth watching 'The Golden Girls' and more recently 'Hot in Cleveland'. Once our laughter subsided, we reminisced on her incredible personality and her "I could care less about fitting in your box" attitude, one that many of us strove to emulate but were not nearly as successful. I loved her "this is me and I don't give a hoot if you don't like me" confidence.

Amy expressed, "I love how she delivered empowering messages, especially for women, cloaked in humor. She really was a very smart lady."

Ronnie piped up, "It should come as no surprise to you that my favorite quote of hers is, 'Why do people say, Grow some balls? Balls are weak and sensitive. If you really wanna get tough, grow a vagina. Those things really take a pounding!' She's not wrong."

We burst out laughing again, and I said, "That really makes a person think. It's funny that someone who's weak or afraid is called a 'pussy', when pussies are tough and durable, not weak at all. A hell of a lot tougher than balls or a penis."

Ronnie chimed in, "Hell, ya!"

Ha! Telling someone to get sensitive and fragile isn't quite the message they're trying to send.

"The English language sure is funny sometimes," Anne added.

Amy said, "Another example of patriarchy in our society. Balls -male- are deemed tough and pussy -female- is deemed weak when the reality is quite the opposite."

"How do we change things like this? They're well-used sayings," Anne pondered.

"Certainly not by using and thereby perpetuating them. There are a lot of weird sayings that don't make a lot of sense. If someone uses a phrase like that, maybe explaining to them why it doesn't make sense and suggesting a better one is the only way to stop their use." Amy suggested.

"Or share the Betty White quote with them!" Ronnie laughed.

Yep, that'll get your point across!

I'd been thinking about the normalcy of sexting ever since the disastrous experience I had with Brad, so I curiously asked the gals, "What are your thoughts on sexting? Do you do it? Love it? Hate it?"

Curiosity killed the cat? My nine lives were long gone, if that was the case.

Ronnie slid her comments in first, "I love it. It's hot AF. Chatting all day long with your lover, getting all hot 'n bothered, working up your sexual energy all through the day. Fucking amazing! Then you meet them after work and BOOM hot and dirty sex. A huge release for both of you. Woohoo!"

"Yes, please! Don't give up," whispered Bridget. Princess said, "Get on it, Daisy!" Shush, you two, I'm trying to listen.

Anne was nodding, "Absolutely! I'm with Ronnie. I enjoy that build up throughout the day. Incredibly hot!"

Amy shrugged, "I haven't had the best luck with it. My ex wasn't into it at all. I tried sending him pictures and texting dirty with him and his response was, 'Don't you have better things to do? Shouldn't you be working right now?' I was trying to spice things up and he wanted nothing to do with it."

What the hell?! Dude!

Ronnie scrunched her nose, shaking her head, "I hope you dumped his ass shortly after that. What a jerk. You're trying to keep the fire alive, and he slams the door on your face. Ugh! Who needs that shit?!"

"Brad and I haven't done much of it, so I tried upping it a bit with pictures and more dirty talk. It was a disaster. I spent a solid hour snapping pictures of me in sexy poses, then sent one to him. Unfortunately, he was in his head that night, so I got a big fat nada for a response. Then in the middle of the night he texted saying my pictures were 'cool'. I'm not sure if I'm being sensitive about it but I felt a bit deflated, well, more than deflated, damn it, I was so hurt. I mean, I guess there's nothing wrong with 'cool', but does it really take that long to type something like, 'Oh, sweetie, you look incredible' or 'Ooh, sexy!' or 'Mmm . . . I want you!'? Honestly, is it really that hard?"

Amy muttered, "And guys wonder why we don't make the effort to do things like this. You try to make is special and sexy and you get a completely boring and benign response, and I get told to stop screwing around at work."

"It's worth the effort with the right guy," Anne mentioned.

"Yeah, I know Brad is the 'right guy' for me but that was sure weird, even if he did have a lot on his plate."

"But that's kinda the point. You went outta your way to send that to him, and he couldn't be bothered to engage with you. Deflating is right!" Ronnie expressed.

I had been looking for some go or no-go experiences and what worked for my friends. I certainly didn't want to dump on Brad, and this is where it seemed to be heading . . . so, I not-so-subtly, changed the subject.

"I have a funny story to tell you, something I was pondering. It's kind a goofy but anyway . . . the other day, I was sitting in our backyard reading and came across some literature on the praying mantis. Did you know that in roughly twenty-five percent of praying mantis sexual encounters, the female bites the male's head off and eats him? It got me to thinking and wondering why the praying mantis might engage in sexual cannibalism."

"Was it bad sex and she wanted to put him out of his misery?"

Amy commented, "That's a bit harsh." Anne's unmistakable laugh rang out and Ronnie snorted as I continued.

"Was the sex so great that she didn't want another woman to have him?"

Twila giggled, "Kill him so you don't have to share him? Hmm . . . but then you don't get to have him again either."

"Did he do something to piss her off, so she bit his head off and then ate him?"

"Ha! I can think of some dudes that I would've liked to bite their heads off after sex!" Ronnie exclaimed, "Some guys are just plain irritating and selfish. Me-me-me! Argh!"

"Is it a turn on for her, devouring him?"

More laughter from the gals.

Only slightly creepy.

"Either way, it's interesting. Scientists have done studies on this, if you can believe it. Apparently, the females who ate their lover produced more eggs and so increased their chances of reproductive success. Fascinating but definitely creepy. And yes, I'm sure there's no thought process for them as to why, but it's funny to think about."

"It sure is!" nodded Ronnie.

"That's super interesting about the egg production. I wonder why?" Amy said.

"I didn't read far enough to discover what they found out, but it's curious that's for sure."

22

coming out to friends and family

RELAXING on my deck sipping a beer after we'd enjoyed Brad's famous BBQ burgers, our kids were playing board games inside, Brad informed me, "On Saturday, Carson and I were chatting with Kyle about how to tell our friends and family about the journey that Carson has embarked on. The three of decided that I'd write an email, with Carson's help, and send it to our friends and family, then post it on Facebook after the email was sent Would you mind reading this for me?

> We have some family news that we'd like to share with you. My oldest child, and Kris's sibling, has recently shared with us that he identifies as male, rather than female. As such, we are no longer using the name Kari. He goes by Carson. We would appreciate if everyone could support Carson, and us, by using male pronouns (he/his/him) when addressing him and using the name Carson.
>
> I've learned through counselling that Kari is his dead name and I under-stand now how hurtful using that name and the pronouns she/her are to him. Of course, we understand that this is new to all of you and that it will take some getting used to. We appreciate your efforts in making the adjust-

ment. I can point you in the direction of some YouTube videos such as Trans101 and Trans Youth 101 that may help shed some light.

Carson is still the same person we all know and love. Aside from using the correct pronouns and name, please don't treat him any differently from how you would have before.

We love you all. If you have any questions, please let me (Brad) know.

Brad, Carson & Kris

"What do you think?"

I squeezed Brad's hand as I replied, "I think it's great. It ticks all the boxes. It's simple, succinctly gets the important content across, provides resources if they want to dive deeper, and tells them who to contact if they have questions. Perfect."

Brad smiled, "Great, I'll send it tonight."

"Please send it to me too. There are a few folks I'd like to circulate it to, as long as you and Carson are ok with it."

"Yes, I was planning to. That would be great. Carson wants shared to everyone we know."

The outpouring support we received from our friends and family was amazing. I wasn't quite sure what to expect, and it was very impressive. There were several we didn't hear from, and we weren't really sure what this meant but that number was far outweighed by the active supporters. The questions and discussion that the email, and the Facebook post generated, were incredible. Lots of very valid and respectful questions. Carson has decided to create a collage for his room with some of the comments of support we received:

"Thanks for sharing the news, we will support Carson (awesome name btw) and his choices in any way we can. We love you guys."

"I admire you deeply for recognizing Carson's authentic self and adapting to embrace him. I love you all so much and am always here - as a family member and an ally on your journey. Big hugs and lots of love to you!!"

"You are, and always will be, cherished members of our family. Our love and respect for you in this moment is pouring from our hearts. Carson is very lucky to have a dad like you and the support of Daisy will be over the top, I'm sure. Let us know if there's anything we can do to support you all. Love you!"

"Carson will of course have my full support, as will you. I'm sure there have been many challenges for all of you, and there will likely be more. In the end though, the comfort, peace, and happiness that Carson will have is all that matters."

"Thank you for challenging me to open my mind and heart and learn more about transgender issues. I'm here for you all."

As time went on, we were impressed by the efforts most people made to use the correct pronouns and name. It wasn't easy and took some concentration to make the switch, like it had been for us.

Brad would get so upset with himself when he slipped.

I hear Carson said to him one day, "Dad, I get it, you've been calling me the same name for thirteen years, it's only natural for you to slip every once in a while. Cut yourself some slack." Undoing what comes naturally from years of practice required a concerted and consistent effort. Old habits die hard. But it was well worth it, as we watched Carson blossom into a vibrant young man.

We corrected those who used the wrong pronoun or name. Most were apologetic and were thankful to learn how this affected Carson. Explaining gender dysphoria became a regular occurrence for us. We'd become educators, of a sort. Typically, the term gender dysphoria seemed foreign to folks. They'd never had a reason to hear it, never mind understand it. Educating people about transgender issues and terms felt really good. I liked helping folks see the world from Carson's perspective. I hoped I was doing him justice.

Chatting on the phone with Twila one night, she asked, "Can you explain gender dysphoria? I've heard you talk about it but I'm not sure I fully understand it."

"I'm no expert but simply put, gender dysphoria is experienced by Carson because inside he is a boy, to his very core; however, his body parts, both sexual and non-sexual are advertising to the entire world that he's a girl. Can you imagine that? Looking into the mirror and seeing breasts instead of a male chest, a feminine-looking face, instead of a more chiseled male angular face? The list goes on. I can't even imagine how much that could mess with a person's head."

"Oh wow, I hadn't thought of that. That must be so confusing and difficult to navigate. Poor guy. I can't even imagine how much something like that would mess with my brain, never mind a teenager's!"

"No kidding! We've learned a lot over the past few months. Carson has struggled with it for years, not being about to understand, never mind come up with the right words to express how he was feeling. Once he figured it out, he and his therapist could help us understand what he was feeling and why. The concept of gender dysphoria is not something I'd had to experience, or even think about either, as a cisgender person. I'm lucky. My insides and how I feel or identify, matches my outsides and my sexual parts. I feel like a woman and my bits and pieces reflect the same, easy."

"I'll say! Being a teenager is hard enough, never mind adding gender dysphoria to that."

"Yes, and that's why it's so important for us to respect Carson's request to call him 'Carson' and to use the pronouns 'him', 'his' and 'he'. By using them, it shows respect to Carson and validates his gender and what Carson he feels inside, thus we are supporting him. Using his old name, or what his counsellor calls his "dead name", hurts Carson, and reminds him of times where he was, in his words, 'living a lie'."

"I hadn't thought of that, thanks Daisy. So much to learn!"

I laughed, "Believe me, we've been learning a ton! Still lots more to figure out too." I love these discussions. Friends supporting us, and Carson. A beautiful thing.

On the flip side, several people, including Carson's mom, purposely refused to use the correct name and pronouns. As time went on, we corrected them more harshly and for some it got to the point where we started misgendering them to make a point. This usually, finally, got the point across as they weren't jazzed at the wrong pronoun being used for them.

Others, we distanced ourselves from. They were belligerent about it. We lost respect for them and began to question whether they were truly important to our lives. We could see the pain the misgendering was causing Carson, so Brad and I decided we didn't need them. If they ever decided to be respectful to Carson, then we'd be happy to let them back into our lives, but not until then.

Carson's mom was a tougher one, she was his mom after all. She refused to adapt, or even listen to Carson or his counsellor about how damaging misgendering is and refused to discuss, never mind respect, Carson's request. She had made her decision to completely ignore his requests and she chose to remain unconvinced that this wasn't just a phase, no matter how much we tried to educate her.

Carson felt unsupported and disrespected by her. He had zero interest in being around her. We could see how hurt Carson was by her flippant disregard and disrespect. It was crushing to watch. Brad tried speaking with her time and time again, but she was unmovable, she refused to look at the situation from Carson's perspective. Not surprisingly, Carson stayed strong in his conviction not to see her. That pissed her off.

23
lay me down in a bed of roses

WATCHING the snow fall from the view of Anne's hot tub, we were on round three of margaritas when Ronnie casually shared, "I had a super-hot dream the other night. I was lying on a bed, one of those big, round romantic honeymoon kind of beds, you know what I mean?"

We all nodded.

Like the one Austin Powers was spinning around and around on as he was hitting on uh . . . what's her name? Good grief. What is her name? I can see her in plain sight. Elizabeth Hurley's character . . . ah yes, Vanessa Kensington. I haven't seen that movie in a while, so funny. Focus, Daisy, focus.

"There were roses everywhere: encircling my body, spread across the bed, draped over me, on the floor."

A sea of roses.

"I was blindfolded and alone, but I wasn't afraid, more like excited with anticipation. After a while, I heard some movement. I had no idea who was there, or how many. And I was horny. My nipples were erect. My pussy wet. Without warning, there was a hand on my abdomen. I hadn't heard a thing. A mouth engulfed my right tit. Another mouth suckled on my left. More lips kissing my mouth. Teeth nibbling and lips kissing the inside of my thighs. And JACKPOT BABY a fifth, yes, a fifth mouth on my pussy, licking and sucking and making me moan."

Princess was salivating.

"Time was irrelevant. I heard a slap and they all switched spots, each one attacking my body with renewed enthusiasm at their new task. The one on my pussy gave me a good lick and then slid inside, humping and pumping me. In no time, I was showering his cock with a solid squirt. The slap again as he slid out of me. This time, I figured it out. The slap was them high fiving to indicate they should switch. My hands were restrained. I moved with glee, struggling against the restraints and enjoying the pleasure. With each struggle, I felt a prick into my skin and blood dripping. That subtle pain was making it even hotter. I was groaning and moaning. A high-level screech escaped my lips as the orgasms overlapped one another. I was in heaven."

Captain Obvious here, there were thorns on the damn roses. Princess Pussy said, "Who cares about the damn thorns, I've gotta grab my vibrator." Bridget giggled uncomfortably.

Ronnie continued, oblivious to the chatter in my head, "I couldn't see anything. Still blindfolded, men were ravaging my body for their pleasure. For my pleasure. Then as quickly as it began, it stopped. The restraints were gone. I removed the blindfold. It was dark. And I woke up. It was a very vivid dream. Now, to make it a reality."

"Wow, Ronnie, that was one wild dream! Talk about waking up horny!" Anne commented.

"I know. I want it for real. I think I can make it happen with Jamie."

Princess was drooling, her vibrator working away. Sending me dirty looks, she wanted in on that action, but she knew I was out. Bridget was shaking her head at Princess, "Dirty girl!" Princess just smiled knowingly, gloating, "Yes, I am."

"Want to hear something odd? I had a dream the other night that involved roses too. Not quite as, erm, steamy as yours. There were some similarities though. I was naked on a bed with rose petals surrounding me, my hands immobilized by something I couldn't see, and Brad was making love to me. It was a very short dream or at least that's all I could remember when I woke up. I remember feeling very turned on. In fact, I woke up Brad for a little morning sex."

Anne nodded and smiled, "That's awesome. Something even more bizarre. Not only did the two of you have rose petal dreams, but I also had a dream I was walking up the aisle at a wedding, throwing rose petals like a flower girl. Suddenly, I was the flower girl. Young, about seven years old, and no longer throwing rose petals but handing out long stem roses to the men and women sitting at the edges of the rows, handing the final one to the bride and groom. Then I was the bride, holding a bouquet of roses. After the reception, my new husband (no clue who he was) and I went to our heart shaped bed to consummate the marriage. There were roses on the floor leading to the bed and petals all over the bed. He made sweet love to me, rolling in the rose petals. Interesting, eh?"

"Ok, so what's with the rose dreams?" Ronnie asked.

"Ah . . . I figured it out. Book club. We finished discussing "Bed of Rose and Thorns" by Lee Hunt last week. Weird that we all dreamt about roses though. Clearly Rose must have made an impression on us."

"Oh wow, I can't believe that didn't occur to me," Ronnie shook her head, "of course!"

Anne served another round of margaritas as we switched topics, moving onto something more serious.

"Oh shit, ladies, I can't believe I haven't shared this yet today. I was so preoccupied by all the weird rose dream stuff. Carson met with a new doctor this week and she prescribed him testosterone! Can you believe it?!"

"Amazing! I remember you saying that he'd likely be stuck on those hormone blockers until he was sixteen, such great news!"

"It's incredible. It's felt like a long time coming. And then it happened so fast. We went in, she asked some questions about why he wanted to go on testosterone and warned us about the side effects, she then spoke with his psychologist and boom, wrote a prescription. Simple. It HAS been ridiculously painful getting to this point but, we made it. He's over the moon about it. We all are!"

"I'm excited for him! Wonderful news!" Ronnie said. "How long does it take for visible changes to occur?"

"Apparently, it sometimes only takes months to start seeing some big changes. It all depends on the dose and how quickly his body adapts. The only bummer is that we have to stab him with a needle weekly. Ugh!"

Ronnie looked like she was going to throw up, "You have to do that?"

"Well, Brad does. But he gets a bit squeamish around needles, so I have a feeling I'm going to be promoted to lead needle stabber. I'm sure that's the official title, right? Ha!"

Anne gave me a hug, mostly not spilling our drinks, and said, "I'm so happy for all of you. Such a huge step forward for Carson."

24

lead up to the big date

OUR RESPECTIVE FAMILIES had spent every weekend together for months now. The kids were truly bonding. My girls were continuing to flourish. Every second weekend Kris was whisked away to be with his mom, and we missed him. Carson was growing and learning and changing. We were figuring out better how to support him. He no longer saw his mom, she couldn't get beyond herself and her misguided beliefs to support him. I knew it hurt Carson that his mom had rejected him, but it was his choice not to see her. It broke my heart.

Unbeknownst to me, Brad had been arranging something special for the two of us. On Saturday morning, he called, "We're going out on the town tonight. Bring something special to wear when you come over today, I have a romantic evening planned for us." Apparently, our older kids had agreed to watch Kris.

We hung out at Brad's all day. Carson, Ang, and Jess were playing board games, reading and chatting, and Kris was hanging out with us in the backyard, playing soccer and enjoying the weather that the chinook had blown in overnight. Jess joined us for a walk to Fish Creek Park, while Ang and Carson decided to hang out on the deck. It was a beautiful winter day and we wanted to enjoy every moment of it. Who knew when the cold and snow would blow in again?

Jess and Kris had run ahead and were checking out some local wildlife, so I took the opportunity to dig. "Where are we going tonight, Brad? I'm dying to know."

"You don't want it to be a surprise?"

I laughed, "Yes and no. I'm excited to go out with you. It's been such a long time since we've had an actual date. I'm looking forward to some one-on-one time."

"I'll let you know where we're going when we're on our way. We should start getting ready pretty soon. We have reservations at six at . . . damn . . . I almost gave it away. We should leave around five-thirty."

"Sounds great, sweetie. It'll take me about thirty minutes to freshen up, so we still have a bit of time to keep wandering."

We continued through Fish Creek Provincial Park to the Bow River, walking hand-in-hand, pausing for a kiss every once in a while. As we neared the river, he pulled me off to the side, kissed me deeply, looked into my eyes and dove in.

"Daisy, I love you so much. I miss you when you go home. I want to spend every waking minute with you, and for that matter, ha, every sleeping minute as well. I want to join our families together and spend the rest of my life with you."

Energy shot through my body. I was instantly lit on fire, from my toes to the tips of my hair. *Is he proposing?*

Brad continued, "I know this is a lot to take in all at once, but we've discussed the idea a few times and I think we should go for it. What do you think about moving in together? Are you ready for that?"

Not a proposal, but the next logical step, shacking up together! *This feels sooo right.*

I looked deep into his eyes, my cheeks burning with the blush of love and excitement, "Yes, Brad. It's time. I'm excited! Best of all, I think our kids will be over the moon."

As we kissed, he tweaked my ass with his fingers and then grabbed it firmly. He moved his hands up my lower back. I felt electrified. "How should we make it happen?"

"I was thinking, with the four kids and us, we need five bedrooms. My place has two bedrooms upstairs and two down, and not much space to build a fifth. With your three bedrooms up and one in the basement and enough unused space in the basement, we could carve out another bedroom and build in a bathroom. Or another option would be to sell our places and buy a new place with five bedrooms. Any other ideas?"

"The idea of trying to sell two houses and coordinate that timing with buying a new one horrifies me, quite frankly. I'm leaning towards renovating my basement. How much do you think it would cost?"

Brad hemmed and hawed a bit, thinking before he spoke, "Well, I can do most of it myself so I don't think it should be too much. Under twenty thousand for sure."

I laughed, "Ok, so between thirty and forty thousand then?" These things never go as planned, often morphing into new projects as new wants and needs miraculously appear, and the total cost skyrockets.

Brad smiled, "Hopefully, we can keep it tight to twenty grand."

"Sweet! Let's do it!" I leaned into Brad, took his face in my hands, and laid a big, wet kiss on his lips.

As I was pulling away, he grinned, grabbed me by the belt loop and pulled me close, "You didn't think you were getting away that easily, did you?" He laid a suck-a-lemon-dry kind of kiss on me. I felt every single ounce of my body's energy move toward his lips. My knees went weak as I felt his hands pulling me ever closer, one on my back and the other on my right butt cheek. Everything around us faded, it was just him and me.

When he finally let me go, I felt a jolt back into my surroundings. Coming back from Utopia, I remembered I had this marvelous man all to myself tonight. I looked to the left and saw Jess standing with her hand on her hip trying to look stern, while shaking her head and tsk tsking. She'd been here before. Kris snuck from behind her and said, "You guys were kissing. And Dad, you grabbed Daisy's bum."

Brad looked slightly uncomfortable as redness moved across his face. I stared innocently, and likely a bit lovey dovey doe-eyed at Jess and Kris.

Could they tell?

Jess laughed, "We're just kidding. But you do look like we caught you with your hands in the cookie jar." Kris giggled as he took Jess's hand and led her down the fork in the path to the left.

I quickly returned to my lovestruck high as I thought of our date, and of my man.

Brad looked at his watched and nudged us toward his home to get ready for our big date. Our hands were intertwined as we walked, not wanting to break the bubble our love and energy had created.

I was probably still a bit dreamy eyed when we got back to Brad's. Bridget Jones was perched on my shoulder, swinging back and forth, humming and smiling. Clearly, she'd experienced the intensely breathtaking visit to Utopia as well.

Hmm, where has that rascally Princess gotten to? She's never too far away from Bridget. Princess has been out of sight for a long time, maybe she's moved on. Nah, she's hiding, patiently waiting. No, that isn't right, scheming is more like it. I giggled to myself. *I bet she pops out after supper tonight.*

Smiling, thinking about the evening, and the prospect of Princess popping up for a visit, I got dressed and put my hair in some sort of semblance for the highly anticipated evening.

Walking out of the master bathroom, I nearly swooned at the sight of my handsome boyfriend in a fancy suit. I gasped as I rushed toward him, launching myself into his arms.

He wrapped me up tight and whispered in my ear, "You take my breath away. You're beautiful, sweetheart."

I cooed, which is something foreign to me, and breathlessly said, "You are too! Handsome, I mean, you're so handsome." I started to giggle, my knees knocking in excitement and anticipation, "See, I'm so breath taken, I can't even string together a sentence." I felt stirring in my loins and knew Princess was stretching as she was waking up.

Not yet Princess, not quite yet. After supper you reign again.

25
the big date

BRAD GRABBED my hand and pulled me toward the bedroom door, whispering, "You, my dear, are unbelievably gorgeous. Your dress hugs your sexy curves deliciously. It's not fair. Far too tempting for me. I can't walk out of here with my pants popping like this. You turn me. I want you so badly."

As Brad's hands traced the outline of my body, a foreign purr escaped my lips. *WTF is that?! Since when do I purr?* My face was beet red, and my heart was pounding with excitement, love, and lust for my man.

Mmm . . . I want you now.

"Oh baby, I want to slip those straps off your shoulders so I can nibble on them, slide your dress down over your breasts, engulf your nipples with my mouth, licking and sucking them as your dress falls to your waist. Then pull it down over your hips, kissing each hip as it becomes bare, then I'd drop the damn dress to the floor, where it belongs. I'd devour you from head to toe. But damn it, we have to go NOW, or we aren't going to make it out of here, never mind our reservation."

Always one to make an entrance, Princess Pussy jumped out of her hiding spot with a triple flip and a la-di-da, clipping her garters into place as she jumped up and down cheering, "Yahoo Brad! Momma's getting lucky tonight!" She pushed Bridget higher and higher in the swing. I could hear Princess whistling and cheering, even Bridget was clapping, as my pussy was dampening, hell, she was dripping. It had been a long time since we enjoyed truly intense sex and I couldn't wait. To hell with supper, let's go to my place and violate every room in the house!

Brad dragged me from the bedroom, my state of arousal slowly dissipating as I floated down the stairs, saying goodbye and goodnight to the kids. Once in the car and headed out of Brad's community, suddenly it hit me . . . *Caesar's Steak House!* "We're going to Caesar's, aren't we?" Brad smiled and nodded as he put his hand on my knee, "Yes, my dear." My blissful evening continued to blossom and grow.

I love Caesar's. And with my man . . . mmm!

Walking through the restaurant, I breathed a contented sigh of nostalgia, my eyes slowly adjusting to the ambiance created by the low lights, burgundy leather seating, and dark wood finishes. Squeezing Brad's hand briefly as the maître 'd led us to a table near the open flame grill, I grinned broadly. I whispered into Brad's ear as we were about to sit down, "Best seats in the house." Brad smiled and whispered back, "I know you love watching the chef charbroil the steaks, sweetie."

Mmm, he even pre-booked our table.

We started with a pinot grigio, beautifully paired with our scampi appetizer. Brad ordered the famous caramelized onion soup for both of us. Enjoying the soup, my eyes rolled into the back of my head, I may have even moaned out loud …

Yikes! Princess Pussy winked at me and grinned her erotic, sex-crazed grin . . . mmm . . . soon Princess, soon. Damn it, Daisy, get your mind out of the gutter!

Next, we ordered our steaks, complete with veggies and twice-baked potato. Our server nodded and went to put in our order. Brad grabbed my hand and looked into my eyes. His gaze made me blush. The server was back moments later to refill our water and wine glasses. Brad and I had made a pact not to talk about our kids tonight. We'd agreed, tonight would about us. Feeling energized and excited, love in the form of warmth spread from the tips of my toes and permeated throughout my body. It spread faster and became more intense as we discussed the timing for moving in.

"It should only take me a couple months to finish the basement. Cory and Mark said they'd be available to help with the plumbing and electrical on the weekends. The outside date for finishing would be the end of September. I'm really excited about this, Daisy."

"Ditto! I'm thrilled too. I just know our kids will be over the moon. Can you move in tomorrow? Ha!"

"I wish!"

"Me too." I knew this was the reality with kids, houses, and dreaded renovations.

Brad took my chin in his hand, tilted it up and laid a sweet kiss on my lips, then said, "On the weekends Kris is at Sara's, maybe we can work it so Carson and I stay over." I smiled.

Why hadn't I thought of that?

"That sounds perfect."

"When do you think I should list my house for sale?"

Tomorrow? Today? Ha!

"The market's strong right now. It'll probably sell quickly but three months is a bit too long for a possession date, maybe the end of August or beginning of September? Why don't we chat with Ronnie, get her opinion?"

"Oh right, I forgot she's a realtor. For sure, let's discuss timing with her." I was enjoying watching the chef pamper our steaks as they sizzled beautifully on the grill. I was salivating in anticipation of our main course. And I wasn't disappointed. Heaven! Every single morsel was delicious. Brad was watching me intently as I thoroughly enjoyed my meal. He had a satiated look on his face, likely very similar to the fulfilled look I imagined I had too.

Sitting back in my chair, I glanced around the room. Out of the corner of my eye, I saw a flicker and a hand wave. Turning to look, I saw Jimmy and his girlfriend, or at least, I assumed it was his girlfriend.

What a good kid, er, young man.

I smiled and waved back. Even from across the restaurant, I could tell Jimmy was explaining the connection to his date.

What's he saying? I wonder. How much detail would he divulge?

I leaned close to Brad as he looked quizzically at me. "Do you remember me mentioning that young man named Jimmy who I . . . uh . . . dated briefly?" Brad nodded. "He's here. I would bet he's going to stop by our table. It looks like they are settling their bill." Brad patted my hand then grabbed it, brought it to his lips and kissed my knuckles.

When I looked up, I saw Jimmy and the woman, hand-in-hand, walking directly toward us. I smiled warmly.

Jimmy proudly introduced us, "Daisy, it's lovely to see you again. This is my beautiful bride, Maria. Maria, this is Daisy."

I stood to shake their hands, "It's lovely to meet you, Maria. Congratulations on your wedding! This is Brad, my beau."

With hands shaken and pleasantries exchanged, I said, "It was wonderful to meet you Maria and great to see you again, Jimmy. You two have a wonderful evening." Normally I would've invited them to join us for a drink, but I wanted Brad to myself tonight.

Jimmy nodded, "You too! Maybe we'll run into you again sometime." I nodded, "I'd like that."

Walking to Brad's car, I felt his grip tighten on my hand. He pulled me into the shadows adjacent to the building in front of his car and kissed me deeply. I felt my knees buckle slightly with the passion of it. I was instantly lit on fire, I felt like gasoline was thrown on the fire Brad had started in his bedroom earlier. The fire went out of control as Brad whispered, "I love you, Daisy. All night long, my mind has been filled with thoughts of ripping your clothes off and thoroughly devouring and pleasing you until you beg me to stop. Even then I might make you orgasm again . . ."

Princess Pussy jumped off the ledge she was on and walked up my shoulder toward my ear, and whispered, "Rip his clothes off and let him take you right here in the parking lot, Daisy. NOW!" Uh, I think we'll wait until we get home, but I can't say the thought didn't occur to me, Princess.

I felt warm and moist EVERYWHERE. Brad gripped me harder and kissed me with the same intensity.

What's that line from Top Gun again? Oh right…

"Hey Brad, you big stud!" Brad's eyes lit up as he caught the reference. "That's me, honey." I grinned, "Take me to bed or lose me forever." He kissed me softly and whispered in my ear, "Show me the way home, honey."

The drive back to my place felt like the slowest drive ever. I seriously don't know how we got there with our clothes intact. I giggled a little thinking about shoes and clothes flying around the car and out the window as Brad drove. I was craving him like I'd never craved before. The connection I felt was soul-wrenching. By the look in his eyes, it wasn't just me. We both felt it. We needed to allow our desires to explode together in the act of making love, a deep and intense love, ignited through feelings and touch.

Drive faster Brad.

You could damn near cut desire with a knife. Running up my walkway, we threw the door open and started making out like lustful teenagers, desperate for one another, before the front door had closed. We paused for a moment, looking left and right, phew, no kids. My shoe shot across the living room as I kicked it off, Brad proficiently maneuvered my dress off and as his mouth was suckling my nipple with determination, he snapped my bra single handedly and launched it toward a lamp. The lamp flew off the table from the force, hit the wall, and landed with a thud on the floor. We both laughed, easing our crazy desire, momentarily.

Moving further into the living room, the intensity peaked again. More clothes were peeled off, mostly his, as I was mostly naked by this point. It looked like a train wreck of clothing by the time we made it to the stairs. He slid my panties off with his teeth as I stood above him on the stairs. Now we were both completely naked. Brad sat me down on the stairs, spread my legs with his hands. As I leaned back, he maneuvered himself between my legs on the stairs below and dove tongue first into my pussy.

OMG!

I grabbed onto his head and held his mouth firmly to my pussy as his tongue was alternating between flicking my clit, licking my pussy lips, and diving right in. "Mmmmm Brad, don't stop, baby, you're winding me up like a top and I'm gonna blow soon." A few more minutes of licking and I was cumming.

Princess was running circles around Bridget, occasionally slowing to give her a high five and scream, "Yaaaaa baby!"

I was moaning and groaning in pleasure as I cummed yet again. Brad licked the inside of my thighs, kissed each of my nipples, then grabbed my hand and led me upstairs to the bedroom. He was hard as a rock, and I couldn't wait for him to be inside me.

But first, I wanted a taste. I could see he had pre-cum on the tip of his penis. As we walked into my room I got on my knees and licked it off, then encompassed his tip with my mouth, then I licked him like he was a lollipop before taking him deep into my mouth. That got him nice and wet and even harder.

Hard like a diamond! Bridget's getting all hot and bothered too. Oh, the intensity!

Brad pulled me up, brought me to the bed and lay me down. He started kissing me, his tongue entering my ear and making me squirm, then to my lips, thoroughly exploring my breasts, then he kissed my lips again as he slid inside me. I squealed as he entered. I cummed again.

Holy fuck was that ever quick. Cumming during entry. Interesting. I'm on fire. Completely lit.

I was having orgasm after orgasm as the intensity between us continued to build.

How in the hell can this get any hotter and more intense? Surely, it's not possible.

We were kissing and making love with a level of passion I'd never felt before. I was swept up in it, like I was being carried downstream by a raging river, helpless to do anything but enjoy the ride, which was just perfect.

He repositioned me on the bed on my side with legs twisted to the right. I giggled as he bore down on me. He smiled and gave my ass a gentle swat as he kissed me. He dove in again, deeper this time, hitting all the right spots. My lady parts were singing. Princess was doing handsprings and back flips.

Oh shizam, *he just hit my g-spot. Don't you dare stop Brad.*

I breathlessly moaned, "Baby, don't stop. Mount Helen's is about to erupt." And blow she did. Just as she started, Brad said, "I'm gonna cum, babe." Boom! Liquid was sloshing inside me, we were both soaked, and my bed was destroyed. It was AMAZING.

We rolled over to the other side of the bed, to get out of the lake-sized puddle, and snuggled in together as Brad brushed my hair off my face. "Mmm, that was incredible. I love you so much, baby." I nodded as I started to drift to sleep, "I love you too, Brad."

According to my alarm clock, we slept for about an hour, cuddled into each other. Wiggling my bum, I gently woke Brad, "I can't wait until we can sleep together like this every night. But tonight, we've got to start thinking about heading back to your place." Brad groaned and nodded as he stroked my face, moving a transient hair out of the way. "Yeah, we should get going. Soon, sweetheart, we'll sleep together every night. I can't wait."

We rolled out of bed, used the washroom, and went downstairs to survey the clothes tornado. We laughed as we attempted to pick up the pieces, finding shoes under tables, socks under the couch and even one on the chandelier. While getting dressed, I replaced the lamp and looked around.

There, it looks like no crazy adult fun happened here tonight.

Nodding to each other, we turned off the lights and locked up.

We tiptoed into Brad's place and discovered all the kids sleeping. *Phew!*

Kris was sawing logs in his bed. Jess, Ang, and Carson were asleep in front of the TV with a movie on repeat, probably dreaming away. I shut the TV off and we went upstairs to Brad's room. We crawled in bed together, happy to have the rare opportunity to sleep together through the night. Positioning ourselves with Brad as big spoon, I wiggled my hips back into him. I could feel his penis starting to grow. As he reached maximum hardness, I tipped my hips up so he could enter me again. He slid in and out of me slowly and gently a few times, a calm and connected love making just before drifting to sleep. We fell asleep with him inside me, I was in heaven.

Brad woke me up the next morning kissing me and whispering sweet nothings in my ear. Then he suggested that I throw some clothes on as his little monkey would likely be dive bombing the bed any minute.

Eek . . . quick! Shoot, where's my shirt? Where had I thrown that pesky thing? Oh, there it is. How'd it get over there? Oh, right . . .

I located and pulled on the rest of my clothes, the comfy ones I'd slipped into at my place, and not a moment too soon. I'd just crawled back under the covers when Kris flew through the door and landed in between us.

26
guess what?

THE FOLLOWING SATURDAY, Brad and I decided it was time to let our kids in on our little secret. Brilliantly executed, at least we thought so, Brad and I broke the news to the kids that we were moving in together. The kids were excited, well, three of them were. *Shit!* Carson was quiet.

Jess gave Carson, Kris, Brad, Ang, and me bone-rattling hugs as she gushed, "This is the best news ever! We spend so much time together now. It's great we're finally going to just do it, not have to flip back and forth!" Ang nodded, "I concur, sista!", as she gave Jess a high five.

My girls are at such an interesting stage. On one hand, they're all ladylike and official and on the other, still playful kids. Kinda cool.

Kris came running and jumped into my arms, "Daisy, I can't wait for us to move into your place. It's closer to my school and I'll get to see Jess and Ang every day. When can we move in? When? When?"

I smiled, "You're so sweet. Probably not for a couple of months yet buddy, maybe by October."

Carson looked somewhat dejected and asked, "Oh, we're going to live here?" I looked at Brad, not sure how Carson would react, as Brad explained, "Yeah, it makes the most sense. Our place would need a much larger reno. So, we'll renovate the basement here: add a bathroom and second bedroom, put our house up for sale then move in here when it's sold. Do you have any concerns with that?"

I held my breath. Carson nodded, "Yeah, I guess. You know, I guess I never thought about how it would work with all of us at our place."

Phew! Big Exhale!

Brad continued, "The timing will be a bit interesting as we'll try to list our house so that the sale coincides with the completion of the renos. Daisy's friend, Ronnie, has already said she'll sell it for us and she'll coach us on the timing."

Carson asked quietly, "How are we going to decide who goes where? I mean, where am I going to sleep?" Carson's privacy and seclusion had become more important to him over the past few months, since coming out. Brad nodded toward me, indicating that I should take the lead on this one. "Well, we'll all talk about it and decide together where everyone's room will be. We'll figure out what makes the most sense. Ha! If need be, we could even draw straws." Carson nodded. He'd been more withdrawn again recently, but at least he was still contributing and participating.

Thank goodness!

"Do you have a preference, Carson?" He nodded, "I'd prefer to be down-stairs but I'm not sure what Jess and Ang want to do. I assumed Kris would be upstairs." Kris was nodding, enthusiastically.

Ang spoke up, "I'd prefer to be downstairs. What're you thinking Jess?" Jess surprised me by saying, "I like my room, I'd like to stay upstairs, if that's ok."

Sweet!

Brad smiled at our four kids, one at a time, and then back at me, "Well, it's settled then, Kris and Jess are upstairs, Ang and Carson are downstairs."

Brad and his buddies started on the renos at once. We hit our first roadblock within a few days. The water meter and inside shut off was in the middle of where we wanted the new bedroom to be, and we needed to shut off the water main to move it. The plumber had planned to shut the water main off himself and when he went to turn it, nada, it just kept spinning and spinning. I called the City, they said they'd be out to turn it off in two weeks. *Ugh!*

The city rep showed up three weeks later (*Oi!*) and, no surprise to us, they discovered that the water main valve was broken and wouldn't turn off.

No shit!

After the City ruled that the main shut off valve was, in fact, broken, we were then placed in the queue a two to three month wait with the City. But there wasn't much we could do until they fixed the valve. *Major bummer.*

In the meantime, the guys ran the electrical and laid out the plumbing as best as they could without the water main being turned off. The good news was that Brad's buddies said it would only take three to four weeks to complete the renos once the waterline was dealt with, now that they had all the prep work done and everything was ordered.

Anne got more than she bargained for when she asked me how the renos were going. I updated her on the goofy valve process and dove into the skyrocketing prices. "Good grief, I can't even tell you the goofy process of getting things ordered, never mind the cost. Supply chain goatshow happening in Canada. Shortage of pieces from abroad, prices skyrocketing, shortage of wood. You know, I don't get it, we have lots of trees in Canada."

Anne laughed, "Maybe it's because of all the damn paper straws. Who in the hell thought those were a good idea anyway?"

"Ha, no kidding. I get the theory, save the turtles, but the fucking things don't work. They fall apart before you're even half done your drink. If you manage to keep the thing in one piece, it's so bloody soggy that it makes you want to vomit with each sip. Am I eating paper while drinking my iced tea? Really? Jeez. I digress."

Finally, everything was lined up and ready to go. *Woohoo!* The City moved faster than anticipated and they fixed the valve just shy of two months. Once the waterline was moved, insulation was reinstalled, drywall installed, tile, shower and fixtures were installed in the bathroom, ceiling sprayed, mudded, painted, electrical completed, plumbing completed, and flooring installed. *Phew!* It was beautiful chaos as things progressed.

In the midst of the pandemonium, Ronnie got Brad's house listed for sale. The first weekend after listing, she held an open house. Kris was at his mom's, and Carson and Brad decided that it would be easier to stay at my place in order to keep the place clean. Friday night before the open house, the five of us made light work of cleaning Brad's place, top to bottom. There wasn't much to do, just a once over really. Carson's bedroom was the one spot where things had fallen into disarray since we'd had pictures taken for the listing.

My girls were up to the task, thank goodness. Jess grabbed some garbage bags and labelled them all, "Ok, this one is garbage, this is storage, this is recycling, donations, and stuff to sell." Jess pointed to each bag as she spoke. They blew through Carson's room in no time. Some of the interesting items found were hidden in Carson's closet and under his bed: half eaten blue and furry sandwich (*ICK!*), a lovely, brown rotting apple, and several beverage containers that had some kind of blue brown blech in them.

Brad dry-heaved at the sight as he said, "Uh, Carson, that's why we have the rule about no food in your room, remember?"

Carson rolled his eyes, "Yeah Dad, I know."

Brad raised his eyebrows, "And yet . . ."

Another eyeroll, "Yeah, I know. Sometimes it's just easier to eat in my room."

"Yes, perhaps easier, but this is disgusting. Just don't, Carson. Food in your room ends up nasty like this."

Carson muttered, "Ok, Dad."

They got the "for sale" items listed on Kijiji, and we dropped off the garbage, recycling, and donation bags the next morning.

Brad and I walked upstairs, and once we were out of earshot of the kids, he said, "Why do I get the sense that I'm going to be having the same conversation with Carson in another six months?"

I looked at Brad directly, entirely poker-faced, "I'll be surprised if the blue sandwiches make it six months before they grow legs and walk out of there on their own!"

Brad put his arm around me and pulled me close, kissing me on the forehead, "Right you are Daisy, right you are!" He spun me around, grabbed my hands, pulling me into a tight hug, "Have I told you how much I love you today?"

I grinned, "You have and I'm over the moon to hear it again, sweetie! Tell me a million times a day and I will love it a million times. I love you too, babe."

We sat down in the living room, looking around and discussing the readiness of the house for the open house. Suddenly Brad sat very still, "Daisy, I get it." His tone had gotten serious, so I sat up in my chair and paid very close attention.

Get what?

I raised an eyebrow quizzically as he continued, "Dead name. I get it. It's not about me and how comfortable I feel with the terminology. It's the terminology that's used. I don't need to question any underlying meanings. It just is. It's understood. Me trying to put it in my own terms, such as "old name" doesn't give it the creed or full depth of understanding that it should." I nodded and gave Brad a hug, "Yes, it's about Carson and his comfort with the words and greater understanding beyond."

27
sociopath sammy

THE NEXT DAY, a discussion with Anne and her friend, Cindy, rocked me. Anne introduced the story, "Cindy had the pleasure, or more aptly displeasure, of meeting with, hmm... let's call him Sociopath Sammy. He had this hard luck story about being a single dad with a couple kids, a boy and a girl, and about how hard it is to raise his two kids on his own. A big story about how their mom didn't participate in raising of them and that he'd been a single dad for years. Cue heartstrings pulling. Carry on, Cindy."

As Cindy's story unfolded, I became increasingly more thankful that I didn't come across too many of the crazy sociopaths out there during my online dating blitz. But the ones that I had stumbled across, man oh man were they good. It's almost like they drill deep into your soul and tell you everything you want to hear, even some stuff you weren't even aware you wanted, or desired, to hear. You just lap it up, or maybe that's just me, ha! They read you like an open book, backwards and forwards. You feel like you have an amazing connection right off the bat because they tell you exactly what you want to hear, for crying out loud.

Cindy explained, "I'm still not sure if there even were any kids. In hindsight, everything is suspect. But I fell for his story at the time. He sent pictures of the kids but none with him in them. The kids were fishing, playing in the park, what have you."

"After chatting for a week or so, I met him one night for drinks and to play a few games of pool at his place . . . strip pool as it turned out. It was super sexy stripping off a layer of clothing at each loss and watching him strip off a layer when he'd lose. Talk about some fun foreplay! Lots of flirtation and fun, his hand brushing against my ass as I bent over to take my next shot, brushing against him while passing by to shoot the next ball."

I nodded, "Oh yeah, that would be a huge turn on."

"Absolutely!" commented Anne.

"Later that week, something struck me as odd about how the night had unfolded with Sammy, but I couldn't put my finger on it. Sammy kept pushing me to drink more. I declined his numerous offers of more booze as I had to drive home that evening."

My eyes squinted slightly, "Hmm, that's a bit odd. Talk about peer pressure."

"I'll say, and there's more. As the evening wore on, I felt increasingly more uninhibited. As you know, I'm not super inhibited to start with so that didn't concern me. *At the time.* I attributed it to feeling turned on from all the flirting brought on by strip pool. The flirtation quickly turned more physical. Our clothes were partially off as we started to make out, heavy petting, with hands and mouths everywhere that wasn't covered by clothes. At that point, my pants were still on and in one fell swoop, he placed me on my back on the pool table and yanked my pants off. I damn near cummed right then."

"OMG, yes!" I was riveted by Cindy's story.

Princess is standing, wide-eyed and panting.

"He forcefully ripped my legs apart, dove tongue first into my pussy, his hands gripping my ass tightly, right there on the pool table. He licked and licked, my body convulsed, my arm scattering the balls everywhere, pool cues hitting the floor. After I came down from the rafters, he yanked me off the pool table and said, "More pool then more hot stuff?" We played another game. The funny thing is that I was completely naked, and his pants were firmly in place. Very odd."

My forehead crinkled as I thought about this, "Why didn't he take his pants off? Most guys want in on the action!"

"I know, eh? Definitely strange. We continued to alternate between licking and pool. That's how the night ended: him with his pants on and me naked and wet, playing pool, but definitely not fucked. That's all that happened that night sexually. Weird naked pool. Some participants more naked than others."

"Well, what the hell was that all about? Did you see him again?" I was baffled by the yellow flags, maybe red, that I was seeing.

Princess Pussy groaned and yawned, "No fucking? No penetration? I got out of my comfy bed to listen to this PG-13 story? I'm going back to bed." Bridget frowned, "There's more to life than sex, Princess. I think something is very wrong with this guy." Princess rolled her eyes as she slid under her covers.

"All very weird, that's for sure. I did see him again, we got together the next evening after I went for a long run. I texted him as I was about to leave.

I'm on my way. Do you need me to pick up anything?

Yeah, thanks, I'm starving. Papa burger meal from A&W, with a Coke.

Text me when you get here.

"I thought, 'Ok then. Supper from A&W it is. So much for a romantic evening out.' I went through the drive-thru and picked up his meal and a mozza burger combo for me. I pulled into a spot half a block away and messaged him."

I'm parked.

He texted right back.

Come in. I'm upstairs. Come on up.

"I went inside, brought our meals upstairs to his bedroom and put our drinks and the bags on the side table. He was locked in the bathroom. I knocked, "Your burger is right here, Sammy." He hollered, "Be out in a minute."

He stumbled out of the bathroom and into his bedroom. He was completely messed up and hung over, maybe still high or drunk. He grabbed his Coke and alternated that with sips of water. He looked like hell. He sloppily removed my clothes and we fucked for a while. Then he excused himself. I heard vomiting through the door. An absolute turn off. I noticed out of the corner of my eye, the sixty of rye that he'd been trying to get me to drink the previous night. It was empty."

"A whole sixty? That's a lot of booze," Anne looked concerned.

"Yeah, as I was staring at the empty bottle, I started to get worried. He'd been in the bathroom for a while. I knocked on the door, 'Hey, Sammy, are you ok?' No answer. Shit, I just wanted to go home. The evening had been a fucked up and bizarre disappointment. I walked into the bathroom. He was passed out with his head on the toilet and there was vomit everywhere, water was streaming out of the shower. When the hell did he turn the shower on? I checked to make sure he was still breathing, turned the shower off, then went back over to him. That's when I noticed it, there was an odd brown thing mashed into the floor and on his leg."

"OMG! He shat himself?" Anne looked ill.

WTF is with guys shitting themselves? This is the second story like this. Is it a thing or just some weird coincidence? At least they weren't having sex when it happened like poor Ronnie.

"Yup!"

"How did you not run screaming from the building like it was on fire?" I was shaking my head, disgusted.

"Believe me, I thought about it. I wanted to make sure he was ok, I guess. Turning the shower back on, I walked back over to the toilet and helped him stand up. He tried to kiss me and pawed at my boob. "I love you, Cindy. Let's fuck." Barf! He stunk. Vomit. Booze. Shit. Not happening dude. He really must've been loaded, the big "L". Helping him over to the shower, I opened the door and made sure he got in alright. He emerged from the shower looking much fresher and cleaner, thank goodness all evidence of barf and crap gone.

He tried to kiss me again. I backed away. "Sammy, I just wanted to make sure you were ok. Now that I have, I'm going to leave now." His face fell, "You're not staying?" I shook my head, "No, this night has been a disaster. Get some sleep.""

"The next morning, I sent him a message, "How are you feeling?" He replied, "Good," then was all chatty for an hour then he disappeared. He ghosted me, which was fine with me as I wasn't interested in another episode with Disaster Dude. I didn't really think much more about him."

"No kidding, good riddance!" Anne shook her head in disgust as I nodded in agreement.

"Three or four weeks later, he contacted me out of the blue. He sent a long text, an essay really, apologizing for disappearing and stating that he had been so scared because he could see a future with me. This was frightening for him, and he didn't know what to do. As you both know, I'm too empathetic, so I tried hard to see his side of things. I figured why not, I'm single, so I gave him another chance, but I insisted we go out on a proper date to make up for the last disaster. We made plans to go for supper. He sent a couple texts delaying when we were getting together, which was super frustrating. I felt like he was wasting my time and that he'd probably bail on me. We finally got together late in the evening and enjoyed a great supper on a patio, with lots of fun discussion."

"After supper, we went for a walk along the lake and then back to his place. We were just getting into it when suddenly, he got visibly agitated and was on his phone texting, texting, texting. WTF?!! He locked himself in the bathroom on his phone, something felt really wrong. When he finally got off the phone he said, "My oldest is sick. My mom is bringing my kids back home now.""

I was feeling red flags from everywhere. Something shady was about to go down. He shuffled me out of the house quickly and walked me to my vehicle, which was a bit weird. As I was getting ready to drive away, he was still watching me. I thought about driving in a circle and coming back and to see who showed up. I thought it was one of two things: he is a drug dealer or has a weird parade of women coming through his house, or one at least. I decided to forget it, he's not worth the effort. As it turns out, he didn't deserve that second chance, at all. Very disappointing. Jerk off."

"It comes as no surprise that was the last that I heard from him, especially since I blocked him. Ha! What a completely messed up human being he is. Playing games with people, not cool!"

"What do you think his angle was?" I asked.

Cindy shrugged, "I'm not sure. Maybe to play a game or maybe he just wanted some female companionship for a minute or two, who knows. Looking back, it sounds like a goofy thing to fall for but at the time, he was so convincing and apologetic and begged me to give him another chance. Hindsight is 20/20. Ugh!"

The more we talked about it, the more we came to realize that he likely spiked her drink with a date rape drug or something else, ecstasy maybe? The bad news for him though was that Cindy isn't a big drinker, so she only had part of one drink but still, it influenced her for sure, loosened her up even more than normal. She didn't realize it at the time but much later it made sense that that might've been what happened. She thinks whatever it was, must have been pre-mixed in the booze itself.

Thank goodness she was driving and didn't get drunk with him. Who knows what might have happened, but we're certain that it wouldn't have been good. I read up on it and it seems that this is a thing people do, both have some ecstasy and then have crazy, wild sex.

The thing is, dude, you must have CONSENT of the other party, you don't just spike their drink, otherwise it is illegal, not to mention dangerous. What a jackass.

Another douche who should be charged except that she wasn't 100% certain that her drink was spiked. If there was a drug in the booze, then it got the last laugh as that's likely why he was so messed up on the second night, he spiked his own drink.

Ha-ha! Karma perhaps? Suck on that, asshole!

28
moving in

FINALLY, moving day had arrived. Kris was running around, dodging boxes at Brad's place, as happy as a clam. He was singing a dandy tune to "Leaving on a Jet Plane" by John Denver, and having a good ole time:

Our boxes are packed and we're ready to go
I'm running loops as you check behind doors
I hate to leave our house and say goodbye

But we're moving into Daisy's
Don't think that we'll be back again
Oh yeah, I can't wait to go

'Cuz we're moving into Daisy's . . .

As Kris sang, I surveyed the main floor for any last minute things we might have overlooked. Nothing. We'd done a good job moving all the breakables already and clearing out a bunch of stuff. The movers were arriving in about an hour. We'd been packing for what seemed like forever.

How is all this stuff going to fit in my place?

I caught myself in my old thinking . . .

OUR place, not MY place.

We'd donated and sold a ton of stuff, there was so much duplication, and still I had doubts as to where to put everything that was arriving.

Oh well, we'll figure it out.

There were two full bed sets for two new bedrooms. We'd moved Ang's stuff downstairs as soon as the renos were complete the previous week, so we could move Kris's stuff straight into Ang's old room.

During my search for any unpacked items, I found Carson downstairs in his room. He was crying. I gave him a hug while he sobbed, "So many memories here, Daisy. Some good, but most of trying to escape the dark cloud."

I hugged him tighter, "Yes, Carson, I know. I'm hoping you'll have a clean slate, a new start, in your new room. New memories, happier ones. But whether they're happy or sad or scary or dark, know that we are all here for you. We all love you."

Carson sniffled and hugged me tighter, "Thank you, Daisy, I love you all too. I'm so happy that my dad found you guys. You're family to me now. You're an awesome lady, you know."

I ruffled Carson's hair, "And you are a very special boy. My oldest son." I kissed his forehead as I spoke those last words.

"I know I haven't been the easiest to understand, or even get along with. Thank you for being patient with me, for your support. I love you."

I smiled, my heart brimming. This was the first time Carson had told me that he loved me. I'd said it numerous times before, but he hadn't been ready to return the sentiment and I respected that completely. It was the right time for him now. "I love you too, Carson."

My girls were busy with volleyball and art classes today, but they would be back home to help unpack a bit later in the day, thank goodness. They had been as excited as Kris at the prospect of us all moving in together.

I loved the idea of our little, or big, blended family. We just worked. Yes, I knew there would be ups and downs, and four kids is a lot, especially when Kris and Carson's mom wasn't always the easiest to work with, never mind having different parenting styles, but I knew we would work our way through it. Brad and I were determined to make this a success. Not only us, but all six of us. We would be successful.

29
butt what?

AFTER WE FINALLY FOUND SPOTS FOR everything and we were all settled into our place, Jen invited Anne, Ronnie, and I over to her place with a very specific topic in mind. Of course, we had no idea at the time, we just thought it was catch up time! Jen enticed us with the promise of tacos, enchiladas, and lime and strawberry margaritas. Who could resist that?

Jen distributed margaritas and chips and salsa, then she sat down with a sigh. "So uh, well, thank you for coming, ladies. Aside from just wanting to see all of you, I have a question. Um…and I wanted to ask it in person. But it can wait. So, what's new with all of you?"

Ronnie looked Jen square in the eyes. "Nope, you're not leading with that and then asking us how we are. What's up? What do you want to ask us? Is it about sex?

"You got a new job?" I asked.

Anne shot out, "Lingerie?"

"Penises?" was Ronnie's suggestion.

"You're pregnant!" I threw out.

"Intimacy?" Anne pondered.

We all giggled, even Jen, although hers was a nervous giggle. She looked down at her feet, "Well, it's kind of embarrassing. I feel kind of gross asking about it. I'm really vanilla and it's just not a vanilla kind of question, it's like strawberry or something." Jen was clearly flustered.

Definitely not a job or pregnancy. Hmm . . . something to do with sex.

Anne touched Jen's knee, "No judgment here, you know that. You're in a safe place. Ask us anything you want. If we know the answer we'll give you as much information as you'd like. . . likely an overabundance of information." She nodded to encourage her to go on. We were all smiling and offering Jen words of encouragement, "We're here for you, girl!"

"Uh, ok, so, I've never done it before, but Chris and I were talking and he suggested that if I wanted, we could try anal sex. And um . . .well, do any of you have experience with it?"

Anal sex? Hmm . . .an opportunity for me to learn something here. I've always been an "exit only" kind of girl. Princess stage whispered, "Pay attention, Daisy. I've wanted anal forever." I shook my head at Princess, "Well, I could listen better if you'd stop your bloody yammering." Bridge just looked uncomfortable as she crossed her legs. "That's not going to protect your ass, sweet cheeks," Princess pointed out. I tuned them both out.

Ronnie was nodding as she laughed, "You're right, that's not vanilla, or strawberry for that matter . . . it's chocolate all the way, baby! Seriously though, I fucking love anal sex with the right partner. Love it."

Jen was blushing profusely, "So, uh, do you mind if I ask you some questions about it? They might seem kind of dumb."

"There are no dumb questions, Jen, ask away."

"Does it hurt?"

"No, not typically. The key to anal sex is lube and slow entry."

"Slow entry?"

"Yes, you have to stretch your ass around his cock. And slowly, or it'll hurt. Don't forget the lube either or it WILL hurt. Your ass is different from your pussy in that it doesn't self-lubricate."

"Oh, yeah, that makes sense. Slow. Lube." Jen was nodding, taking it all in.

I jumped in, "Ronnie, isn't it messy and gross? Doesn't poop get everywhere?"

"It's not usually messy and definitely not gross. If a guy is very large then it will be messier than with a man with a smaller cock, that's for sure."

"Oh? I hadn't even thought about that."

"If you're really concerned about it, you can give yourself a water enema, but it's not necessary."

"Oh? That's a thing? Ok, that makes sense."

"Yes, you can buy it at any drugstore," responded Ronnie.

"And you're sure it doesn't hurt?"

"The enema or anal?" Ronnie joked.

Jen blushed, "Uh, anal sex."

"It shouldn't hurt, no. If it does, you're going to fast or too rough or not enough lube. If you're slow, gentle, and lubed, it shouldn't hurt at all. It felt a little weird the first few times I did it but then after that, I wanted it big time. It feels amazing. I can cum with anal rather quickly."

"What? You cum? Cum where? Not in your ass?"

Giggling, Ronnie responded, "No, I cum in my pussy with him in my ass. It's a different kind of cum. He hits my g-spot from inside my ass, or at least, I think that's what happens. Regardless, fuck, does it ever feel good."

"Different how?" Jen asked. I was fascinated. Listening to their volley of questions and answers, learning about something I'd never endeavored to try.

Princess Pussy had an eyebrow raised at me, "Uh, Daisy . . . why haven't we done this? It sounds amazing." I turned and looked at her, "Shush, I'm learning here. Exit only remember?! Exit only!" Bridget was continuously crossing and uncrossing her legs and shaking her head, "No entry, nope."

"It's hard to explain. But different from any cum I've had from pussy sex. It just touches different things. It's a hard, deep cum. Feels great. My 'oh fuck' meter goes off the charts."

"Oh? Well, that's pretty wild. I had no idea." Jen was smiling in wonderment.

Anne joined in the conversation. "Another thing with anal sex is that he needs to switch condoms or go clean off with soap and water before his penis goes back into your pussy. You don't want ass bacteria in your pussy."

"Ass bacteria?!! Nasty!" Jen shook her head, "I hadn't thought of that."

"Fuck, I sure as hell don't!" I exclaimed.

Oops, did I say that out loud?

Ronnie glanced oddly at me for my outburst. "Same thing if he's got a finger in your ass. Once it goes in your ass, it doesn't go back in your pussy."

"Finger in your ass?" Jen asked.

"You've never had a finger in your ass?" Anne asked.

"Uh, nope?" Jen looked uneasy, thinking that maybe she should've by now.

"Ok, start there. See how you like it. Get Chris to lube or suck his finger and then slowly put it in your ass. If he can do it while you're on top riding him, that's always fun."

"Oooh, that sounds like an easier place to start. And it feels good?"

"You bet it does!"

"Ok, cool, thanks Ronnie!"

Anne looked over at Jen, "Another thing to prepare yourself for is that when he's entering your ass, he's in control so you need to trust that he'll go slow enough not to hurt you."

"Oh yeah, that's true for sure!" Ronnie said.

"I know Chris would never hurt me. He's never done it before so I'm sure we'll be so slow and cautious. Ugh, so, uh, what kind of positions do you find best for anal?" Jen bravely asked.

"My personal favorite is me lying on my tummy with my ass in the air. He has full control, and he can see and feel how I'm stretching. A second for me is when I'm doggy but my ass is pretty tight with this one, so it takes a bit longer to stretch. Anne?"

Princess Pussy was salivating, "Daisy, I want some. Please!?!" she whined. Good grief. Bridget was shaking her head back and forth with her arms in an "X" position muttering over and over, "Exit only. No entry. Wrong way. Exit only. No entry. Wrong way." I gave my head a shake. They were giving me a bloody headache, "Enough girls! To your rooms. Now."

"Yeah, I like lying on my back with my legs up and he's standing beside the bed. He lifts my hips up and slides in my ass. That's my favorite alright. I like to be in spooning position too, there's something super sexy about my man sliding from inside my pussy and right into my ass in that position. Mmm . . ."

I reached for my strawberry margarita, realizing I'd sucked it back during that informative discussion. "Wow, ladies, I've learned a shit ton tonight. We've never talked anal before."

Anne and Ronnie smiled while Jen said, "Yeah, thank you, ladies! I knew you were the right ladies to ask!"

I love our girl chat. Never a dull moment. Always learning.

30
dark days

Brad

BUSILY WORKING AWAY in my office one Wednesday afternoon, my phone rang. It was Kyle. "After Carson's session on Saturday, I'd like to see you for half an hour."

I nodded, not that he could see me nodding. "Yes, of course." I felt like I'd been summoned to the principal's office. My stomach dropped.

Something very serious is wrong. And it has to do with my kid. Fuck!

"Is everything ok? Anything I should be preparing for?"

Kyle responded, clearly not his first rodeo, with, "We'll discuss the details and go forward plan on Saturday. I have to run. I have another appointment in five minutes."

Fuck! I hate this. I had a knot the size of my fist growing in my guts.

The damn tightrope was back. I felt the wind pushing me back and forth as I tried to balance. I don't want to fall. I looked down at my phone, still in my hand, dialed Daisy and raised it to my ear. I told her about Kyle's call. She unknowingly helped steady the tightrope as she said, "We'll get through whatever it is together. Try not to worry about the unknown. If Kyle felt it were urgent, if there was imminent danger, he'd have called you in to see him earlier."

I nodded uselessly, clearly a habit, but I knew she was right. "Yeah, I'm sure he would."

Throughout the week, the knot in my stomach grew larger and larger. By the time Saturday rolled around, I could barely eat, the bloody thing had taken over my guts. I was feeling downright sick to my stomach. Whatever Kyle needed to share with me wasn't good, I knew that much.

The important part of the conversation went like this, "Carson has been having some serious thoughts about harming himself and ending his life. Yes, this is extremely serious. I didn't call you in here urgently because, so far, it has only been thoughts, an idea. I'm sure you're wondering what I mean by that. Let me explain. It's extremely positive that he hasn't thought so much about it that he's come up with a plan on how to do it. We'd be having a very different conversation if he had. Carson and I have worked through a plan for him when he has those dark thoughts, who to reach out to and when."

I nodded. *Fuck!* This confirmed the thoughts that I'd been rolling around in my head for months, but I hadn't wanted to put words to or even allowed them to be fully formed in my brain. I didn't want them to be real, I wanted to be wrong. *Damn it!*

Trying very hard to keep the tightrope out of mind and remain logical I said, "Yes, it makes sense with everything Carson has been dealing with gender dysphoria, his mother completely rejecting him, being misgendered nearly constantly, depression and anxiety that are still not fully managed medically. It's no wonder he's having some serious thoughts about harming himself. Ending his life."

I knew this. Carson didn't tell me. He didn't have to. Kyle didn't have to tell me. I knew. This conversation confirmed it for me. Made it real. FUUUUUUCK!

On one hand I had these very thoughts about him myself but was hoping I was out to lunch. On the other hand, I didn't actually know how bad things had gotten for him. I was there to support him every step of the way but there are some things a person just has to go through and experience on their own, others can't always make it better.

Kyle had asked Carson if he would talk to me about part of his safety plan for when he was spiraling down and seriously thinking that suicide was a viable option. Carson had said yes. Kyle and I discussed my role in the safety plan and what I could do to continue to support Carson. There was hope. A plan. A way out.

The plan made sense logically, but suicide isn't logical. I was sick with worry about my son. It made me nauseous every time I thought about it, it still does.

As I explained the safety plan to Daisy, I couldn't shake the feeling that it was familiar to me somehow, in some way. When I mentioned this weird familiarity to Daisy, she suggested that it reminded her a bit of an Emergency Response Plan, something that we prepare and do practice runs for all the time at work. Of course, that was it. A weird comparison but that was why it felt familiar. But this was so different, so much more real, and scary, because it was Carson, my kid. Daisy's hug kept the tightrope at bay.

Even before my discussion with Kyle, I can't tell you how many times I stood at the top of the stairs, dreading that walk downstairs, praying that my son would answer my knock on his door. The thoughts flying through my head as I tread down each stair made me catch my breath. Horrified that there would be no answer to my knock, to my call, to my pleas. I prayed as I held my breath, my mind taking me to unimaginable, gut-wrenching thoughts. Thoughts that my little boy wouldn't answer the door. That he was no longer with us. That his little body was hanging or lying somewhere in the basement, lifeless, having overdosed or done some other action to end his life.

Still not daring to breathe, I reached his door. I knocked. It sounded so hollow. So empty. My voice caught in my throat and came out as a hoarse whisper, "Carson?" My ears straining for any sound of movement, shifting in bed, or even his voice. Some signal to let me know that my son was still alive.

Please let him be safe.

I don't hear anything. Panic was stirring through my body. I was starting to vibrate. *Maybe he hadn't heard me.* Speaking louder this time as I knocked, "Carson?!"

"Yeah, Dad?" he casually said. An enormous weight of was lifted from my shoulders as I exhaled at Carson's words. I chided myself, *see, he's fine*. But, until I felt he was completely on stable ground, those fifteen seconds spent walking down those stairs each day, praying he was still with us, was the most horrifying experience I've had in all my years.

Knowing that my child has contemplated suicide, thought of it as a possible potential option, broke me at the core. It's unbelievably scary. You aren't sure that they won't attempt it and really, when it comes down to it, there's not much you can do about it besides letting them know you're there for them and that you love them.

On the drive home after meeting with Kyle that day, I told Carson, "I can't bear the thought of living a life without you in it. I'm not interested in that. At all. I love you so much, son." I'm not sure my words were all that helpful for him or for me, but it was truly what I felt. Straight from my heart.

Carson turned to me and put his hand on mine and in a soft, almost little boy voice, he said, "I know, Dad."

I started to cry. I pulled over and gave my son a hug. We were both sobbing, not just crying but sobbing… ugly crying from our guts, goose honks, snot, and all. But it was a much-needed release for us both. We talked about "the plan" and he assured me that he would reach out. I knew it wasn't that simple but it's all we had.

I felt so helpless. I couldn't take away the pain for him. I would've gladly taken it on myself to help keep my oldest son safe and healthy. But that wasn't an option. I continued talking to Kyle about other things I could do to support Carson. Kyle was working with Carson to text or call if the self-harm feelings became very dark for him. Discussing solutions and continuing to work through the feelings, depression, and anxiety related to gender dysphoria and transitioning would be the solution, it just took time.

Junior high students are the worst at picking on others at the best of times. For my kid to be going through such a monumental change in the midst of junior high seemed cruel. Thank goodness he had switched schools and he had Jess and Ang the grade above him, for this year at least; they were off to high school in the fall.

One of the amazing things I'd learned, even during this dark time, is that this next generation is much more sexually liberated, and gender liberated than my generation. Honestly, it makes me feel a bit disappointed in myself and my fellow Gen Xers. Why didn't we think about things like this? Why didn't we push the limits and open our minds more to the possibilities relating to gender and sexuality? But I guess they were all steppingstones to supporting this new generation. Lots of learning for Daisy and my generation.

Carson

Sometimes everything backs up on me and I feel like there's nowhere to turn. I get all wound up and spiral into a black pit of despair. Kyle's helping me work on this. Putting "tools in my tool kit" is how he puts it. It happens less now and sometimes with the positive self-talk methods that Kyle's taught me, I can actually remove myself from the spiral once it starts or even refuse to engage with the spiral. But other times, I can't pull free. It has a grip on me. I have some anger that I need to get out. I hate that. I hate that I can't control it. That it manifests inside me.

I know that I scare my dad and family sometimes when I go silent, turn inward, and especially when I go dark. But sometimes, I just can't face the world. I know my dad supports me in any way he can but he's right, there are some things that I have to work through on my own. There are times when I just can't. My room becomes my sanctuary, where I can pull the covers over my head. That helps to block the bad shit and keep more from entering my body and brain. Sometimes I just write, the writing takes some of the bad out of my head. Then I delete it, remove it from this world, erase it or throw it in the bonfire. That feels good. Sometimes I go and do sports, I throw a ball or practice lacrosse. That gets some of the crap out too. But I can't ever get it all to leave my body. Some simmers, waiting for its next opportunity.

My school has been especially bad about misgendering me and calling me the wrong name. My dad got it fixed in one layer of their system, but the administration couldn't change it on a deeper level until we got my name and gender changed legally. My dad is working on this but as a minor, my mom needs to sign off on the change and she won't even call me the right name, so I'm sure as hell not holding my breath on that happening anytime soon. My dad said there is an option to go to court as a work around, but it's not the greatest path and I may have to testify. I'm not sure I'm ready for that quite yet.

In my darkest thoughts, it's true, I have thought about committing suicide. Sometimes this world and the pain is too harsh for me to deal with. But in those times, I often cling to the love of my family and what my life could be, when I feel rational enough anyway. I don't want to leave my family and friends. And besides, what if I'm put on this earth to do something great? The pain that I feel is real. But it too shall pass. I heard that somewhere recently and it kinda stuck with me. Fitting, I thought.

Kris

Carson is an amazing brother. He plays board games with me, helps me draw and paint. He gets sad and grumpy sometimes. I don't like being around him when he's like that. It makes me feel yucky. It's like his body gets taken over by a symbiote, like Venom. I don't like when those demons reach for him and try to steal him from us. Bad demons! Go away! We don't want you; you're not welcome here.

Sara

Brad told me that he's concerned for Kari's wellbeing. Apparently, she told that counsellor, Kyle, or whatever his name is, that she's thought of ending her life. If she'd just suck it up, put on her big girl panties, and forget all this "I'm a boy" bullshit, then life would be so much better. It's embarrassing. Until she sorts herself out, she isn't welcome at my house. In fact, I'm converting her room to a crafting room. When she smartens up, I'll convert it back, but until then . . . nope.

Daisy

Carson has become a very important part of my life, our lives, just like Brad and Kris have, of course. Carson is a true hero to me. The amount of crap that kid has gone through, and the strength required to continue to bash his way

155

through a seemingly never-ending stream of bullshit along his path, is simply amazing. I'm in awe of him most days.

I do my best to support Carson, Brad, and Kris, especially when Carson has those days where he's really down in the dumps, depressed, and seems filled with anxiety. That's a huge understatement, those days when we're scared that we might lose him, days when we can't get him to come out of his room and talk with us, days when he goes so far inwards that I'm scared he may never resurface again. But he does, thank goodness, he does. My insides quiver and I feel ill when I think about it. I wish I could transfer some strength to him on those days, when he's tired of being strong, tired of fighting the good fight. But I can't. I feel helpless.

As a mother, I can't understand Sara's stubbornness and unwillingness to even attempt to comprehend what Carson is going through. I try not to judge, as we all have our own path, but damn it, I'm going to judge. What kind of parent abandons their child when they're at their most vulnerable? A heartless, selfish bitch, that's who. *Shit, was that out loud? Ah, fuck it.*

Jess

Carson scares me sometimes when he's really depressed. I'm scared he's going to hurt himself. I've come to love him like a brother. In my heart, he is my brother. I feel so helpless some days though. He knows we all love him and that we're here for him. I hope it's enough.

Ang

When I think of Carson, I want to spread my wings and protect him. When the darkness sweeps in, I want to hug him tight until it passes and he feels better. But he won't let any of us in when it's at its darkest. I wish he would. We all love him so much and want him to be all he can be.

156

31
speed dating

FRIDAY FUN NIGHT. Sipping on beer one evening after a long week of work, us gals were immersed in conversation. Feeling like a fly on the wall, I listened as Anne and Twila exchanged their latest dating stories. Anne was frustrated, "Online dating won. Or lost. Depending how one chooses to look at it. Five hundred for online dating and zero for me, if we're keeping score. Either way, I give up! Spun up and thrown out is how I feel about dating sites. They're all the same, really, same with a different name. Same people. Same lines. Same lies. Same process. Same result. Utter bullshit".

Twila and Anne continued chatting, well bitching if you must know, about online dating and the lack of eligible men. The guys were either married, scammers, liars, disgusting, emotionally unavailable, or a combination thereof. You'll be aware of this if you heard about my dating adventures or if you, yourself, has dared to venture onto a dating site. What a mess!

"Anne, there must be a better way to meet men. What are we missing? I want to get married again. I want someone to spend my lonely nights with," Twila whined desperately.

"It's just the way people meet these days. The day of the organic meet has all but disappeared. Friend referrals have gone by the wayside. It's almost like people think you'll hold them accountable, and perhaps even sue them, if it doesn't work out," Anne laughed.

Twila was shaking her head, "I know. So, what in the hell do we do? I want a man but frig, I can't handle the crap being thrown at me on dating websites. I think my 'swipe left' has been so overused that they're going deactivate the button for crying out loud. I've tried updating my profile pictures and story, but nada. I'm still attracting the same bottom feeders."

"I did the same on my profile but to no avail. The thought crossed my mind that maybe I'm too picky. But then I'm reminded of my latest yawn session, I mean, date, when buddy unzipped his fly at the table, reached down into his pants, and started scratching his pubes like something was on fire or maybe he was trying to start a fire. I didn't ask why."

Twila choked on her wine, "What? He did what?"

Anne laughed and shook her head, "Yup. Lucky me. I stood up abruptly, excused myself, and headed quickly for the door. The jackass chased me out of the pub. I could hear chairs being tossed as he exited."

"I could imagine cookies being tossed," Twila muttered.

Laughing, Anne said, "I sure wanted to! If you can believe it, it gets worse. He caught up with me at my car. As I was saying goodbye, again, he pinned me against the door. His tongue was coming at me like from a possessed demon, flicking like a snake. He was trying to kiss me with that disgusting thing. I had my hand in front of my face and my other hand pushed him away to avoid that. I seriously felt like prey with him coming at me, the mouse. A toy for the snake. Blech!"

I'm so glad I met Brad and I'm off those bloody sites. Hearing my girl-friends' stories made me want to retch.

Twila's eyes were bugging out of her head. "Blech is right! That makes my stomach turn. How did he misread the sign that you weren't interested when you left the pub?"

"Hell if I know. I was relieved we were in a public place. With him acting like that, can you imagine what would've happened behind closed doors?"

Looking disgusted, Twila said, "I don't even want to think about it. Dude, have you heard of consent? Gross Mr. Snake Tongue. Uh, on that note . . . where are the good ones? There are good ones still, aren't there? Jen and Daisy can't have gotten the last ones."

My sweet Brad.

"Oh, I'm sure there are. They're just hiding under a rock or something!"

"Where does one find the map to those rocks? There must be guys out there who are frustrated with the whole online dating saga, too." Twila pondered.

I recalled an email I'd received the other day. It was advertising a different kind of dating. Why the hell do I still get these things? It's creepy when stuff happens like that.

Damn you, big brother!

Anne mentioned, "Oh, I'm sure there are."

I spoke up, "Hey, here's one avenue that I've never tried, although I've heard mixed things about it. Have you ladies tried it? I flipped my phone around so they could both see the ad.

Twila cocked her head, "Oh?"

Anne read the ad aloud. "Speed dating! The organizers sell tickets, get a bunch of men and women in a room, and you have a series of mini dates throughout an evening."

"That could be interesting. At least you have your five senses working for you at an event like that. Rather than judging a dude on his texting abilities:

Hey, you DTF?

Twila was laughing, hard!

No dude, I'm looking for a long-term relationship, I'm not 'Down To Fuck'.

But thanks for making this easy for me. See ya! No mystery there man, I'm out!"

Anne grabbed my phone out of my hands, "I'm so tired of that garbage. Here check this out . . . it's sixty dollars to register, there are spots available for twelve men and twelve women at this event. Oh look, it's in two weeks. Hmm . . . you have twelve dates over the evening, a break in the middle and it looks like seven minutes to chat with each person. What do you think?"

"Honestly, I'll try anything at this point. Well, almost anything. Seven minutes seems like a long time to talk to a stranger."

"I'm sure you get into a rhythm after the first one, I hope!" Anne laughed heartily.

"Well, what do we have to lose? Let's do it!"

"Yup!"

After the event, I met with Anne to debrief.

"The day of the speed dating event finally *(unfortunately?)* arrived. Twila and I met just before the event for an 'ounce of liquid courage'. After downing it, we each took a deep breath shaking our heads, onwards and upwards. 'Let's do this!' I laughed. 'Hopefully it's better than we anticipate.' Twila crossed her fingers and grinned."

"They weren't joking when they named it 'speed' dating! My head was spinning by the time we reached the halfway point. A steady stream of men, a new one sitting down every seven minutes. I could hardly keep their names straight, never mind what they did for a living, how long they'd been single, what their hobbies were, how many kids they had, and so on.

The first dude started out like this: "Two kids, four ex-wives, all selfish, greedy bitches. Wanna be wife number five?"

Hell no! Winner, winner, chicken dinner.

And the second: "I'm pooped today. Was up all night playing video games. I'm almost to stage five. Stage five, can you believe it?"

Stage five of what? I seriously don't get video games. Next!

"Two kids, ex-wife I get along with, dog we share, looking for work."

"Oh, what do you do for work?"

"Yeah, I'm figuring that out?"

What? Are you switching careers? So I asked and the response was, "I don't know what I wanna do when I grow up." *Uh, what've you been doing up until this point? You are in your forties. Odd.*

I thought to myself, 'Am I attracted to any of them? Nope'."

"Sitting down and chatting for seven minutes at a time with a person felt a bit daunting before I even got there. But I was surprised how quickly it flew. There were some very interesting people searching for love, or at least, I assumed they were searching for love. But maybe not. Who knows? After each person, we had to mark 'yes' or 'no'. These choices meant 'yes – exchange our contact information' or 'no – not interested'. Both parties had to check 'yes' before the organizers would share anyone's information. By the halfway point, I had a stream of 'no's checked. It wasn't looking promising."

Yikes! Hopefully not a complete waste of time! My fingers had been crossed for Anne.

"And that dreaded bell, I could definitely do without that. I'd be just getting into a decent conversation and 'ding ding' echoed in my eardrums. There must be a more dignified way of letting us know time is up. Next!"

"At the break, I chatted with Twila and one of the guys we'd both chatted with already. I wasn't interested, there was an aroma that was rather unsettling coming off of him. It reminded me of that stinky meatball metallic guy you dated for a while, Daisy. Blech!"

"Eww . . . I didn't actually date that guy. I only went out with him twice." Why I felt I needed to defend myself, is beyond me.

Chuckling, Anne continued, "I wondered if it was the same guy, but no, it was a completely different person."

Ugh!

"It was crazy. Ding! Break's over. Back to our stations to meet six more guys. Here we go! About two minutes into the second half, I heard a screech, 'All you men are trash. How are you going to be my sugar daddy and give me everything I want and deserve making the blue-collar salary you do?'"

In shock, I asked, "Holy hell, some chick said that?"

How rude!

"Yup, can you believe it? Talk about gross. My eyes wide, I looked at Twila as she mouthed, What the fuck? I shook my head and shrugged. The room was silent. Queen Bitch Sugar Baby abruptly stood, wrapped her fur around her shoulders, grabbed her friend, and stormed out of the event. Crazy much? What the hell just happened?"

"What happened next?" I wondered aloud.

Anne shook her head, "The poor host stood up, 'Well, with that sudden exit, we have two empty female tables. Please continue to rotate as before, unfortunately the men will have two tables to simply hang out at when they get to them.' An opportunity to check their phones, in other words. That broke the rhythm for them though. Jeez."

"Speaking of checking your phone, the friend of the QBSB had been heavily monitoring her phone all evening long, emailing, texting, shopping, and at one point she was on a call as some poor guy was trying to get to know her. Extremely fortunate dodge, dude! Talk about rude! Leaving in the middle, and that outburst, very uncouth! It seemed it wasn't just crazy men who were looking to date, there are plenty of crazy women, too."

"Halfway through the second round, I was having a fun conversation with a gentleman named Tom. He was engaged, made eye contact, asked questions about me, and appeared to not lose interest when I responded. He was also pretty cute. I don't know how I missed him when we first arrived. Delicious."

"Tom was mid-sentence, 'I have two boys and . . .' when we heard sobbing. I searched the room for the source of the noise. It was an older man, speaking through his tears, 'I can't do this.' He got up, grabbed his coat and headed for the door. The lady he'd been speaking with looked stunned. There was a sadness about her. The host went to chat with her and we overheard the conversation, 'He started talking about his deceased wife and then completely broke down. That poor man. My heart aches for him.'"

"I looked back at Tom, 'Oh my goodness, he's sure not ready to date yet. Poor guy.' Tom nodded, 'That's for sure!' I shrugged, *best get back to it*, smiled, and looked into Tom's eyes, 'You were saying?' He looked thoughtful for a moment, 'Oh yes, I have two boys and two girls: a twelve-year-old girl, ten-year-old twin boys and an eight-year-old girl. They're great kids.' Oh my, four kids. That would flip my life upside down nicely. Would I be interested in that? Hmm . . ."

"Ding! The dreaded bell. 'Very nice to meet you, Tom,' I subtly batted my eyelashes as I gave him my most charming and sexy smile. He smiled back at me, 'Yes, you as well, Anne. I hope we'll have an opportunity to chat more in the future.' I checked a 'yes', my only one of the evening."

"After the event, Twila and I compared notes. Twila commented that four kids, added to her one, were far too many for her to stomach. I was still on the fence about it but was happy to see if we matched. I had to wait until the next evening to see if I would get Tom's number. Twila checked 'yes' for two people, neither of which was Tom, thank goodness."

"Ok, then what happened? Did you hear from him?" I had a hunch she had.

Anne nodded and smiled, "The next night, Tom texted me.

Hi Anne, this is Tom. I'm so glad we matched. I was praying for it.

I smiled. I'm happy we matched too.'

We chatted that night and then he invited me out for dinner and drinks the next night.

I'm excited to learn more about you and have a real date. Shall I pick you up at six?

Ooh, chivalrous, that's something not so common anymore.

That sounds wonderful, Tom."

32
strange dreams

BRAD WAS AWAY on business for a full week and I'm not sure what the heck was going on in my mind, but I woke up recalling the most vivid and bizarre dreams that week.

The first seemed so real that it took me a minute or two to remember if it was a memory or a dream. Definitely a dream. I call this one "Flashback to Christmas 2020". And typical for my dreams, it started in the middle of something that had happened already. I pieced together that I'd been sent for professional photographs by my company. That part was a bit warbled in the dream but the next was crystal clear.

Our public relations specialist asked if we had any strong feelings or concerns about Fred, our corporate photographer, posting our management pictures on his website. I shrugged my shoulders, then responded clearly and strongly, "I strongly feel that he SHOULD use my pictures on his website." Heck, I squished and prodded and sucked in and stuffed and rolled my poor COVID-19 body into a sausage casing-like thing to fit into my fancy business suit I haven't worn in two years. There has got to be some athletic award for the gymnastic performance that was required for me to get into that outfit.

Where ARE my sweats? And who put those goodies on the table? Oh right, ME, it IS the Christmas season after all. And on top of all that, Fred and I really bonded as we discovered that I truly DO have a much better and more photogenic side. Who knew?!

Damn it, now to remember which side it is. "Oh Fred?!" That mirror image picture thing is throwing me right off."

Weird, right?!

The second dream hit me beautifully and fully in the heart. It was sweet and warmed my entire body. It was Adam. He came to me in my dreams again.

"Hi Daisy, my sweet girl. I've been watching over you and our girls. They're growing up big and strong. You're doing a wonderful job with them, you're a great mom, as you always were. I've enjoyed watching you fall in love with Brad. You two really are a great match. Being I can't be there for you, he's the one I trust to take care of you. Not that you need taking care of, but you know what I mean. You'll be a wonderful stepmom to Brad's boys. Watching you with them has been heart-warming. I love you so much, sweetie."

"Adam?" I could feel him on the bed beside me, stroking my hair like he used to.

"Yes, my darling. I have but seconds left. I must be gone before you're fully awake."

"Adam, I love you. I always will," I mumbled, still not quite awake.

"I know, my darling. But now I must go. I will be watching out for you and our girls. I love you, always."

And with that, he was gone. I fully woke up and felt happy and sad. My heart hurt and felt full all at once. I remembered every word that Adam had said.

Oh, how I still miss that man. My guardian angel. My first love. Always my soulmate.

The third night, I awoke with a start. Horrified that my dream might be true. Carson was dead. It couldn't be. Could it? I had to know. I rushed down the stairs, two and three at a time, skidded along the main floor as I wound around and sprinted down the stairs to the basement. I slammed into the door as I started pounding on the door like a crazy woman and calling out Carson's name.

No! Don't let it be true.

Behind me, I heard a very groggy Ang say, "Mom? Are you ok?" I pounded harder on Carson's door, "No!" I spat. "Carson, are you ok?" I heard a groan from inside. Ang raised her eyebrows and looked at me funny, "Uh, Mom, he was out late last night, remember?"

I looked sideways at Ang as I recalled, yes, he'd been out late celebrating his lacrosse team's provincial victory. By this time, Carson had sauntered out of his bedroom and was looking at me bleary eyed. I rushed to him and threw my arms around him, "Thank God you're safe, Carson."

Carson stretched his neck to peek around me at Ang, hoping for a clue. She shrugged and shook her head, as if she said, "no clue" without uttering a word.

Now that I confirmed he was safe, I explained, "I had the most terrible dream that something happened to you, Carson. It was a horrible nightmare." I finally let him go. "Ok, you can go back to sleep." He looked at me and then Ang, and muttered, "Ok, that was weird. See you around noon."

After the third night's horror of a dream, I was concerned what the fourth would bring. Unfortunately, it was a bit of a doozy but at least no one was dead in it.

But fuck!

It was about Brad. He was away at a conference. The beginning was true, even in the dream I knew that. What happened next, I hoped was just some weird thing that I conjured up. *A few of the guys decided to go out to the strippers, including one of the ladies from his work,* who I'd met briefly at their Christmas party several months back. She was gorgeous. That much I remembered. *They both got drunk and horny at the rippers and then things got a little handsy as they were walking back to the hotel. I saw her take him by the hand and lead him to the elevator and up to the floor where her room was. In the elevator they were making out, her hands all over him and his all over her.*

Even in my dream I felt like puking.

Once she got him to her room and they were naked, she told him how long she'd wanted to fuck him. They slept together.

Thank goodness I was spared the intimate details in my dream, but still.

The dream cut to the next morning, Brad with his head in his hands, swearing and clearly upset that he'd had sex with another woman. He was shaking his head. And crying. Fuck.

I think the last part was the worst for me as it seemed too real. It was just a dream.

But could it have happened? Did it? Shit.

This was the first time that I had felt even remotely uneasy about Brad remaining faithful to me.

It was killing me. I had to talk to him.

Please let this just be a dream. Don't let it be real.

I thought back to my girlfriends and the men who'd cheated on them, and all the married guys we'd talked to on dating sites. Surely Brad wasn't to be lumped in with these guys.

Fuck! This bloody dream is killing me.

I dialed the numbers with my stomach in knots. Brad picked up, thank goodness. I asked him what he'd gotten up to the night before. He told me that he'd gone to the gym and then hit the pub with two of his buddies who were at the conference. I told him about my dream and how much it had upset me.

Brad said, "Oh baby, no, no strippers and no other woman. I'm so sorry that you had such a terrible dream. I only have eyes for you, sweetheart. Drunk or sober. There isn't enough drugs and alcohol in the world to cloud my judgment that much, honey. I love and miss you so much."

This man, my man. He was so worth the wait. Able to express his thoughts and feelings and support mine, make me feel better. He is a dream.

"I love you too, Brad. I can't wait to see you."

33
date with tom

Anne

AT SIX ON THE NOSE, Tom pulled up in front of my house in his black Corvette. The drive to the Cattle Baron was short but made shorter by the rev and acceleration of his muscle car. I was looking forward to some great wine and a delicious meal with whom I hoped to be a fantastic guy.

As we enjoyed wine and appetizers, Tom told me about his previous relationship's demise. "We were never a good fit. We rushed in too quickly and never really had much in common, no shared interests. We were so busy getting married and having kids that we didn't make time for one another, and neither of us really cared that we didn't. She got herself a boyfriend quickly after we split. I was still living in the basement, which got uncomfortable when she had her boyfriend over and the kids and I were hanging out in the basement. We could hear them banging upstairs, all the way in the basement."

Lovely! Thanks for that image.

"Oh my. That doesn't sound good at all. How long until you moved out?"

"I moved out a year ago. Got my own place."

"Your split was amicable and mutual then?"

"Well, yeah, I guess you could say that. We aren't divorced yet and separation agreement needs to be signed yet. So far so good though."

Oh, oh, he still has a ton to get through with her. Lots of opportunity for the amicable to turn plain nasty as money and assets get thrown on the table to be split. And with four kids! Shit!

"There's no getting back together with her, if that's what you're thinking."

It's not. That's the least of my worries.

"How are your kids doing with your separation?"

"They've been pretty good. The back and forth seems to be working ok. I have them every second weekend and Wednesday nights."

"That works for you?"

"Yeah, it's great. Best of both worlds. I get to see my kids and I get a lot of me time. I've been spending a lot of time at IKEA lately, getting my place all set up with furniture. It's really coming together now, great to be on my own."

Hmm . . . I thought you moved out a year ago. Seems odd to be purchasing furniture a year later.

"You're just buying furniture now?"

"Yeah, I just moved."

"Oh, a new place? Where were you before?"

"Yes, I have a new place. I was living in the basement at our family home until just recently."

"I thought you said you moved out a year ago."

"No, you misunderstood me. I moved to the basement a year ago. I moved to my own place just recently.

Hmm . . . what'd he say again? "I moved out a year ago. Got my own place", which is certainly not the same as, "I moved to the basement where my wife and kids lived above me." Back away Anne, back away. I bet this isn't the only thing not adding up. As Daisy would say, "TSN turning point". I'm out. Huge red flag. Should I walk out? No, that would be rude. We've already ordered. Ride it out, Anne, ride it out.

"Oh, interesting. You feel like you're ready to date?"

"Definitely. She's dating someone else. There's no going back."

That's not what I asked. Just because she's dating, doesn't mean you're ready to date. You could still be completely hung up on her. Emotionally unavailable.

"Understood but have you . . . never mind."

Don't get invested, Anne. You already know you're out. Keep the talk superficial.

"What do you like to do when you don't have your kids?"

"I game. I'll stay up all night long playing with my buddies. I've met people from all over the world playing. It's awesome. I even met some chicks on there. Chick gamers, can you believe it?"

Chicks? Really?

"Hmm, any plans to meet them in person at any point?" I was trying to grasp any sort of commonality. I'm not sure why though. Clearly, we weren't going to have a second date.

"Nah, gaming is good enough."

He keeps checking boxes in my "I'm not interested" area.

The rest of supper was relatively uncomfortable. He talked more about his ex-wife, and it was easy to tell that he was still head-over-heels-in-love with her.

I'm not interested in him and he's not ready to date, at all.

I couldn't eat my meal fast enough.

"Would you like dessert or another drink, Anne?"

"No, I think we should wrap things up, I need to be up early tomorrow."

"Ok, I'll just have another drink."

I stared blankly at him. Was I not clear?

Is this guy missing a brain cell or five? Maybe it's all the gaming?

I took a deep breath before saying, "I need to get going."

"Just one more," he pleaded as he waved down the server and ordered another drink.

Now this was getting irritating. My patience had run thin with this guy. He was being rude, completely disregarding my need to get home.

And damn it, he drove me here so it's not like I can just go. Why didn't I wear more sensible shoes tonight? If I did, I'd just walk home. Wait a minute. How many drinks has Tom had? Can he even drive safely? Let's see . . . oh, this is number four. Nope . . . I'm texting Daisy.

Hey sweetie, can you pick me up? I'm at the Cattle Baron.

Be right there!

Thanks, gorgeous!

"Ok Tom, I need to get going. My girlfriend is on her way. I'll just settle up my drinks and food with the server."

"Nah, we can just split it down the middle."

"I'll flag our server down. Oh hi, Tammy, please separate our bills for us if you don't mind. I need to settle up with you. Thanks, sweetie!"

As I was leaving, I saw Tom smack Tammy on the ass. I turned and looked at him, shook my head and mouthed, "Really?"

Ugh, what a mess.

I was shaking my head and giggling as I slid into Daisy's car. "What a disaster!" I didn't have to go into any more details than that. We were both laughing all the way back to my place.

"Thanks for the ride, sweetie! See you tomorrow!"

"Looking forward to it!"

34
girl talk – raindrops on roses

SPRING HAD OFFICIALLY ARRIVED. Tulips were coming up around Anne's deck. Jennifer, Amy, Twila, Ronnie, Anne and I had finally found some time to get together. It had been far too long. I relaxed into the comfort and love of my gals. It always felt great when we were together. We had so much to catch up on that it was hard for us to know where to start.

After serving some appetizers and pouring wine for us all, Anne started the discussion. "You all have a ton happening in your life and I can't wait to hear it. Let's get my updates out of the way as they're quick. Boyfriend, no. Dating, not successfully. Career, same ole same ole. That's all I have to update. Daisy, you're up. I want to hear more about Brad and the boys moving in and how Carson's doing."

"Settle in and hold on tight ladies! This could be long! The big move just happened . . . we've been renovating for a couple months, and it was finally done a couple weeks ago. Brad's house sold, thank you, Ronnie!"

"It's what I do! But, yes, you're welcome. It was easy to sell, it's a great house for a family to raise their kids in and a wonderful location."

"Brad, Carson, and Kris moved in last weekend. Ang moved downstairs so her room was open for Kris to move into and I'm busily sorting through my closet trying to make some room for Brad, still. Poor guy! Where did all those clothes come from? I've completely taken over the closet. Clothes are exploding everywhere. Holy Hannah!"

Anne laughed, "I use all three of the bedroom closets here plus I have a dressing room, right?! Believe me, I know!"

"Yeah, but you're a fashionista! I'm not. I have no clue where it all came from. Oh well, purging is good for the soul. I'd forgotten about a number of things I had in there. My wedding dress gave me a good little cry. I moved it to the back of the closet. I'm not ready to part with it. In fact, I may keep it for my girls." Twila gave my shoulder a little squeeze. I nodded and smiled.

"I'm really excited for all of us to be under one roof. The reality is amazing. There's been so much back and forth between our two houses that it's a bit surreal to just all be together. It'll be nice to have one we share as a family."

"That's awesome, Daisy! I'm so happy for you. What about Carson, how's he doing? Coping?" asked Jennifer.

"Overall, he's doing well. We've certainly experienced some unsettling times with him where we've been scared for his wellbeing. Kyle is fantastic, Anne! He's helped Carson and us through all of this. Provided us with a lot of educational material and given Carson some skills to help him work through the tough times. The schools are frustrating as they keep messing up his name and pronouns. And don't even get me started on his mom. I could smack her."

"What do you mean?" Amy asked.

"She refuses to call Carson by his name, and she uses the wrong pronouns on purpose. He hasn't seen her in months. He refuses to. Then she went on a tirade about how she converted his room into a craft room as her kid no longer exists in her mind. I can't fathom how a parent could behave like that. It's disgusting. Brad has been so supportive of him, and all our friends too, thank you all by the way. I'm happy that I can be there for him, whatever he needs."

"That's shocking. I never would have thought that Sara would behave like that. Disappointing. So much for the unconditional love she has for her kids," Twila shrugged and shook her head.

"Yeah, it seems pretty conditional and self-serving, doesn't it?" Ronnie mentioned.

"I forgot that you know Sara from way back, Twila," I nodded in her direction.

"Yeah, I don't know her anymore really. Just met her when our kids were in 'mommy and me' classes. We hung out for a while but then lost touch."

"I remember, from years gone by, Kyle telling me about a large number of transgender youths who are alienated by their parents and kicked out of their houses at fourteen, fifteen or sixteen. Zero support from their parents. It crushed me to hear things like that. Teenagers are already dealing with so many things growing up and then for their parents to toss them out on their ears." Anne let out a huge, disappointed sigh, "The gall of those so-called parents. I'm sorry but parenting isn't just about the easy stuff. You prove your worth as a parent when things get tough, and you have to dig deep within yourself."

"Oh, I agree, 100%. I can't imagine turning my back on my kid. I'm here for life and he knows that," Twila shook her head.

"Brad had a hell of a time trying to get Sara to sign off on Carson's official name- and gender-change paperwork. It got to the point where he spoke with a lawyer about going to court to get full custody and full legal rights over Carson so her signature wouldn't be required."

"How'd he get her to sign?" Twila asked.

"I don't know what made her finally agree to sign off. I don't think Brad mentioned court to her, but it might've come up. All of a sudden, she just relented," I shrugged.

"Even without the struggle for signatures, it was a ridiculously painful process to go through: multiple forms, a psychiatrist letter was required, and several other steps including going to the registry office twice and to the police department for fingerprints. All very odd."

"That sounds like a royal pain," sighed Jennifer.

"A royal pain in the ass, you mean," Ronnie pontificated.

"Oh, it was for sure. But what a relief it was when we finally received the Certificate of Name Change and then shortly thereafter, Carson's birth certificate. We had a little supper celebration the night that came in the mail. All Carson's favorite foods: pizza, Pepsi, garlic rolls and chocolate cake. And then the real work began! Updating his passport, banking info, Registered Education Savings Plan, school, Social Insurance Number, Brad's will, any beneficiary information, the list seemed to be never ending but with each successful change, I saw weight come off Carson's shoulders. It's been simply brilliant to witness."

"That's fantastic news, Daisy! I'm so happy for Carson, and for all of you!" Jennifer smiled, as she hugged me.

"Thank you! One more step on the way to minimizing, and hopefully eventually eliminating his gender dysphoria. Another thing that's helped is that Carson switched schools so that he's with my girls. The timing was perfect with his official name change and the move. He was able to start fresh at a new school with his new name and gender. Much easier transition for him. No one at the school, except my girls and one of his old friends, know his dead name."

"Now that IS brilliant," Amy smiled.

"You know what ladies? My heart is so full with my family and my friends. So much love." A single tear escaped my eye and streamed down my face. My gals and I all stood and hugged, one giant hugging circle.

Twila kicked off the next round of discussion after Anne refilled our drinks and we helped ourselves to more appetizers. "Anne and I went to a speed dating event. It was a bit odd, odd yet fun. I ended up making a match. Not my normal type. He's 57, much older than I'm used to, but he's a sweet man, very intelligent and kind. He treats me like gold."

"What's his name, Twila? What does he do for work? Does he curl your toes?" asked Anne.

"His name is Carl. He's a financier. And yes, he definitely curls my toes. It turns out that I'm sapiosexual."

"Sapio . . . what?" asked Amy looking extremely confused. I hadn't heard this term either, so I leaned forward to hear Twila's response.

"Sapiosexual. To put it simply, it means that intelligence turns me on."

"Oh, wow, that's cool. I've never heard of that," smiled Amy, "but it makes sense that would be a huge turn on. I've never experienced it myself, but I sure can imagine."

"It's a new thing for me too. We're taking it really slowly but so far so good. I'm smitten, that's for sure."

"Aww, that's awesome, Twila. I didn't know that you and Carl had matched, so happy for you!" Anne smiled.

Ronnie took center stage now. "Jamie and I are going strong, and I absolutely love having an open relationship. I know it's a tough concept for some folks, but you know what, I feel like I'm made for an open relationship. Jamie too. It just works for us. We've had all kinds of luxurious fun together, apart and together. We share all of it. When we play apart and get back together, we rehash everything and it's a huge turn on for us both. Sometimes we swap, sometimes we do threesomes, but ALWAYS we communicate with one another.

That's the key. I'm so in love, ladies. Jamie is my man, my soulmate. We were made for each other."

"Aww, that's incredible Ronnie! Sounds like you've found a perfect match. You're built so differently from me in that regard, but I love that you've found exactly what works for you. I'm over the moon happy for you, girl!" Twila expressed.

Ronnie grinned, "I'm over the moon happy, myself! I can't believe it really." We all smiled, basking in Ronnie's glow. The glow of love, sweet love.

Amy took the stage, "I don't have much to update you ladies on. I've been off dating sites for about six months now and just focusing on rebuilding me, exploring me. It's been a great journey. I've gotten into yoga and meditation. An unexpected journey into awakening my inner Amy. It's been pretty cool. Jen, you're up, girl."

"Yes, I guess it's my turn," Jen said, timidly.

Hmm, that's a bit unlike her. She's often quieter, but not timid. Something interesting is coming.

"Chris and I are doing really well, and we've decided to buy a house together. My condo isn't big enough for us and his house isn't really suited for a baby."

"A baby? What? You're pregnant?!!" We all screeched.

Jen blushed a million shades of red before nodding. "I am! Due in September. Chris and I are really excited! We're planning to get married in the summer. I know, I'll be as big as a house by then, but I really do want a lovely June wedding in Kananaskis."

"Oh sweetie, you saved the best news for last!" Anne crossed the room to give Jen a gigantic hug. She stage-whispered in Jen's ear, "Great idea with the apple juice. The gals didn't expect a thing, did you ladies?"

We all shook our heads. We were clueless. Anne had done a wonderful job seamlessly covering for Jen's non-alcoholic "wine" drinking.

"Bravo ladies, well done!" I smiled, "But why'd you wait until the end to take your turn, Jen? That's such exciting news!"

"I figured we'd get all sidetracked to babies, houses and stuff after I went, and I wanted to hear the latest and greatest on everyone else first. By the way, Ronnie, we'd like to hire you to list both Chris's place and mine. Clearly, we'll also need to find a new place. I'm thinking somewhere close to Anne and

Daisy. They live in such a beautiful area, so close to schools and parks and there's the lake too, of course."

"Absolutely, Jen! I'm on it!" grinned Ronnie.

"Oh, and one thing I wanted to ask you ladies as well. Erm . . . Chris and I are still having sex and uh, I'm a bit dry. Have any of you used any lubricant that you like?"

Anne chimed in, drowning out the rest of us, "Fuck Water, baby, Fuck Water. Get the water-based lube. It's the best."

The look on Jen's face said it all: bewildered, confused, "Fuck Water? You must be joking?!"

"No, I'm dead serious. It's awesome stuff. The company has a great sense of humor too. The slogan on the bottle cracks me up: 'When spit and courage aren't enough.'"

We all giggled and nodded in agreement. There are lots of brands out there, but that one did the job for me when required.

35

top surgery

ONE SUNDAY MORNING when the girls were out at volleyball and basketball, and Kris was at his mom's, Carson called Brad and I into the living room. Clearly alarmed, Brad firmly asked, "Is everything alright, Carson?"

Carson nodded. I sat down on Carson's left side and put my hand on his knee. I beckoned Brad to sit, patting the couch with my hand. He was just standing there. I gave him a head nod, *sit your ass down, sweetie.* Finally, Brad sat on Carson's other side.

Carson took a deep breath, "I've thought long and hard about this, done a bunch of research and Kyle and I have been exploring the idea for months." What idea? "Dad, Daisy, I've decided that I'd like to have top surgery. Kyle and I have been discussing the benefits, the side effects, and how it all works. It's the next step for me now that I'm taking testosterone." I patted his knee again, nodding, while Brad said, "Tell us more about it. How does the process work? What do we need to do?"

"Top surgery is basically removing the breast tissue and creating a flatter chest that looks like a typical cisgender male's chest. Kyle is up on all this with all his clients, and he said that there aren't any surgeons in Alberta who'll perform top surgery, or even discuss top surgery plans with, anyone under seventeen."

What the fuck?! Why?

"What about discussing it with their parents?" I asked.

Carson shook his head, "Nope! Not with parents either. It's like your rights relating to your body don't exist until you're seventeen."

WTF is wrong with Alberta?

Carson wouldn't be seventeen for a few years, he only just turned fourteen. There must be another option.

Brad shook his head, "So, what does that mean? What are our options?" Carson sighed, "Here in Alberta, we need to have psychiatrist assess my needs for top surgery and then have them recommend me for top surgery. That's the only way to get on the waitlist right now." I can't even imagine the look on my face at this, "What?"

"Yeah, I know. Apparently, the Metta Centre will hook me up with a psychiatrist. So that's good."

Brad and I were nodding, "Ok, how long is the waitlist?"

Carson's shoulder's drooped, "Well, it's eighteen to twenty-four months wait time before I'm seventeen, but I'm not even eligible to go on the waitlist until next year. Then, when I finally turn seventeen, we'll be able to speak with a surgeon. Kind of. Kyle said the timing is a bit of a shot in the dark as no one can provide a definite timeline to meet the surgeon, never mind how long it'll take for the surgery to be booked and how far out the booking would be."

Sounds like a lot of unknowns! And a lot of bullshit.

I shook my head. Brad said, "This is ludicrous. Are there any other options?"

We were well aware of the effects gender dysphoria had on Carson and his mental health. We knew that Female to Male ("FTM") top surgery would hugely lessen the effects of gender dysphoria for him and we were willing do just about anything to support this process. We felt sure that once he had a more masculine looking chest that he would be misgendered far less as well.

I can't imagine walking around having people say to me, "May I help you, sir?" or "Pass this to him," or "There he goes,". It would seriously mess me up.

"In your FTM top surgery research, did you look into bottom surgery at all? Is that something that interests you?" Brad asked.

"I did. Most of the stuff I read said that FTM bottom surgery hasn't really been perfected yet. On top of that, I'm not sure whether I'm planning to do it at all, even when it has been perfected. Time will tell."

While reflecting on this, it occurred to me that it made perfect sense. Male-to-female bottom surgery requires a bunch of extra stuff moved, removed, and shaped (*yes, I'm very technical*) to form a vagina. Female-to-male bottom surgery requires some serious work to form a penis, one that actually moves and behaves like a penis, one a cisgender male is born with. Getting hard and soft, cumming.

How do they do that? Hmm... I can see clearly how difficult this would be.

During one of our discussions with the doctors about top surgery, I had a hilarious thought. What if I made a query with a straight face and a very serious tone, "Do you think it might be possible when Carson is having top surgery, for me to be in the bed next to him? They could just move his excess breast tissue into my breasts. You know, to make them firmer. After having twins, my boobs are rocks in socks."

The thought of this made me want to burst out laughing. I was dying inside, forcing my giggle down, desperately trying to not smile. I managed to set my face in an innocent, curious look, quizzical even.

I imagined the doctor mortified. The nurse disapproving with a hint of unsure. Imagining the look of shock and disbelief on their faces was making it harder and harder for me not to burst out laughing.

I envisioned Carson snorting, "She's joking!" Then the nurse laughing so hard she was squealing and snorting. Me laughing uproariously. The doctor stone-faced for a moment and then a rumbling belly laugh.

Honestly, you have to have some humor in these situations, they are way too tense and serious.

After we left the doctor's office, I told Carson what I'd been thinking, quickly adding, "I'm sorry, that was inappropriate."

Laughing, Carson shook his head, "Nah, Daisy, that was just fine, hilarious in fact. On top of it, it might have made that pole-up-the-ass doctor laugh, or at least break a smile, although his face might've cracked."

I laughed and then nodded, "Phew, ok, when I was telling you, I thought maybe it was in bad taste but I'm glad you see the humor in it." Carson turned to me and smiled, "Daisy, you added some color to the sitch, it's all good."

It was extremely frustrating trying to get information on top surgery timing and the process, beyond what Kyle and the Metta Centre had given us. Alberta's Health Minister was useless. Kyle suggested we reach out to another jurisdiction if we could afford to fly and pay for the surgery. We reached out to Ontario and BC. There was a clinic in Ontario that had a shorter waitlist and was slightly less restrictive on age requirements. At least the surgeon and nurse would talk to us. We asked a ton of questions and received a boatload of answers. We were prepared to move forward with the process once the surgeon gave the nod. Whenever that might be.

Brad discussed Carson's wishes with Sara. It went about as well as you'd imagine. Something along the lines of, "over my dead body." All I could do was shake my head along with Brad on that one. I'd love to sit down and chat with her and explain what her son has been going through. There are a couple reasons that wasn't going to happen: 1) Sara had taken to calling me "Dandelion or whatever." *Holy hell.* Pretty clear where her respect level was with me. And 2) I knew she'd never hear me. She didn't hear Brad or her kids, why would she listen to me? I didn't think it was worth the effort.

Talk about slamming my head against the wall. No thanks. The best I can do is just keep supporting my family.

Carson didn't need his mom's permission. But it sure would be nice to have her support.

36
single life

TWILA, Anne and I were hanging out one Friday night in Anne's hot tub. Twila was grumbling about the dating scene. Same shit, different pile. nothing had changed since I'd been single. Their frustration was real.

After a few drinks, Twila exclaimed, "I'm so tired of being fuck-zoned."

"Fuck-zoned? What do you mean?" Anne asked.

"You know how guys say they get friend-zoned? When a woman won't date or fuck them, and just wants to be friends with them? Guys get super pissed at that."

"Uh huh."

"Well, fuck-zoned is pretty much the opposite. It happens when a guy won't date you, they just wanna fuck you."

"Hmm . . . never heard that before but it's damn accurate. Not even FWB, just fucking?" Anne seemed intrigued by the term.

"Yup. It keeps happening to me. It was fun for a while but now it just makes me feel like shit. It's like I'm on call all the time, on call for sex. I wait for the call, then jump to attention and rush over to the dude's place when it comes. It's getting old."

"Fucking booty call! Oh yeah, I get that for sure. That's how I felt sometimes with David years ago, jeez how long ago was that? Two, no, three years ago. It felt all fucked up to me."

"It is. It's the thing these days, and it drives me nuts."

"Wait a minute. I thought you were dating Carl, the financier?"

"Yeah, turns out he was seeing three of us at once."

"Oh, for fucks sake. Is dating not monogamous anymore? I don't get it. How are you supposed to properly get to know a person when you're distracted by two others?" I was bewildered.

"Well, I thought we were. Apparently not. He broke up with me in favor of one of the other girls. The fucker invited the three of us over one night and interviewed us all through the night, making us compete. I don't know why I stayed, morbid curiosity maybe, or perhaps just complete disbelief at the situation. It was awful. Answering questions, kissing, an all-out competition. I guess I stayed thinking I'd win. Looking back though, what a fucked-up situation. Oh and he gave me the runner-up prize, a blue second-place ribbon."

"A second-place ribbon? Holy fuck. That whole thing is completely messed up!" Anne exclaimed.

"Did the winner get a trophy?" I giggled.

Twila laughed, "No, she got the fuck-nut financier."

"Score! You escaped that disaster! You won the real prize, freedom from that whackjob!"

"That's for sure."

Anne was laughing, "Speaking of disaster, one of the guys I was trying to unsuccessfully date contacted me the other day, hmm . . . now that I think about it, I think he fuck-zoned me. Argh! Anyway, he invited me over and said, 'Hey, I've gotta warn you, I'm so horny that I don't think I'll last long. Oh and I don't have much time.' I grunted, 'Uh, that's not the best-selling feature, you know?!' Ya sure, I'll warm up my car in this frozen hell of ice and snow, drive up Deerfoot for half an hour to come join you for average sex made terrible cuz you last seven seconds. Hard pass! Ya I love cumming but at least my vibrator lasts longer than a cowboy on a bull at a rodeo . . . Yeehaaa! You not making it to the horn 'aint gonna make this girl cum!" Anne said with her best cowgirl twang.

We laughed uproariously. Yeah, not the best way to entice a woman to join you for a romp in the hay. "Ok so you probably won't cum but I will. When can you be here?"

Ha-ha-ha . . . try never!

The conversation shifted as Twila asked how Carson was doing. I was happy to report that he was doing really well. "One thing I never thought about before is the difficulties Carson encounters simply trying to find a washroom." My girlfriends look puzzled and I continued, hoping to clarify, "For example, the school is a bit messed up on the whole washroom situation. Carson has to go into the teachers' lounge to use the single stall there."

"What? How uncomfortable would that be?" exclaimed Anne, "Isn't that against policy?"

"Apparently, they can't make the washrooms 'unisex' until they can renovate. The sides of the stall need to go all the way to the ground."

"Hmm, that seems weird. What are they worried about?" Twila puzzled.

"No clue. Maybe people checking out other people under the stalls? But it's a pain when we go to the mall. Carson wants to find a single stall and they don't have any there. His anxiety soars when he can't 'hold it' any longer. I can't even imagine the stress as he gets misgendered going into the washroom. Jeez. Poor kid just wants to pee."

"How irritating! They should all be unisex. We're in stalls for crying out loud, who cares if a guy or girl is next to you. That show *Ally McBeal* was way ahead of its time."

It sure was!

Anne nodded, "Right?!"

37

mainstream pan

ONE EVENING, Brad and I were sitting on the couch, munching on popcorn, and watching my new favourite show, *Schitt's Creek*. That particular episode seemed to really hit home for us.

David—male—and Stevie—female—are good friends. It's a unique relationship but they are good friends. One night they drink a bit (a lot) too much, which leads to an interesting encounter in the bedroom. No surprise here, they end up sleeping together. Except that up until this point the viewers are led to think David is gay.

The next day they're in the liquor store buying wine for a dinner party. Stevie ("SB") gently nudges David ("DR") for some clarification about his sexuality as she's a bit confused. They're picking out bottles when this conversation ensues:

SB - So, just to be clear, um . . . I'm a red wine drinker.
DR - Ok that's fine.
SB – Ok, cool. But, uh, I only drink red wine.
DR – Ok.
SB – And up until last night, I was under the impression that you too only drank red wine. But I guess I was wrong?

DR - I see where you're going with this. Um . . . I do drink red wine. But I also drink white wine.

SB – Oh.

DR - And I've been known to sample the occasional rose. And a couple summers back, I tried a merlot that used to be a chardonnay . . .

SB – Uh . . . ok.

DR - . . . which got a bit complicated.

SB – Yeah, so . . . you're really just open to all wines.

DR - I like the wine and not the label. Does that make sense?

SB – Yes. That does. Um . . . this is just very new to me.

"Brad, they're talking about pansexuality." I paused the playback, "Wow, that makes a whole lot of sense. That hugely simplified pansexuality for me. It's all about not limiting the choices of who you love based on gender."

Brad laughed, "Absolutely! I didn't actually realize that David's pansexual. I'm sure Stevie was confused too after the two of them slept together."

No shit! That's enough to confuse a gal.

I was nodding as Brad was speaking, "One hundred percent! What a fantastic way to explain it. Where was this when we needed it when Carson first came out?" I laughed.

Brad was nodding as well, "No kidding. Although, I'm not sure the light-bulb would've gone off for me back then. Now that I understand more about pansexuality, it's beautiful to see it discussed and framed in a mainstream TV show. I love that they're helping to normalize the term by not pussyfooting around it, rather they're discussing it in a direct and straightforward way."

"Me too. I love the transgender discussion too with the merlot and chardon-nay. Very simply put."

We called the kids in to watch that one scene. The kids looked at us with a slight expression of "duh" spread across their faces. Carson said, "Uh, yep. That's it in a nutshell. Pretty simple."

"But don't you think it's great that they're talking about it in a show?"

"Yeah, but it's pretty normal for our generation. There are exceptions of course but for the most part, everyone just gets it. It's your generation and beyond that need to figure this stuff out," Jess said boldly.

"Ok, I agree. But don't you think it's good to have it in a show that attracts folks from our generation? Isn't that helping to educate the generations that need it?" I queried.

"Ya. But most probably wouldn't get it," Carson stated.

"Right, but don't you think it's it good to have it in there to open the dialogue though?"

"I guess," Carson and Jess relented.

The kids left the living room and went back to whatever they were doing before. "Hmm, that's not quite how I thought that would go," Brad said.

"Yeah, me neither. I thought they'd think it's great. Hmm . . . are we really that not with it?" I laughed.

"I think you might be right, sweetie."

"You know what?"

"What?" Brad responded.

"It's weird that people who are gay or bi or transgender or pansexual have to 'come out'. Why is that? Why don't you have to 'come out' when you're straight or cisgender? That's just weird. I hope in my lifetime that I experience a time when people can just be. There's no assumption about gender or sexuality. Let's face it, as long as you aren't trying to date someone, what does it matter. Hmm . . . even then. I'm trying to break down these crazy assumptions in our society, but it's ingrained in me too."

Brad smiled at me and said, "Yeah, it is weird. I hope we see that too, sweetie."

I snuggled into Brad as we continued to chill in front of the TV, his left arm around me and his right on my knee. I snuggled in close. *Heaven.* After the show ended, Brad took me by the hand while I mumbled something about the dishes. He nudged my hand harder. "They'll still be there in the morning." I nodded.

When we reached our bedroom, Brad closed the door and took me in his arms. I sunk into him deeply, with complete surrender. We kissed, gently and slowly at first, his lips slowly sucking on my lower lip, his tongue tracing the outside of my lips. The passion started deep inside me and permeated outward, our kissing becoming more intense, almost urgent. Passion exploded. We were making love, eyes locked, seeing into each other's souls. Completely connected. He was holding me in the palm of his hands, and I was holding him. We were one.

38
chance encounter

MCKENZIE MEADOWS WAS CALLING my name one afternoon, so I booked a tee time for Anne and me. The day was gorgeous, and the greens were exquisite. Brad was playing golf with some of his buddies at Kananaskis, another course I loved to play. We checked in well ahead of our tee time and grabbed a quick bite in the restaurant. Walking to the starter's shack, where we'd start our game, I heard a familiar voice. I grabbed Anne's hand and hissed, "Anne, that's David's voice. I'd recognize that voice anywhere." *Shit!*

As we rounded the corner from the pro shop and checked in with the starter, there was David, strutting around the corner from the driving range, chatting with another man.

Fuck. Fuckety. Fuck.

I pulled my shit together and put on my best smile. David looked over at me, his face lit up as he beamed in my direction, "Daisy, it's been forever, how are you?" He scooped me up in his arms, swung me around, and gave me a kiss on the cheek. He held out his hand to Anne. "Hmm . . . let me guess, you're Anne?"

Always couth, Anne held out her hand and smartly said, "Yes, I'm Anne. And you are?" I recovered my senses, but David beat me to the punch, "I'm David. A pleasure to meet you." Anne tipped her head, nodded, and smiled, "You as well."

"When do you tee off?" David queried.

"Six-thirty, how about you?" I responded.

"Cool! We're at six-thirty, too. Oh, and this is my buddy, Doug."

"Great to meet you, Doug!" Anne and I said in unison as we each shook his hand.

"The privilege and pleasure are all mine," Doug responded with a wink, "shall we?"

David and Doug teed off first from the blue tees, the second furthest tees from the hole. Anne and I followed up from the gold, the closest to the hole. We'd decided to golf the white/gold combo.

The conversation flowed easily amongst the four of us. David told us he'd proposed to his girlfriend recently, the one he'd been dating when we were FWB.

Yikes! Not that I knew, though.

"She's a nurse and I'm head over heels in love with her, Daisy. It's been wonderful."

I smiled and felt more comfortable with this than I thought I ever would. He'd broken my heart, but time, and putting in the work, heal all wounds, and I felt good.

"Congratulations, David. That really is great!"

"What about you, Daisy? Are you seeing anyone? You must be. You can't have stayed on the market long, you're a great catch."

But you didn't want me.

That flicker only lasted for a second or two.

I'm pretty sure I blushed a crimson red. "Yes, I'm living with a wonderful man named Brad. He has two boys and I have my two girls, of course. It really has been great. I'm truly happy."

"Daisy, I'm happy for you."

"Thanks, David. I'm happy for you too."

Great, we're all happy and happy for each other. Good grief, we sound like a freaking nursery school rhyme or something. "I'm happy that you're happy and you're happy that I'm happy." Well, that's stuck in my head now. Holy jeez.

I looked over to see Anne and Doug chatting away.

Ooh, that could be interesting.

"David, is Doug single?" David glanced over at the two of them, smiled and said, "Yes, he is. And Anne?" I smiled at him, "Yup! He's a good guy?"

David nodded, "The best!" I grinned, "Good! Shall we do a little match making then? Let's switch golf carts so they can spend more time together."

David winked at me, "Consider it done." He rearranged the clubs, so we were paired together, and Doug and Anne shared the other cart. They were oblivious to anything, anyone, and everything going on around them, they were so intent on their conversation. I smiled, watching them.

Anne deserves a good man. Please let Doug be a good man.

Our evening continued, David and I focused on golf and chatting, Anne and Doug were only half golfing, not really paying much attention to the game. At one point, David awkwardly rearranged his legs and looked uncomfortable. He was always sure of himself, so it was a bit odd seeing his body language shift. "Daisy, there's something I need to say to you. I've thought about it a lot and should've reached out to you. I'm sorry I wasn't honest with you about seeing someone else. That wasn't fair to you. I knew you wanted more with me, but I already had my eyes set on Rose-Marie."

"Thank you for acknowledging that, for your apology, and for being honest with me at the time about not wanting more. You were clear on that. You did break my heart, but you'd been clear that your heart wasn't available to me. It was something I couldn't comprehend, so I take some ownership in that for sure. I'd like to also thank you for teaching me so much in the bedroom. You helped me open up a bit between the sheets and I appreciate that. When I think about you it's with fondness."

"Daisy, I did grow to care a great deal about you as well. But my heart was always for another."

"Yes, I understand that now. I was destined to be with Brad. And you, with Rose-Marie. But we sure had all sorts of orgasmic fun in the meantime."

David laughed and nodded, "We sure did! We had a blast."

"Or seven! Eruptions, that is."

As our round ended, Anne pulled me aside, pressing her keys into my hand, "Would you mind driving my car home? I've had a few too many and Doug has invited me over to his place for drinks and snacks."

I hugged Anne and whispered in her ear, "Of course, sweetheart!"

"Thank you! And I hope it wasn't too awkward for you with David. Thank you for switching our clubs around, by the way," Anne winked while grinning.

"No problem at all. We could see early on that you two were hitting it off. And surprisingly, it wasn't awkward at all. He's engaged and happy. I'm so happy with Brad and our family. It was nice to catch up with him. He really is a great guy."

Anne nodded as she snuck glances at Doug behind me. The sun was settling down in the sky and soon the mosquitos would be out.

"Have a great night, sweetie! Call me in the morning. Don't do anything I wouldn't do!" I laughed as I hugged her and kissed her on the cheek. "Oh, and I want details!"

"Thanks again, Daisy, and of course! Always!"

Brad got home late that night from Kananaskis. I was snoring away when he snuggled in beside me in bed. I let out a contented sigh as he wrapped his arms around me. The next morning I awoke to him nuzzling my ear and playing with my nipples. I moaned, "Mmm . . . baby, yes please." He started kissing and sucking each breast and nipple, then he lowered himself on me as his penis entered me. I groaned, "Oh . . . mmm . . ."

He slid deep inside me, my pussy instantly getting wet with each pulse and push. "Ohhhhh … Mmmmyyyyyy . . . Gaaaawwwwwwddddd babe! Faster . . . mmm . . . deeper . . . mmm . . . harder." And comply he did. I was cumming in no time, one of those deep guttural ones. "FUUUUCCCKKKKK!" Brad started to moan too as he cummed inside me, "Aahhhhhhh, Daisy, baby!" We collapsed together. The heavens had opened and swallowed us whole for a moment or two as we enjoyed the bliss we'd created.

As we were cuddling, I said to Brad, "How was golf yesterday?"

"I played pretty average, an eighty-five, but I had a great time with Neil, Frank and Sean. We had a blast. I haven't laughed so hard in a long time! How was golf with Anne?"

"That's great sweetie! I golfed reasonably well, a ninety-five. But the big news of the night . . . guess who Anne and I golfed with yesterday? Completely bizarre, total fluke."

"I'm not sure hun, who?"

"David and his friend, Doug."

"David, David?"

"Yes! He's engaged. To the lady he was dating when I knew him. I know, it seems like it might be kinda weird. But shockingly it wasn't uncomfortable at all. And Doug and Anne hit it off big time, she even went to Doug's place last night. I drove her car home for her 'cause she'd had a few. I can't wait to hear the details. They looked like they instantly connected. It was very cool to watch."

"Oh, well, that's good, exciting for Anne."

"It is for sure!"

"And nothing weird with David you say?"

"Not at all. It was like we were friends who'd lost touch. That's it." Brad kissed me on the forehead and rubbed my back as we lay in our bed together.

Mmm . . .

39
new love

AROUND ELEVEN THE NEXT MORNING, I sent a text to Anne, Hey gorgeous, how'd it go? Or maybe it's still going? *Mmm . . .*

At noon, I heard a ding, AMAZING! ONGOING. Will text later. Love you! I smiled as I read Anne's message out loud to Brad. We were in the kitchen, making noodles and a salad for lunch. Brad was out on the deck, barbequing the chicken for the salad. He came up behind me, wrapped his arms around me and kissed my cheek, "I love you, Daisy!"

I turned to face him so I could give him a proper kiss. The passion zinged as we kissed. *Wow!* When we came up for air, I breathed, "I love you too, Brad. It's hard to believe, but I love you more each and every day. I really don't know how that's possible."

Brad tousled my hair and combed it out of my face as he kissed my hairline, "I know! I feel exactly the same way, sweetheart." He kissed my lips gently, patted me on the butt and went out to the BBQ to check on the chicken.

Mmm . . . what the hell was I doing before that sweet encounter? Oh right, chopping veggies for the salad. Get your head out of the clouds, Daisy. . . nah!

Oh crap, I better respond to Anne too! I completely forgot. Holy hot distraction from my lover.

"Excellent, I can't wait to hear the details!"

Around nine that night, I answered a breathless call from Anne, "I just got home. OMG! I have so much to tell you. Can you come over or are you busy with kids?"

"You bet I can! Kids are all well in hand. Kris is at his mom's and our other three are self-sufficient. I'll just say goodnight to them and pop over. What can I bring?"

"I've got wine so if you want something else to drink, bring that. Oh, and bring your suit, we're hot tubbing! I'm a touch sore today. There were some . . . um . . . hard core gymnastics going on last night."

"Gymnastics, eh? Right! Cool, hot tub and wine sounds great! Be there in about ten minutes." I grabbed a bag and threw in my swimsuit and a couple cans of Okanagan peach cider, my fave, and left my bag at the front door while I made my rounds saying goodnight to Brad and the kids.

"I know it's only been about thirty hours, but Daisy, I AM IN LOVE! We hardly slept last night, we talked and talked and talked. We kissed and talked all night long when we weren't sleeping. We have a ton in common from movie choices to activities to authors to travel to retirement goals. It's uncanny! He has one daughter who's eleven, fifty-fifty custody with his ex. They've been divorced for five years. No drama."

"That sounds fantastic, Anne! Very exciting!"

"This morning he woke me up with a kiss as he served me breakfast in bed: eggs, bacon, fruit, and toast. We sat together chatting and eating in bed. When we finished eating, he cleared away the dishes and trays. When he returned, he took me by the hand and stood me up. Kissing me deeply, oh so passionately, he removed what remained of my clothes and his. His lips were on my neck and his hands, well, they were everywhere. His touch felt incredible."

"Oh, Anne, that sounds amazing."

"He laid me down on the bed and we got to know each other inside and out. It was one long sex session, broken up only by breaks for food, washroom, and water! At one point he sat in an armless chair and had me face him and straddle him, sliding up and down on him, while he manipulated my hips with each thrust. It was sooo fun! And in the shower, we soaped each other up and rinsed each other up, pausing on our sexy parts, thoroughly enjoying each other's touch."

"Oh, Anne, you're making me want to rush home and jump Brad! I'm so excited for you! When are you seeing him again?"

"Mmm . . . not soon enough. Tomorrow night after work he's picking me up and taking me out for supper. Some fancy new organic farm-fresh restaurant a friend of his just opened."

"That sounds great! You're glowing, Anne! It's so great to see you all giddy and head-over-heels for Doug."

We continued chatting and chilling in the hot tub until well after midnight. All Anne's sexy talk had made me horny.

I wandered home and true to my word, I disrobed completely before sliding into bed. I pressed my naked breasts into Brad's back as I cuddled into him and kissed his cheek. He reached around and grabbed my naked left cheek, ass cheek that is. I reached around and stroked his chest and down to his penis. I could feel him starting to get hard for me. As I grabbed hold and started to stroke, he jumped to attention, eager to please. He licked his finger and traced the outside of my pussy with his finger, just dipping inside to taste and feel how wet I was. Tickling my clit lightly with his fingertip, I got even wetter.

Suddenly he stood beside the bed and whipped me sideways, so my feet were resting against the wall at the side of the bed, with him between my legs. He started to flick my clit with his tongue while his finger slowly circled and then penetrated my pussy. I could hear my wetness sloshing against his finger. A mini clit cum rose and exploded on his finger as he was playing with my g-spot, getting it good and ready. He bent down and gave my pussy a big lick, lapping up the escaping cum, then his tongue dove deep inside to capture some more. Then his finger dove in again, playing with my g-spot, deeper and harder and faster until, OMG, I was squirting, liquid spewing everywhere. I was on fire.

Then he grabbed my hips and pulled me even closer to the end of the bed and drove his cock inside me. I grunted and groaned. He stretched me good and hard. A few hard thrusts and I began to cum and squirt again, all over him. Liquid was escaping and running down my ass. My orgasm had several waves and Brad caught the very last one as he released inside me. We shoved over in the bed, out of the wet spot and collapsed together, for a deep and sexually gratified sleep.

40
wedding bells

THE DAY BEFORE HER WEDDING, Jen and I met for lunch. Anne was the maid of honor but she had a work engagement that she couldn't get out of, so I agreed to step in. Anne would join us when she could. Today was all about Jen and making sure everything was ready for the festivities the next day. Our plan was to eat, Jen wanted to try on her dress and veil to be sure everything was perfect, then spend the afternoon relaxing, napping (for Jen) and getting manicures and pedicures. That evening the remaining bridesmaids were set to arrive for a pre-wedding celebration.

Upon returning to the hotel, Jen stepped into her dress and pulled it up, inch by inch, the material stretching over her large baby belly. She pulled the straps up over her shoulders. "Help me zip it up, Daisy. I can't get my arms around to reach the zipper," she laughed.

"No problem, sweetie." I pulled together the material and started the pull up the zipper.

Oh, oh! Houston, we have a problem. There's no way this zipper is going more than one third of the way up.

I kept trying, gently, to stretch the material and ease up the zipper. It wouldn't budge. *Shit!* There was an inch gap at least and the material was stretched to the brim across her glowing belly.

The dreaded words a bride never wants to hear the day before her wedding. "Um, Jen, the zipper isn't going to go all the way up. We're going to have to alter your dress a bit."

Jen was near hysterics, "But I tried it on last week and it fit, there was even some room to grow. How can it not fit now?" Tears were streaming down her face.

I came around her and held her in my arms, combing her hair, as she sobbed. "Sweetie, your baby had a growth spurt. It happens. We'll get it fixed. My grandma can do it, I'm sure. We have twenty-four hours, that's plenty of time. Now, let's see about your shoes. Where are they?"

She pointed to the right side of the closet. I reached up onto the shelf and pulled down the box. I slid off the box top and removed each shoe carefully from the box. White flats with all sorts of fun lacy and jeweled decoration, to match her dress perfectly. "These are gorgeous, Jen!"

She smiled and said, "Yes, Anne's stylist nailed it, the perfect shoes for my dress," she sobbed. "The dress that doesn't fit! Damn it!"

I draped one arm around her, "We'll fix it, honey." Jen sat on the chair by her makeup table, tears streaming down her face.

"Shall we do this? Cinderella style?" Jen grinned through her tears. I fell to my knees and slowly and gently slid each shoe on Jen's feet.

"There. Gorgeous! Stand up and walk around a bit to make sure they still feel good."

Jen walked around; zipper not quite done up at the back of her dress, busting out of the unzipped portions, squishing her belly in an attempt to free up enough material so the zipper would catch. She tripped on a corner of the rug, her shoe fell off, and the zipper slid down ever further. She laughed, hugging her belly, beaming, with tears running down her cheeks, "Daisy, I'm a train wreck." I grabbed her by the shoulders, hugged her, and walked her over to the mirror, holding her dress together for her, "See, you're gorgeous! You're going to be a beautiful bride tomorrow, Jen."

She grinned, tears ending, "Yes, I am. Thank you for being here, Daisy!" I looked into her eyes, "Always Jen, anytime! When's your sister coming?"

Jen rolled her eyes, "Zara has been here for a couple days. She texted me yesterday to let me know she'd be by around eight o'clock tonight, maybe."

"What? She's been here since Wednesday, and she hasn't come to see you yet?"

"Nope. That's Zara. She's a touch selfish."

"What's she been doing?"

"Ha, you mean who?"

"What?"

"Yeah, she has a couple boyfriends that she sees when she's here."

"Oh, I thought she was married?"

Jen looked at me, raised her eyebrows, and gave a quick nod, "Yup."

"Oh, jeez."

"Yeah, pretty much. I try to stay neutral. I figure it's none of my business and quite frankly, I don't want to know."

"What time is everyone else coming?"

"Anne and Twila said they'd be here after work, around five."

"Ok, cool. Should we run your dress over to my grandma's now? That way you can have a nap before having your toes and nails done, and the gals arrive. If you'd like."

"Let's go!"

My grandma was excited at the prospect of fixing a wedding dress in short order. She said it spiced up her life for the minute. "What else am I going to do on a Friday night? Do you think I have a hot date? Maybe I'm playing the championship match in bingo?"

I laughed, "Grandma, who knows with you!"

She laughed, "Right, Daisy. Jennifer, we'll have your beautiful dress altered and ready for you by nine tomorrow morning. We'll do another fitting then, and that will still give me time to do any last-minute adjustments."

"Thank you so much, Sophie, you are truly a life saver."

"It's my pleasure, sweet girl. I'm happy to help for your special day."

Upon returning to the honeymoon suite, Jen crawled straight into bed and passed out, hard. I could hear her snoring softly as I read my book in the other room. Feeling refreshed from our relaxing afternoon, we were both raring to go at three, well maybe not raring but definitely excited, when the lovely ladies from the nail salon knocked on the door of the honeymoon suite. The rest of the afternoon was glorious. The four ladies brought foot and hand baths, lathered us up, massaged and pampered our feet and hands.

I hardly ever take the time to pamper myself like this. I really need to do this more often.

Anne and Twila were right on time. Jen's supper request was Chinese food. We ordered dinner for the four of us. I asked if we should reach out to Zara to let her know that we were ordering. Jen shook her head, "Nope, she's late. I'm sure we'll have tons of food anyway, if she does show up." We watched a couple of funny wedding movies and had sparkling apple juice and wine. Between movies, we chatted about marriage and love and keeping the spark alive.

Zara never showed up.

What a piece of work.

We drove back to my grandma's the next morning to find Jen's dress was perfect. It hugged her in all the right places, her belly bump glowing. "Thanks, Grandma! You saved the day!"

My grandma hugged Jen, "My pleasure."

"Well, Jen, let's get going. The altar awaits."

"Thank you again, Sophie!"

The three of us shared a giant hug and said our goodbyes.

We got back to the hotel by ten thirty. Still no Zara.

What the hell is with this chick? Newsflash! Your sister is getting married, you're in the wedding party, but you can't bother to show up when the bride asks you to be there?

Jen took a nap while we laid out her dress, shoes, makeup, stockings and undergarments. The wedding was scheduled for two o'clock. Jen asked us to wake her at noon so she could have a bite to eat before we helped her with her hair and makeup, and then helped her get into her dress.

While she was asleep, the three of us got dressed and finished our makeup and hair so we could focus solely on the bride at noon. Anne was slightly wringing her hands, one look and I knew she was concerned about the two-hour window to get Jen ready. That was heaps of time for me, but I was sure Anne would prefer four hours or more.

We joked a bit about the bridesmaid dresses.

Is there really such a thing as a nice bridesmaid's dress?

Likely on purpose, the day is all about the bride, not the bridesmaids. The somewhat meh dresses make the bride look even better.

Jen had picked a peach color (*ugh . . . completely the wrong color for me*) for the dresses and they were strapless to boot. My poor rocks-in-socks-boobs weren't large or perky enough to hold the bloody thing up. Anne to the rescue with some kind of magic superglue boob tape.

What, that's not the official name? Whatever do you mean? Sounds right to me. Ha! Thank you, Anne!

I hope this sticky crap comes off later. Eww . . . it better not be the same as when the sticky part on a bandaid gets exposed and gross black goo remains stuck to your skin after the bandaid is removed. Blech!

The clock struck noon and Jen rolled out of bed. Her hair was almost dry from the shower she'd had earlier. With Jen wrapped in a special bright pink honeymoon bathrobe—cheesy yet perfect—Twila and Anne got to work on her makeup and hair. Twila removed the last bit of moisture from Jen's hair before moussing and curling. Anne applied foundation, eyeliner, blush, mascara and lipstick to Jen's glowing face.

At one thirty, Jen was ready to don her dress. I lent a hand for balance as Jen stepped into her newly altered and exquisite wedding dress. Anne and I gently pulled dress her dress up and over her belly, firmly attached the straps, and Twila zipped her up. We all murmured various compliments, "Beautiful, gorgeous, a princess, you look absolutely perfect, the beautiful bride."

We were helping Jen step into her shoes at one forty-five, when her cell dinged. It was Zara. Then there was a knock at the door. Again, Zara.

Nothing like cutting it close. What the hell chick?

Jen's shoes seemed a bit tighter than they were yesterday and we were struggling to help her feet into them. Twila answered the door, "Hi Zara, cutting it a bit close, no? You do know the wedding starts in fifteen minutes?"

Zara stormed in with a "pishaw", with arrogance and self-importance wafting behind her. It seemed to say that the show could now go on, "now that Princess Zara had arrived". *Barf.*

But we had bigger problems than Queen Zara. How to stretch Jen's shoes out a bit so the bride wasn't limping down the aisle.

How in the hell had her feet swollen up over night?

Anne to the rescue! Again. "Feet up my darling!" Anne called, "Twila, grab some ice and a large bowl, please. Daisy, in my bag there's a shoe stretcher. It won't help much over the next fifteen minutes, but every little bit helps."

Anne is the best person to have around in a shoe crisis. She knows every trick in the book.

Anne glanced up at Zara, standing there waiting for the world to stop and notice her, "Zara, my dear, get dressed, touch up your makeup, and get your hair combed out and reset. We are expected downstairs in exactly thirteen minutes. We shan't be late."

Don't fuck with Anne around a wedding!

Jen's feet were soaking in the cold water in the hopes of reducing the swelling and the shoe stretcher was doing its thing. After seven minutes of calm, it was time to give the shoes another try. Twila and I removed Jen's feet from the frigid water and thoroughly dried them off, while Anne removed the stretchers from Jen's shoes. Tights reinstalled securely; we crossed our fingers . . . magic! "Thank you, thank you, ladies! Shall we go? My groom awaits!" Jen announced proudly.

I popped my head into the other bathroom, "Zara, we have to go." She was just stepping into her dress and rudely blasted, "Ya, ya, give me ten minutes."

I backed into the bathroom and shut the door. "Zara, today is your sister's wedding day. We are NOT going to be late to her wedding because you chose to arrive fifteen minutes before it was scheduled to start. Get your shit together and be by the elevator in the next two minutes or we're leaving without you. Today is not about you."

Zara's eyes got very large, and she nodded, "Be right out."

True to her word, Zara was out in time for us to go to the ceremony together. The five of us drifted along the hallway, down the elevator and popped out in the wedding waiting room. We were ushered to the start of the aisle. It was GO time. Each bridesmaid walked individually up the aisle doing the fancy wedding step slide tap, step slide tap, and waited at the front expectantly for the music to change and Jen to emerge. I peeked out into the audience where I connected eyes with Brad and our kids, giving each of them a quick wink. Anne found Doug in the audience, smiled, and when he beamed at her, she blushed.

Ooh, he is special to her, I've never seen Anne blush before.

The first notes of the Wedding March played, and Jen floated up the aisle, a gorgeous bride. I stole a glance at Chris, he was beaming as he watched his love walk toward him to join him at the altar. I felt a tear fall down my cheek as I watched the scene unfold. *Just beautiful.*

The ceremony was precious. They wrote their own vows, which were personal and lovely, magical really, talking about their unborn child and their commitment to each other and their family to be.

The reception was fun, and we had a fabulous time, well except for the drama. I spent much of the evening dancing with Brad and our kids, chatting and dancing with Anne and Doug.

It was only mostly good because Zara's drama crept in to disrupt the evening. Her husband, Mike, had flown in for the wedding, but no one was sure whether he'd show. I can't even imagine how gross that felt. I'm sure it was hard for her. He was a big wheel attorney in Vancouver and often missed family events. He walked into the reception like he owned the place and Zara's face fell. It was obvious that she wasn't at all pleased to see him.

He took her by the hand, walked her to the dance floor, dipped and kissed her. They continued to dance for three or four more songs when I saw Zara pointing at her shoes and motioning back toward the table. About an hour later, Zara's face lit up and then she looked alarmed. Her husband turned to see where she was staring, as did I. The man striding toward her stopped in his tracks, retreating quickly back toward the door. Zara's husband looked sternly at her and then I heard raised voices but couldn't make out what they were saying.

Mike took off like a shot after the man, and Zara took off after him. The dance floor was split by the three of them running through it, one after another. Near the edge of the floor, Zara's husband caught the man, grabbed him by the arm, roughly turning him around, then yelling into his face, "What's your business with my wife?"

You could hear a pin drop. Everyone was staring.

What the hell happened to the music? I thought this kind of stuff only happened in the movies!

The man looked bewildered, looking at Mike, "Your wife?" then turning toward Zara, "Stephanie?" Mike was hot, steam was rushing from his ears,

"No, her name is Zara." His right hand was by his hip, fist cocked, ready. *Oh shit.*

"Zara? Wh...who's Zara?" The man was clearly baffled.

Zara looked blankly at her lover, almost right through him as though he meant nothing to her. She grabbed her husband by the hand. "Mike, let's go sit, or better yet, take me for another spin on the dance floor."

The silence was deafening. After what felt like a solid minute, Mike's fist relaxed. He turned his focus to Zara, patted her on the rump, and nodded in the direction of the door.

The man looked at her in disbelief, calling after her, "Zara? Your name is Zara? And you're married? But I love you, Stephanie, uh . . . Zara. You lied to me. Who are you? We had plans for the future. And you're married? I can't believe it. How could you?"

Zara looked heartlessly and blankly at the guy as she walked past him. Mike was forcefully pulling Zara toward the door. Trailing behind, Zara turned slowly toward her lover, she silently mouthed, "I'm sorry. I can't. Not like this."

Holy shit. Did anyone else see that?

Zara's lover fell to his knees, sobbing, as Mike whisked Zara away, leaving the reception immediately.

I can't imagine the discussion those two will be having this evening. Oh, to be a fly on the wall.

The music started up again and soon the memory of the bride's sister's lover had all but dissipated into thin air. *Poor guy.* Smartly, the DJ threw on the bird dance, flooding the floor with dancers, all of us doing the goofy bird dance.

You know the one! Don't even pretend you don't.

After a few more song, he laid on Cadillac Ranch, my all-time favorite line dance. I kicked off my uncomfortable shoes, *damn heels*, and jumped onto the dance floor with my girlfriends, dancing and singing our hearts out.

Not surprisingly, the bride was worn out by ten. The bride and groom made their exit, retreating to the honeymoon suite. We danced for a while after they left but the helium had been released from the wedding party balloon, and it had been a long day. Brad and I did one final slow dance, as our kids looked on. Brad swung me around the dance floor, swaying and kissing and enjoying one another in PG. At the end of the song, he dipped me and planted a big juicy kiss on my lips. When we came up for air, we saw Kris and Jess clapping. Ang and Carson were avoiding eye contact.

Good, we can still embarrass some of them!

Oh, and I can report that the superglue boob tape came off beautifully. I was a little concerned what Brad would find under my dress that night!

41

young love

ONE AFTERNOON AFTER SCHOOL, Carson came rushing through the front door. Brad wasn't home yet. Striding up to me with purpose, Carson exclaimed, "Daisy, I'm busting at the seams, I have to share my news and I'm glad it's with you. I'm dating a boy named Tim. He's so cute and he plays the guitar. Can you believe it? I met him at the school dance a month ago. I didn't want to say anything until it felt like it might stick. I really like him Daisy, I do."

I smiled and ruffled his hair as I reached in to give him a hug, "Congratulations Carson! I'm so excited for you! When do we get to meet Tim? You know, we're planning to have a BBQ on the weekend for the girls' birthday, perhaps he could come then? Would that be too overwhelming for him, you think?"

Carson grinned, "Ya, that might work, Daisy. I'll ask him if he's free and ready to meet my family."

"Poor guy!"

"You know, Daisy, I couldn't think of a better group to introduce Tim to. I love you all so much! I know I don't say it much, but I do. Do you think Jess might bring her boyfriend too? At least then there's two non-family members."

"You should ask Jess, but yes, Jared is welcome to join us too, of course. He seems to be busy playing basketball a lot, but hopefully he's around."

Carson ducked in for another hug, "Thanks, Daisy!"

That night, Carson shared his news with the rest of the family. I smiled knowingly, as did Jess. She'd already confirmed Jared was able to join our Birthday BBQ on Saturday. Brad was encouraging, as anticipated, "Carson, buddy, that's awesome!" Ang smiled, "I thought you two might've been dating." I found out later that Jess and Ang knew about Carson and Tim already from school and that Carson had confided in them weeks before.

Of course he had, duh! High fives were exchanged all around the table.

Later that night, Ang texted me, "Mom, can we go for a walk? Just the two of us."

"Sure thing, hun. Just give me five." I snuggled into Brad and whispered in his ear, "I'm going to go for a walk with Ang." Brad nodded, looking up from his crossword, "Sounds good, sweetie. See you soon." As I was getting up, he said, "Not so fast!" He grabbed my hand, pulled me close, and kissed me. Then as I turned, he swatted my ass as I grinned and mouthed, "Bye, bye baby bye, bye," and winked.

Putting my shoes on, Ang snuck up behind me. I damn near jumped out of my skin. She casually slid her shoes on, giggled, and we walked out the door together. I gave her a little squeeze on the shoulder. We wandered down to Fish Creek Park. Once we were by the river, Ang started to talk about what she had on her mind, "Mom, I know you're pretty perceptive so you may already know this, or at least have an inkling, but I wanted to tell you outright. I'm gay, I'm a lesbian."

I stopped Ang and put my arms around her. "Oh sweetie, I'm so happy for you. I didn't know for sure, but I suspected that you might be into girls."

"And Mom, I didn't want to mention it today as I didn't want to steal Carson's thunder, but I'm dating someone too. A girl. You know her. You remember my friend, Ina?" I nodded. "She's so very beautiful and kind and talented. You know, she plays flute in the school band."

"Oh wow, Ang, that IS exciting. How long have you been seeing each other?"

"Well, that's a little hard to tell precisely. We've been friends for about six months and maybe two months ago, she let me know that she wanted to date me. We explored that for a while because I wasn't sure right away, and then it just felt right. So, maybe six weeks ago."

"Oh, wow, amazing! She's a great girl."

"Do you think Ina could come to our Birthday BBQ on Saturday?"

"Of course, sweetie! She's welcome at our house whenever you'd like."

Saturday arrived and the weather was perfect to celebrate Jess and Ang's fifteenth birthday. We were expecting four guests: Ang's girlfriend, Ina; Carson's boyfriend, Tim; Jess's boyfriend, Jared; and Kris's buddy, Sean. The kids arrived mid-afternoon for games and snacks. We played volleyball, basketball, catch, and cornhole. A few of the kids had never played cornhole before and it was an instant hit. The kids were giggling and cheering as each beanbag hit the board, most inevitably sliding off the board.

Around four thirty, Brad turned on the smoker to warm it up for the burgers. As the burgers cooked, Brad and I cut up the tomatoes, avocados, buns, and cheese, and placed the spinach, lettuce and condiments out. The kids were sitting around the picnic table chatting and munching on chips, salsa, veggies, and pickles.

It was great watching the kids interact and learning about what makes them tick. The kids talked about their sports and dove into hockey discussions: Flames vs Oilers. It was pretty funny to listen to them chat about their favorite players. Brad and I exchanged a few glances as we looked at our kids and how happy they all seemed. We brought out the cake for the girls, singing Happy Birthday. Chocolate, their favorite. They blew out their candles and we enjoyed cake and ice cream. The ice cream was melting like crazy, so I tucked the carton back inside the freezer while we devoured the delicious dessert.

After the BBQ Brad nuzzled me and said, "Our kids sure have a great group of friends." I smiled and nodded, "They do indeed. It was nice to see them in their element, conversing together."

42
anne's loves

ANNE HAD JUST GOTTEN BACK from an adventure with her new love, Doug, and she was excited to tell me all about it.

"Daisy, I'm a changed woman. I went on a motorbike ride with Doug, and I loved it! A motorbike ride! Can you believe it? I had an amazing time. Truth be told, I could've done without the bugs and wind messing with my hair, but the actual ride was a blast. So fun!"

I was smiling and nodding along with Anne. She was bubblier than I'd ever seen her. Refined and poised Anne had become like a giddy child, exploring the new wonders of the world. It was great to see.

"Doug has one of those big, fancy Gold Wing Touring bikes. A travelling couch is how he affectionately refers to it. And he's not wrong. We drove down to Montana through the mountains and then circled down to Oregon and back up the coast. It was amazing. I was concerned my rear end would hurt but honestly, my biggest worry was that I'd fall off the bloody thing."

"Yes, Anne, I recall that being a . . . um . . . concern."

Anne smiled as she continued, "But as we started to ride, it became clear to me that it would be pretty difficult to shake me out of my comfy seat. I was in there tight, I wasn't going anywhere, unless we ended up upside down, but that would've been a whole different issue.-We had headphones so we could chat with each other, and I even nodded off a few times to the hum of the bike. It was so freeing. I've never experienced anything quite like it."

"That's awesome, Anne! I'm glad you had an amazing time exploring the world from the view of a motorbike. Do you have any interesting riding stories?"

Laughing, Anne commented, "You know, there was a funny incident that happened. Doug had no idea, but as we were speeding down the highway in Oregon, a rather large bug hit my face shield square in the middle. I popped the visor up a bit, hoping to shake it off, but in that same moment, I got hit in the eyeball by another bug, and the darn thing dislodged my eyelash. How? I have no clue. There I am bouncing around on the back of a bike with my damn eyelash flapping in the wind. All of a sudden, a tornado-type gust of wind hit us, went inside my helmet, and ripped the bloody eyelash off. I shut my visor in an attempt to contain the bloody thing, but it was flying all over the place: whacking my eyes, the visor, my forehead, the visor again, my cheeks, the helmet, and back to my eyeball."

I was laughing hard imagining Anne's eyelash fiasco.

"I know, funny scene! Naturally, I was squirming around so much, Doug asked what the hell was going on. I'm sure the little shriek I gave when the bloody thing fell off gave him a bit of a start. Anyway, this goofy thing is flapping around and when I couldn't stand being beaten by my eyelash, I lifted my visor again, in hopes of some relief and poof, the bloody thing got sucked out the side of the visor. There went my eyelash, flying down the road behind us. A couple hundred dollars gone in a jiffy. Damn!"

I was laughing my ass off visualizing the bloody eyelash flapping around inside Anne's visor. Whack! Whack! Whack! Her trying desperately to save the thing. Then in the blink of an eye it's free! Flying, ricocheting, and tumbling toward someone's window. At the mercy of the wind.

Can you imagine that hitting your windshield? Plunk. "Boy, that's a weird looking bug. That's not a bug. What the hell is that thing?" As the super glue attaches to the car, the window wipers swiping back and forth, unable to remove the fluffy eyelash, not that they know it's an eyelash.

"Did you rip the other one off?"

"Yeah, I knew I'd never find a perfect match so a complete re-do was required. Thank goodness the hotel we stayed at had a spa with all kinds of esthetics treatments, including eyelashes. They did a good job. We were back on the bike again the next morning heading down to California. Ha, eyelash intact. The rest of the trip was amazing. The scenery was breathtaking, miles of beach and ocean flying by us. Daisy, I'm falling hard for Doug. He's a sweetheart, so kind and does he ever curl my toes. What a man!"

"I'm over the moon for you, Anne! It's been a long time coming. You so deserve it."

"Aww, thanks sweetie. Speaking of romantic adventures, I have more exciting news to share with you."

"Oh? What's that?"

They didn't get engaged, did they? Hmm, I wonder . . . no, she would've led with that.

"Oooh, I really can't contain my excitement about this one. Kyle and Benjamin got engaged! Oh Daisy, they're so absolutely adorable together."

"They finally got engaged? Amazing! I'm pumped for them. They're great together. How did it happen? Where? I bet they did something romantic, knowing the two of them. Give me details!"

"Kyle took Benji out to Banff for the weekend and they went hiking. At the top of the Johnston Canyon Falls hike, they took a rest. Kyle laid out a blanket and they snacked on a little charcuterie plate along with a glass of wine."

WTF is with that damn charcuterie popping up everywhere? Ha . . . I'll always smile when I see or hear about one, remembering when I was part of one. Princess Pussy started playing boom chicka boom music in the background while doing a sexy dance. Bridget shook her head, but smiled nonetheless. I giggled. Oh shit was that out loud?

Anne looked at me sideways with an eyebrow raised. Then she remembered. "Daisy! That brings you back to time with David, eh?!"

I nodded, still giggling, "Yup, and it always will, I think. Keep going, I want to hear about Kyle's very romantic wedding proposal."

"Kyle was wearing a GoPro so I got to see every minute of it when they got back. Hmm, where was I? Right . . . after they finished and packed up their lunch, Kyle took Benji by the hand and led him to see the waterfalls. You may recall that Benji is quite the photographer. He was snapping away, focusing and refocusing, changing lenses. While Benji was distracted, Kyle reached back into his backpack, removed two rings from the side compartment, and put them in his pocket. He asked Benjamin to put his camera away for a moment so they could enjoy the falls together. They both described feeling at one with nature, and with each other. At one point, Kyle extracted himself from the hug and slid beside Benji."

"Kyle told me how nervous he was. Taking a deep breath for courage, he swept Benji up into a kiss, took his hand, and then he went down on one knee, 'Benjamin Walter Smeltly, I've adored you since the moment I first laid eyes on you. Over the past few years, you have been the center of excitement, fun, love, and the rock in my life. I don't want a minute to go by without you in my life.'"

"Benji said he was crying as Kyle pulled out the ring, 'Benji, will you marry me? Can we officially be each other's forever?' Hell, I was crying when he got to this point of the story!"

"I would've been too. In fact, my eyes are feeling a bit wet right now."

Anne continued, "Through teary eyes, Benji said, 'Kyle, yes, of course. I want to be yours forever. I love you so much.' Kyle slid the ring onto Benji's finger. 'Did you bring the ring that we bought for you?' Kyle said, 'Of course I did.'"

I was smiling and nodding, enjoying the story, and I encouraged Anne to continue, "What happened next?"

"Kyle said that Benji asked him to stand up, that he wanted to kiss him. After they kissed for a while, Benji said he took the ring from Kyle and fell to his left knee, 'Kyle, I feel so fortunate to have found you. My rock and my lover, for all time. Will you marry me?'"

"Kyle smiled broadly, 'Yes, Benji, I will. My forever.' Benji slid the ring on Kyle's finger. They intertwined their fingers and stared lovingly at the rings on their fingers, then back at each other."

"'We better get off this mountain and back to the cabin. And tout suite. We don't want to pull off into the trees to do something that scares the bears!' Benji laughed."

Ooh, sexy time!

"Kyle smiled, 'We have a perfectly romantic log cabin with a burning fireplace, in which to explore each other, let's get the hell down there and enjoy it!'"

"They walked hand-in-hand down the path, utterly glowing, even running. That night, they enjoyed a passionate evening making love in front of the fireplace. Thank goodness they stopped the recording at this point, or at least that's all they shared with me. Ha!

But Kyle explained that there was lots of kissing and exploring and caressing, more kissing and touching every square inch of each other's bodies. Teasing each other. Loving each other to the full extent of the word. They made sweet love in front of the fire on a blanket on the floor. Kissing and nibbling until their rumbling stomachs forced them to stop for a bite."

My eyes welled up. Kyle had been so lost trying to find his soulmate. *And now he is going to marry that sweet boy!*

"Around eight that night, Kyle called me, 'Anne, we have news.' I knew right away that they'd gotten engaged, finally. It really was overdue. They are truly perfect for each other. Kyle found happiness and I am so thrilled for him. 'We went for a hike today at Johnson Canyon Falls and guess what, we got engaged?!!' Benji squealed. I giggled, 'Congratulations both of you. I'm very excited for you. Now go and have fun! Don't do anything I wouldn't do!'"

"Kyle laughed, 'No promises!' Both Benjamin and Kyle echoed, 'We love you, Anne!'"

"Isn't that awesome? I love that story. So sweet and romantic. And I am SOOOO happy for them. They're incredible together."

"Aww, Anne, that story warms my heart. They are so great together. I can't wait for the wedding. They aren't eloping or anything like that, I hope?"

"No, they'll get married in or around the city."

Excellent!

43

camping

ALONG WITH OUR regular camping adventures to Banff, Canmore, Dinosaur Provincial Park, Waterton, and Radium, this year we decided to take a trip down to Idaho to stay at the campground across from the Silverwood Theme Park and Boulder Beach Water Park. The cross-border excursion required Kris and Carson's mom to sign off to give consent for us to travel with them into the USA.

In April, Brad started the process with Sara as soon as he booked our campsite. It's a good thing too, as it took several months for her to finally sign off on our August vacation. I breathed several deep sighs, and thought numerous unkind and frustrated thoughts, through the process. I purposely kept out of it and kept my mouth firmly shut. This was Brad's fight to fight. He knew I had his back, but this was not my battle to fight. That Sara would even think of holding it up, or refusing a fun trip for the kids, got my blood boiling. What an unbelievably petty form of control and manipulation.

Oi! That woman!

Remaining patient (*were we patient? Hmm . . . probably not*) and the passage of time, paid off. Finally, we received Sara's written consent. Brad and I had a quiet little celebration the day we received it, from the lawyers of course. *OMG!*

The kids, of course, had no idea what we struggled with to make our vacation to the States a reality. These were adult problems; they didn't need to know. They shouldn't know.

Why people drag their kids through all the adult crap is a mystery to me.

The week of our Idaho adventure had finally arrived. As was typical, I had some pressing matters at work so needed to work straight through Thursday. That evening, we packed up the fifth wheel and Brad's truck in anticipation of leaving first thing on Friday morning.

Our kids were blurry eyed and half-asleep when we packed them into the truck and started our journey at six a.m. All but Ang were asleep again almost immediately, as Brad started to drive. Ang had her head buried in her latest novel *Hypnotized* by Alberta author, Don Trembath. She was on a local author kick and was demolishing books left, right, and center.

The six-hundred kilometer drive, which included a stretch through the Rocky Mountains, would take us approximately seven hours. Traffic was light as we wound around the great mountains through Crowsnest Pass. Always in awe of the majesty of the mountains, as we passed the Frank Slide memorial, I felt humbled by the mountain's sheer power. Gigantic boulders still line the highway where a portion of the mining town of Frank, the CPR rail line and the mine itself, had been buried by a massive rockslide. In the wee hours of April 29, 1903, roughly 110 million tonnes of limestone rock slid down Turtle Mountain, obliterating the eastern side of Frank within 100 seconds. That's just over a minute and a half! Can you believe it?! A jarring and sobering reminder of the power of nature. I always felt a brief shiver driving by the site. One minute the town was there and the next it was gone, buried by rock.

As we neared Fernie, BC, I roused the kids, "Wakey, wakey! Anybody hungry? We're almost in Fernie." Groans sounded from the back seat. Even Ang had fallen asleep, her head against the window and book upside down in her lap. Kris's hand shot up and he sounded almost chipper as he exclaimed, "I'm starving! Let's eat!"

Jess giggled at that and said, "Me too, Mom!" Ang wiped the drool from the right side of her mouth and mumbled, "I could eat," as she gently shook Carson, who'd fallen asleep leaning against her. He lurched, "What?" We all burst out laughing. "Good of you to join us, Carson! We're going to grab some breakie in Fernie." Carson groggily laughed, "Oh good, I'm starving."

After filling our bellies and the gas tank, we grabbed some coffee and hit the road once again. The border crossing went seamlessly, and we pulled off the road just across the border and bought some fruit and other things we hadn't been able to bring across the border. We pulled into Athol, Idaho in midafternoon and searched for our campsite. The kids were visibly excited as we pulled in. We could see the rides and waterslides right from where we parked our trailer.

The kids piled out of the truck while Brad and I attached hoses and the waterline to the fifth wheel. Once the trailer was balanced and sturdy, I made sandwiches and soup for a late lunch. The kids pulled out chairs, moved the picnic table around, pulled out the cooler, and helped themselves to drinks, while Brad set up the BBQ and hooked it up to the propane.

Day one, we floated down the Elkhorn Creek lazy river, our tubes attached together with rope to make a giant raft. We kept going around and around, just floating and bathing in the sun. It was a wonderful way to spend the day. Every once in a while, one of the kids would slide off and swim a bit or float behind the raft. We stopped at lunchtime for some sustenance at the burger joint in the park. Brad's eyes nearly popped out of his eyes at the price, "Holy crow, talk about overpriced hamburgers and fries! At least it comes with giant vats of pop, or soda as they call it here."

I nodded in agreement, "Not sure the pop makes up for the price, but at least the burgers are good." Jess laughed, "Good and greasy!" As grease dripped down her chin. She was enjoying every morsel. After floating for the rest of the afternoon, we returned to the campground where Brad grilled chicken along with veggies and we cooked rice for supper. The kids and I downed water like it were going out of style.

Mental note: pack more water tomorrow.

On day two, we hit the rollercoasters, er the older kids and Brad hit the rollercoasters. Jess nudged Ang and Carson, "Have you seen the Aftershock? It looks awesome!" Carson nodded, "I saw it yesterday, I can't wait to hit that one." Ang only nodded.

Personally, I avoid rollercoasters like the plague. Ever since I had the girls, they gave me vertigo. I used to love them. Such a bummer! Kris and I enjoyed the Bumper Boats, Roaring Creek Log Flume, the Scrambler, and the Krazy

Koaster. Those were more our style and speed. Kris and I high fived a bunch of times that morning, thoroughly enjoying our slower paced adventures. We all met up again for lunch back at the trailer. We'd learned our lesson the day before with that expensive lunch. Brad made us a choice of tuna or ham sandwiches. Those sandwiches hit the spot *And they were less of a barf factor!*

When we got back to Silverwood after lunch, Kris and I beelined it for the Tilt-a-Whirl. "Come on Daisy, let's go!" Kris exclaimed. We'd spotted that ride as we were leaving, and it had long been a favorite of mine. I really hoped my vertigo was kept at bay. But we were turning and spinning, and I felt great!

Brad, Jess, Ang, and Carson headed back to enjoy the Aftershock, Corkscrew, Panic Plunge, Round-up, Spincycle, Tremors and Timber Terror. *I feel green just thinking the names of those rides!* The Round-up was very similar to the Gravitron, a ride I used to love as a teenager, but I knew my sandwich would be going for a different kind of flight if I went on that one, these days.

We met up around three to go on the Krazy Kars, Thunder Canyon, and the Roaring Creek Log Flume together. We were all tired out and ready for supper by five. The kids tossed around a ball in the campsite, while Brad and I chopped carrots, mushrooms and potatoes, wrapped them in tinfoil with some butter and spices, and threw them on the BBQ. As the veggies cooked, I added spices and oil to the steak, allowing the flavor to sink in. One of our new friends came over and asked if we were interested in half a dozen cobs of corn, they couldn't finish them, and they wouldn't be able to take them back across the border in the morning. We happily accepted and got some water boiling. The kids shucked the corn and threw them into the pot. Supper was scrumptious that night. We were all stuffed.

Day three, we headed back to Boulder Beach where we took on the waterslides including Avalanche Mountain, Ricochet Rapids, and Riptide Racer, where all six of us lined up to race each other. We hung out in the Boulder Bay Beach wave pools for the afternoon and suntanned. We read, relaxed, and napped the afternoon away, content in the warm sun, with water glistening off our drenched bodies.

On our last day, Brad, Jess, and Carson decided to split the day between Silverwood and Boulder Beach. Ang, Kris, and I decided to sit out the morning adventures to hang out at the campsite, reading and chilling. Our fearless adventurers returned at noon, and we all supped on homemade turkey soup (*Eek . . . don't tell the border guards we snuck it across!*) and sandwiches. Then we all got into our swimsuits and enjoyed our last afternoon in Idaho at Boulder Beach, swimming, floating the lazy river, and screaming down the waterslides. A great day!

The next morning, after breakfast, we packed up the trailer for the long trek home. We'd been there for four heavenly nights. The weather was gorgeous and there was peace and quiet. There were a ton of Canadians in the campground, and even some Calgarians. We felt right at home. We were all a bit sad at leaving the fun of the amusement and water parks. But the weather was changing, and rain started to fall just as we finished tucking all the hoses under the fifth wheel.

"Just in time for us to head home!" I commented. Ange nodded, "It must be a sign. We stayed exactly as long as we were meant to!"

Brad backed up the truck and we got everything all reattached for the drive, locked into place, safe and sound.

The drive home was perfectly uneventful. We were all tired, so Brad and I switched off driving a few times while the other nodded off in the passenger seat. We stopped at a pub by the border, where they make a mean fish and chips, for lunch.

We didn't run into any issues crossing back into Canada either, just a slight delay as the border guards wanted to know what we were bringing back. "Just a few souvenirs, mostly shirts and a hat or two," Brad responded.

After looking in the back of the truck, and staring at our passports, they asked, "What's the story with all the kids. How does everyone fit in?" It was a natural question with two different last names and four kids. Brad presented the consent letter, explaining, "The two boys are mine and their mother signed off on the consent letter, here you go." The guard looked over at me, "The girls are mine." The guard nodded, "And the consent letter for them?" I turned to the guard, "Their dad is deceased." The guard nodded and went back to his shack to review the information we presented. He came back out and asked for the death certificate for Adam.

Holy man. I guess it's good they're thorough.

After several minutes, he returned, "Here are your documents. It all checks out. Welcome back to Canada." We both smiled, "Thank you, sir."

44

the rock

A MULTIPLE DAY business trip took Brad out of town, and we decided that it would be best if Carson and Kris stayed at our place while he was away. It was easier, as Sara wouldn't have to be involved.

I tell you, that woman has a way of making the simple request extremely complex and expensive. With her it is always a trip to the lawyer with a hefty bill, that Brad usually ends up paying, argh!

Besides, Carson would be staying at our place anyway. He and his mom still weren't on speaking terms. I really couldn't blame him.

We'd a couple of regular days: kids going to school, me going to work. Everything was moving along tickety-boo. Brad and I chatted a bit before I hit the hay each night. Finally, it was the night before he would be home and he'd be holding me in his arms. I couldn't wait. I was fantasizing about him kissing me as I drifted off to sleep.

Smash! Crash! Scared and startled from my cozy nest by the sound of glass shattering at two in the morning, I leapt out of bed to see what in the hell was going on. Lights were flipping on throughout the house as my daughters and

Brad's boys were awakened and just as curious, shaken, and disquieted as I was.

The culprit, a rather large rock, was sitting in the middle of our living room floor. On it was written the words "Your In Are Sites Trans Fuck". *Fuck!* Great, just what we need, transphobic slurs on rocks being hurtled through our window at all hours.

What's wrong with people?

My blood pressure went through the roof. I threw a sheet over the rock, so my family didn't have to stare at the disgusting words. I gave the kids a big hug, and then I picked up the phone and called the police. As soon as I hung up with the police, I called Brad and let him know what had happened. I was vibrating I was so mad. *How dare they!*

"Hi sweetie, sorry to wake you but I wanted to let you know that some asshole, fuckhead, backwards hick just threw a rock through our front window." I was blustering. Probably not helping the situation but my mama bear instincts had kicked in and I was pissed.

I could hear the creak of the bed as Brad sat up straight and said, "What? A rock through the window?"

"Yes, and the worst thing is there are transphobic slurs written on it. Clearly written by some imbecile as the bullshit is all misspelled."

Brad's voice went up an octave as panic entered his voice. A panic cause by being away from home when something like this had happened. I could hear his footsteps as he was pacing around the room. "Is everyone alright? I'll head to the airport right now and catch an earlier flight. Oh shit, did Carson see it?"

I smiled, comforted by his concern. "Unfortunately, yes, all the kids saw it. I covered it with a sheet, so we don't have to look at the fucking thing."

"Good thinking. Everyone is ok though? No injuries?"

"Yes, we're all fine. I called the police already and they're on their way. No, you absolutely don't need to head home right this instant, we're shaken but good. You're home tomorrow night and we'll be fine until then."

"Yes, I'm sure, we'll be just fine. I love you, sweetie."

I could hear the helplessness in Brad's voice when he said, "Yes hun, I know you have it handled, you've got this. I love you too. If you change your mind and want me to come home early, I'm happy to do that. Family first. Oh, and remember that I installed those cameras last spring. Maybe those will help identify the morons who did this. May I speak with Carson?"

"Of course, sweetie. Carson, your dad wants to chat with you, buddy."

I could only hear Carson's side of the conversation, "Hi Dad…Yup… Nope…Ya, we're good…Daisy's got it handled…Love you, too. See you tomorrow night."

Carson handed the phone back to me. "Ok hun, try to get some sleep. You have a long day tomorrow. We can't wait to see you."

When I hung up the phone, I saw our four kids standing there staring at the sheet covering the rock.

Almost like it's a dead body. Ick!

Carson looked completely shaken. "Don't worry, sweetie, we'll get to the bottom of this. You need to feel safe at school and everywhere. I'm sorry you have to deal with this garbage. Some people are just completely uneducated, not empathetic, and downright cruel. Come here." I gave him a big hug and tears started streaming down his face. "Do you want to call your dad back? I'm sure he won't sleep another wink tonight."

Carson gave me a small smile and said, "No, I'm just hurt and disappointed in some humans." I nodded, "I know, sweetie, unfortunately these animals exist, and we just have to focus on your safety and making sure our circles are filled with kind and supportive people."

The police arrived, lights flashing, dogs sniffing the flowers at the front of our house within fifteen minutes. Why they had the lights blaring and dogs sniffing and growling, is beyond me. But the ruckus sure brought our neighbors out to their lawns to check out what was going on.

Nosy Nellies! Great! I'll be answering curious questions all day tomorrow.

A big burly police officer pounded his fist on the door. Our house even shook.

Really dude? Do you think we missed the sirens?

As he came inside, I noticed his partner, previously been hidden by the large skyscraper-like stature of the man. She was rather mousy looking and appeared to be about twelve-years-old. I smiled and welcomed them both in while thanking them for coming, then offered them coffee. They both accepted my offer and settled themselves at the kitchen table.

I served the coffee and relayed what little I knew of the incident, explained that our oldest son was a transboy hence the vile words on the rock. I saw the mousy cop bristle when I mentioned my son being a transboy.

Hmm, it's the middle of the night. Did I just imagine that? Who knows?

I shrugged inwardly and informed them my boyfriend had installed security cameras somewhat recently.

The burly cop asked if I could get the tapes for them, and they'd review them back at headquarters. "Yes, of course but I'd prefer that we take a quick look now to see if we recognize the jackass who did this."

Mousy got a little punchy and her tone turned condescending, "Now ma'am, we're going to take them and view them at headquarters. If we need your assistance, we'll let you know."

Um, excuse you? I know it's the middle of the night but no need to be a condescending bitch.

I stared at her, raised my eyebrows in disbelief, and then I turned to the burly cop, "These are our tapes. We're going to watch them right now and then I'll let you take them. I have a strong suspicion that this was done by someone Carson goes to school with. Before he goes back to school, I want to ensure he's not in stepping into harm's way, what if it's one of his classmates?"

Burly cop nodded his head and grunted. "Sure, we can take a look with you now and then take the tapes with us for further evaluation." Mousy got all red in the face, she looked like she was going to lose it. Steam was damn near coming out of her ears. I ignored her.

What the hell, be professional, chick.

The seven of us, the two cops, me and the four kids, gathered around the computer in the office to watch the tape. To begin with, it was grainy and dark, so it was hard to see much of anything. We could see two people moving in our bushes and we caught the glint of red on the jacket of the taller one. Unfortunately, we couldn't distinguish much as far as facial features were concerned. Carson thought he recognized the sneakers of the shorter person but said he couldn't be sure. *Damn!*

Oh wait, something interesting . . . Angela's face did an almost imperceptible flicker of recognition as her face went slightly red and then white. Something struck a chord for her, but I kept quiet.

I removed the tape and handed it to the burly cop. "We may be able to clean it up at the lab so it's less grainy and who knows, we may even get so lucky that our techs can clean it up to the point where we see a face. But nothing is guaranteed. Are there any other details you can recall?" I shook my head, wondering what Angela may have seen on the video. I'd ask her later, but I was determined not to put her on the spot without talking to her first. "No, nothing. I didn't hear anything until the rock hit the window. I rushed downstairs but didn't see anything except the broken glass and the rock on our living room floor." I looked at the kids, "How about you?" All four of them shook their heads. Nothing.

Mousy cop advised as to the next steps, "We'll have the forensic team dust the rock and then take it to the lab to see if we're able to grab any fingerprints or DNA. Are you sure no one here touched the rock?"

I shook my head, "No, we didn't touch it. I threw the sheet over it and called you guys."

Mousy cop nodded her head and replied, "Good. Ok, we'll be in touch once we have a bit more information. In the meantime, you have my card. Call if you have questions or concerns. Have a good night."

By the time they left, it was five o'clock. We were all exhausted. As the door closed, I asked the kids if they were ok. They were all just tired. The drama of it all was enough to choke a goose. I said goodnight to each of them and got Kris settled back in bed. Soon he was snoring.

I texted Brad to let him know how it went with the police and that our plan was to stay home and sleep in the next day. I emailed the kids' schools and my work to let them know we wouldn't be in. There was no way in hell we'd be functioning properly. Besides I was a bit nervous about sending Carson to school before we had any clue who had fired that rock through our window.

Damn bullies! Hmm, I wonder what Ang saw.

45

best pals

EXHAUSTED AFTER THE ROCK INCIDENT, I rolled into bed. My head hit the pillow and I stared at the ceiling for a while until I drifted into a restless sleep, tossing and turning. Once I settled into a deeper sleep, I flashed back to an evening, not that long ago, when Anne and Doug had just met. Anne invited me over for wine and hors d'oeuvres. Let's face it, it was for a girl's chat. Lots was going on for both of us, so there was never a dull moment. After we were settled on her couch, she made a big ask, "How is everything going with Carson? How's he doing?"

Smiling and with a tear in my eye, I said, "Most days he's doing so much better. There's just so much that guy is dealing with. And so young. Things I've never fathomed." I explained about top surgery and what a complete and utter clusterfuck the process is. There were so few specialty surgeons, and the insurance coverage was all messed up and then there were the wait lists.

Anne nodded. She'd heard all about how broken the system was from Kyle over the years. They're still best buddies. That thought made me smile.

I continued explaining some of the hurdles Carson faces on a daily, or monthly, basis, "Fuck, Anne. Carson started his period a couple months ago. Can you imagine being him and having to deal with menstruation FFS? A monthly reminder that his physical body and his internal being are not aligned."

A horrified look came across Anne's face, "Oh my God, I've never thought of that. It's a pain the vagina to get a period monthly as a woman. I can't even imagine it as an adolescent boy. Talk about fucking with your head."

"No shit!"

"The testosterone didn't wipe it out? You'd think it would."

"Yeah, it's supposed to. But I guess it has something to do the amount. At a certain level, it knocks out the bleeding. I guess it has to be slowly introduced."

"Oh, sure, that makes perfect sense."

I let Anne know more about Carson's dark days, the fear our family felt, driving the point home when I explained the tightrope that Brad had told me about, the falling part. So much to deal with.

Embracing me in a huge bear hug, Anne squeezed, and a tear slid down my cheek.

"Daisy, you've been so strong and supportive over the past five years, well for your whole life really, but it's been tested big time and you've shone. You've been there for Carson and Brad and Kris and Ang and Jess, unwaveringly. Looking after your girls after Adam's death, you were a pillar of strength. And now for Carson. You've been a powerful force for everyone. Sweetie, you must be exhausted."

I sobbed. My shoulders shook and Anne squeezed tighter, "Aww honey, don't forget about taking care of you. You carry a lot, superwoman. But even *you* need to decompress sometimes, go get pampered. You're so busy taking care of everyone else that you're forgetting about you sometimes. Let it all go, just for a little while."

Anne wiped a tear from my face as I nodded, "I know. I know. You're right. I'm not good at that. But yes, I need to take care of me sometimes."

I understand. Yes, Anne is right.

I changed the topic.

"Soooo . . . remember that night that you told me all about the day you and Doug met? I don't think I told you, it really lit my fire. I totally woke up Brad when I got home."

"Awesome, I love it!" Anne cooed, "and he was into it."

"Ha! Of course. It was amazingly fun. Short and perfect and just plain great!"

46
bullies learning

I CRASHED hard around six a.m. and slept right until noon. I checked in on Kris, he was still fast asleep. I smiled at the sweet little snoring sound emanating from his room. My heart felt a little flutter just watching him sleep. So sweet. So innocent. Precious. I then wandered downstairs to the kitchen. Carson was munching on cereal and reading an article on improving your lacrosse shots. He'd taken up lacrosse recently and his water polo expertise gave him a huge advantage over the boys he played against. As he started to transition, water polo had become uncomfortable for him. He still had breasts, rather than a chest, so the swimsuit aspect of water polo just wasn't cutting it for him.

"Good morning, Carson. How'd you sleep?"

Carson startled, he'd been deeply ingrained in the article and hadn't heard me come down the stairs. "Good morning, Daisy. Alright, I guess." He looked back at his article.

"Girls' still asleep?"

Carson looked visibly uncomfortable at my question, "Uh, I guess. I haven't really seen them."

Red flag. Oh shit.

I flew down the stairs to check on Angela. I knocked on her door rapidly and powerfully. No answer. The door creaked open under the strength of my knocking. Gone. *Fuck.*

What had she seen on the video last night? Or rather, who? Why hadn't I talked to her last night? Fuck. Fuck. Fuck. We were all so tired though. I didn't expect Ang to take matters into her own hands.

I knew I didn't need to check Jess's room, but I did anyway as I rushed to pull on some clothes. They would've gone together. They better not be doing some vigilante bullshit. There would be hell to pay if they were.

Bridget was on my shoulder wringing her hands, "What if they get hurt? What if they hurt someone else?" Yeah Bridget, got it! Holy hell.

I texted both of my girls, "Where are you? It's not like you not to let me know when you go out."

No response.

Once dressed, I confirmed with Carson, "Are you ok to watch Kris while I go out and look for the girls?" He nodded, "Yeah no problem."

"Do you know where they went?" Carson shook his head.

"Hmm, ok. I think I'll go straight to the school. That seems like a logical place to start."

Carson nodded and shrugged his shoulders. Looking at me sheepishly, he said, "Uh,

Daisy, Ang took my lacrosse stick with her."

"What?"

Fuck! My girls better be thinking more logically before they find Ang's suspect.

Carson was red in the face, hands up, "She didn't ask. I just noticed it as she was closing the door behind her."

"Shit! Thanks for letting me know. Hopefully we'll be back shortly." I walked over to the school. The admin staff looked at me like I had three heads when I asked if they'd seen Jess or Ang today. No, they hadn't seen my girls. They had weird scrunched up eyebrows as they responded. Yes, I had in fact called in to say they weren't coming in.

Holy hell. A lot of good that did. But I had to check.

I charged outside and circled around the school. When I got to the back, I saw them. Shit, Jess and Ang had two boys up against the wall. I could see wrinkled scrunch marks where the girls had had the boys by their shirts recently. They were just standing and talking now.

Phew, no blood and no physical injury that I could see.

The lacrosse stick was abandoned on the ground not far from the scene. I glanced at it, picked it up. My hand was white as I clenched it. Mama bear was raging inside me.

Bridget and Princess both shook their heads, "No Daisy, that's not the answer. They're just kids." Yes, but kids who fucked with Carson, with my family.

I wasn't really going to use it, but the thought was there.

As I stormed towards the group, I noticed the shoes of the smaller boy. They were exactly like the shoes in the grainy security video. The shoes Carson thought he recognized.

Now I am mad. Mama bear is out in full force. Fuckers! How dare you!!

I took a deep breath as I covered the last few steps toward them.

These are children. Yes, they hurt Carson.

I dropped the lacrosse stick at my feet.

But is there a silver lining here? Can we educate these boys so they're more empathetic towards others in the future? Especially transgender humans, but all humans really.

I could hear Jess talking quietly, in complete control. She was explaining everything that Carson had been through over the past few years. The pain he'd experienced. The effect the rock had on our family.

I could see that the younger boy had been crying.

Did she break through to him? Or was he just scared that he'd been caught?

He looked at me. Jess and Ang turned around and saw me standing a few feet away.

Ang looked over at the lacrosse stick and then back up at me and her face on fire, "I'm sorry, Mom," she whispered. I looked at my two girls and then at the boys. "Are you done here or is there more to discuss?"

Jess looked at me, "They thought it was all a funny joke and they say they meant no harm by it."

I nodded at the boys, "And do you understand the depth of those harmful words and what doing something like that causes?"

Both boys nodded, "Sorry, Mrs. Flannigan. It was a really dumb thing to do. We were trying to impress our friends," Billy, the big one, said.

The smaller one, Scotty, was still nodding and then looked down as a light-bulb went off in his head, "I guess they're not very good friends if they egg us on to do mean things like that."

Looking at each boy, I said, "You're right, they're not. Have you learned your lesson?"

The boys nodded and spoke in chorus, "Yes ma'am. We've learned our lesson."

I cocked my head, "Have you now? I appreciate that. Thank you for apology but I'm not the one that you need to apologize to, well aside from breaking my window."

The older boy's eyes grew very large, "Yes, we need to apologize to Carson, don't we Scotty?" Scotty nodded.

"And the window? How will you be handling that? Making us whole."

"Making you whole?" Billy asked.

Scotty nodded, "She means, how are we going to pay for it. We broke it, we buy it."

"Oh," Billy frowned, "I guess we have to talk to our parents." Both boys became even more white faced at the thought of telling their parents what they did. Scotty nodded, "Yup. My dad is going to freak."

Consequences.

"You can come and apologize to the rest of our family tonight after supper around seven. Bring your parents. Clearly you know where we live."

The boys nodded solemnly. Scotty eeked out," See you at seven." Billy nodded.

Inwardly, I shook my head. How thoughtless and unnecessary and hurtful. No. Hateful. Cruel. Were these hateful instincts buried in these boys, ready to come out when allowed? Or just boys not thinking, being foolish, and not really understanding the harm it caused?

"Girls, let's go. Don't forget Carson's lacrosse stick." I was still seething about the lacrosse stick and the show of force I imagined my girls had been ready for, if they had encountered any resistance.

Yes, it worked out well and cooler heads prevailed but frig. A lacrosse stick, really? I shook my head. *The girls know I am pissed.*

Ang ventured first and an apology tumbled out of her. "Sorry for not telling you where we were going out, about taking a weapon and for not telling you that I had a pretty good idea that I knew the guys. We should have told you."

"Those are pretty big things, Ang. Yes, you should've told me you knew who they were, last night. You should've told the cops. You know, life is a whole lot easier if you tell the truth from the get-go."

Ang hung her head, "I know, I should've. I was just so mad."

"I'm thankful it ended the way it did but you both could've been hurt. That kid, Billy, is massive. He could've hurt you both, badly. Violence is never the answer."

Their heads drooped, "Yeah, we decided against the lacrosse stick when we got to the school yard. Dumb!"

"Yeah, not your smartest idea, Ang. But, from what I heard when I got here, it sounded like you did a good job of getting across the absolute hell that Carson has been living and struggling through."

Both girls nodded, but Jess responded, "Yeah, I know Billy pretty well. When Ang told me I was shocked that he was bullying Carson, he's usually a decent guy. It sounds like they were dared to do it, a so-called 'funny prank' that a bunch of teenagers thought was hilarious after they got drunk. Billy said he felt like shit this morning after he remembered what they'd done."

I nodded as we walked up to our house, "Good! Jess, what about your role in this?"

Jess looked at me, "Sorry, Mom. I know, I should've tried to talk Ang out of it. I think I egged her on and we both got madder and madder together. We should've come to talk to you. That wasn't very smart of us."

"You're right, Jess. It wasn't. Thank you both for your apologies. Remember, we live and die by respect here in this house. Don't disrespect me or do things you know aren't smart. You're good girls. One thing I wanted to mention as well . . ." I stopped walking and turned to face my girls. Thank you for sticking up for Carson. I really appreciate that and I'm sure he and Brad will as well."

"Mom, he's family. Our brother. We'd do anything for him, defend him, protect him," Ang stared at me hard as she spoke those words. Jess nodded, agreeing with what Ang said.

I had a tear in my eye, hearing the bond that my girls felt for Carson. I said, "Taking a bullet might be a bit dramatic, but I absolutely love the sentiment. I love you both so much."

We hugged for a minute or two on our front step before I shook my head and mumbled, "Now, what to do about the police. I don't suppose there's a choice. I'll give them a call as soon as I chat with Carson about the kids coming over to apologize, make sure he's ok with that."

Once Ang and Jess explained how the schoolyard encounter had gone down, Carson was visibly relieved. He nodded in agreement, "That'd be ok."

I called the cops and explained the entire situation. "We aren't concerned that Carson's life is in danger. It was a hurtful, ill-thought-out, stupid prank-gone-wrong stemming from some teenagers drinking from their parents' liquor cabinet on a Wednesday night." Because of the words written on the rock, this was deemed a hate crime. I told the police that the kids were coming over to apologize tonight and that I'd let them know how it went.

A very concerned Brad arrived home shortly before six. It took about fifteen minutes of us talking for him to visibly relax and for him to recognize that everyone was ok. He must've hugged Carson twenty times, at least. Carson finally said, "Dad! I'm good. Really."

Brad got tense again when I told him about the schoolyard and that the boys were coming over to apologize at seven. "Likely their parents will come too so we can figure out the window replacement."

At seven on the nose, Billy and his dad, Norm, arrived, along with Scotty, who looked slightly sheepish. After we invited them in, Norm started off, "Brad, Daisy, Carson, and all of you, I'm so sorry for the pain that my son has caused by his . . ." Norm shot an extremely if-looks-could-kill-you'd-be-dead glare in Billy's direction, ". . . hateful, immature and disgusting actions. I didn't raise my son to spread hatred or behave like this and I'm extremely disgusted and disappointed in him. Know that he will be punished."

Brad and I walked over to Norm and shook his hand, "Thank you!"

Carson nodded, a bit embarrassed by the whole scene, "It's ok."

Norm looked at Carson, "It's most certainly not ok, son. What my son did is damn near unforgiveable. However, in time, I hope he can prove to you that that stupid transphobic shit he wrote on that rock is not truly who he is."

Carson shifted uncomfortably from one foot to the other. Norm looked at Billy, "Son?"

Billy walked over to Carson and said, "Carson, I'm so sorry about being such an asshole. I really didn't mean anything by it. I mean I guess we were trying to be funny, but this morning I felt sick to my stomach about it. It was wrong and cruel. Then when Jess and Ang talked to us, well, I couldn't even eat supper I was so torn up about it. I'm truly sorry, Carson. I feel like such a jerk."

Carson nodded his head and followed our lead, "Thank you, Billy. I appreciate that."

"If you can find it in your heart to forgive Billy eventually, we'd be extremely grateful. No rush or pressure. I'm sure it will take time, but please think about it."

Carson nodded again, "Yes, I will."

Scotty walked up to Carson, "I's really sorry for what we done. It were wrong. It won't never happen again. Sorry, Carson." Scotty held out his hand. Carson shook it and then pulled Scotty into a hug. They'd been friends years before and had lost touch, I had no idea. Scotty was crying again.

Carson was crying, "Thank you, Scotty. It made me so sad and disappointed to know that you were involved. I'm happy you understand more now about my life over the past few years."

Carson turned to look at Jess and Ang and said, "Thank you! I know Daisy wasn't very happy with what you did but thank you."

Jess and Ang ran over and gave Carson a giant hug, "Of course, little brother," teased Jess.

From the other side of the room, Kris said, very loudly, "Hey! I'm your little brother." Ang, Jess, and Carson all laughed. "Of course you are, Kris!" said Ang, as she ruffled Kris's hair, "You're our little, little brother and Carson is our big, little brother."

Watching the kids interact with each other and pull together, and laugh about it, I damn near forgot that Norm, Billy, and Scotty were still standing in our living room.

Norm reached out his hand to Brad and then to me, shaking our hands warmly. "Again, I'm so sorry about this. We'll pay for the window replacement, of course. In fact, if it's ok with you, one of my buddies is a window guy and he can replace the glass for you, to your specifications." He nodded over to Scotty, "Scotty's dad can be a bit of a prick, excuse my French, so I'll deal with him. I'll make sure you're not out of pocket a penny and that you have a window the same quality or better than the last one. In fact, I'll get Scotty and Billy to help, so they get a glimpse of what it is to put in a day's work. If that's ok with you."

Brad and I nodded and thanked the threesome as they slid their shoes on. Both Billy and Scotty apologized one more time and thanked us for giving them with the opportunity to apologize. Carson shook both of their hands, smiling.

That ended way better than I thought it would. Phew!

I called back Mr. Burly police officer and told him what happened and their commitment to replace the window.

Even though the event itself is resolved, I have a feeling that this incident will stay with all of us for a long time.

47
baby shower

AFTER OUR FAMILY trip to the States, my gal pals and I hosted a baby shower for Jen. She was glowing and absolutely exploding out of her maternity clothes. She was hot and uncomfortable and counting the days until her due date. Of course we were having a heat wave, something not all that normal for us in late August.

Twila asked Jen, "Are you having a gender reveal party? Or maybe you're going to tell us today?"

Jen shook her head, "No, we just want a healthy baby. His or her gender will be a pleasant surprise after all the work on his or her birth-day! Ha-ha!"

I nodded. Gender reveal parties had always made me uncomfortable. I wasn't quite sure why. I had run into Kyle at Anne's place the other day and he'd enlightened me about his aversion to gender reveal parties. We'd chatted in depth about it, especially as it related to his work with transgender youth. "A doctor announcing, based on the sum of sexual body parts, the gender of a child, is really not quite right when you think of it. The child should have the opportunity to figure out his, her, or their gender as they grow, what feels right."

I understood what he was saying but that didn't seem to help me with my discomfort.

Is that the reason "why" for me? No.

The more I thought about it, the more I thought that, for me, it had more to do with the fundamentals of it all.

Really, why does it matter what gender a baby is? A boy. A girl. Why does it matter? It doesn't. It shouldn't. Our society is still a bit interesting about boy versus girl children. Yet, what's the first thing people want to know about a baby: Is it a boy or girl?

To me, kids should just be kids. Be how they want to be, wear what they want to wear, love who they want to love.

Nail polish on girls or boys is just fine with me, pink or blue as a favorite color is good enough for everyone. Heck, my favorite color is royal blue. Boy, I sure went off on a track there for a minute. Back to the baby shower . . .

Anne brought a journal for us all to write in. A note to mom and dad, and to baby. It was pretty cool to write a note to the parents to be. Mine went a little something like this:

I have every confidence in the world that you'll be great parents. Remember: every child is unique. No one knows what they're doing as a new parent. Hell, half the time we don't know what we're doing as experienced parents. There is no manual. There couldn't be. Every child makes their own way in the world. Us gals know some tips and tricks, ask us. Just love that baby. There is no wrong. And, most importantly, have fun! Continue to date each other. Make time for one another. Have sex, no matter how tired you think you are. Be lusty and sexy together.

Daisy

48
las vegas baby

CHILLING in Anne's hot tub one night, we hatched a plan to head to Vegas the following week for three to four days. Any of our friends who wanted to come were welcome. After much interest and discussion, the list was confirmed and finalized: Anne, Doug, Ronnie, Jamie, Brad and I were in like Flynn. We booked some shows and events. I was especially excited to see P!nk.

The first night we headed through a smoky, '70s decorated casino on Fremont Street, making a beeline towards the buffet. Casinos are always interesting spots for people watching. I could sit there for hours watching folks push buttons on the loud, flashing slot machines. There were lots of characters to watch, some pumping their life savings in at the hopes of a big return. Others throwing in a few dollars to give it a spin. Others so drunk they have no clue what's going on around them. The casinos know who wins big. And it's not you or me.

The folks playing poker at the tables were always fun to watch as well. Some were very sneaky in their moves, with the sunglasses and costumes like on the poker shows. We were able to catch some of the various scenes, and even pumped some of our own money into the slots, while waiting in the buffet line.

Once inside, I was distracted by Typhoid Mary, coughing away at the salad bar.

Ugh! I'll skip salad today, thanks.

I headed straight to the prime rib, potatoes, and cooked veggies.

Hopefully she hadn't gotten to those yet.

All six of us ate way too much. I had a flashback to Banff fondue adventure where I needed a wheelbarrow, ha! Jamie mentioned that he felt like a stuffed pig meandering back to the hotel. We all laughed, planning to sleep off those enormous plates of food.

The night of the P!nk concert had finally arrived. Anne helped me with my make-up and hair. We looked like sexy divas if I did say so myself. We just might fit in at the concert. Anne always would, but I was another story, it was a stretch for me on a regular day! Brad and Doug were heading to play poker. They whistled at Anne and I as we stepped out of the bathroom. We kissed them goodbye to groans that we were going out without them looking that hot. Ronnie and Jamie had been mysterious about their evening plans.

I can only imagine!

The P!nk concert was worth every penny. She put on an amazing show, filled with acrobatics and, of course, her amazing costume changes and hold-nothing-back singing style. I loved every single second of it.

We were staying in a suite with three bedrooms and bathrooms at Mandalay Bay. Each room was very private, *or so we thought*, almost in its own wing. Anne and I came back in the midst of Ronnie and Jamie's sexplosion. They hadn't heard the door when we walked it. I snorted. We heard the head-board banging against the wall, the rhythm of the bed creaking and moving beneath them and the sounds of ecstasy exclaiming from their lips. Creak, creak, bang! Creak, creak, creak, bang! "Fuck ya, baby, harder, harder, pound me!" That was Ronnie.

Anne and I giggled as we helped ourselves to more wine, listening intently, but also trying to not listen.

Princess Pussy was purring, "Get in there, Daisy!" I shook my head sternly, "Are you nuts?" Princess replied with a pouting lip and a whiny, "Please?" I shook her off, "It's out of the question." Bridget was shaking her head, "Very bad girl, Princess!"

Creak, creak, creak, creak, bang! Creak, creak, bang! The bed continued. Smash! Thud! Crash! "Fuck!" exclaimed Jamie. Crack! Boom! Smash! "OMG, fuck!" giggled Ronnie.

What in the hell was that?

Gales of laughter escaped from the bedroom.

At least they're ok.

I walked over to the door, "Knock, knock, are you guys ok?"

Ronnie's laughter hit a higher octave, "Yup, we're good. We broke the fucking bed. The damn thing splintered and fell apart. Our mattress is on the floor now, so at least we'll be quieter!" She was gasping, sucking in air between laughs, "We didn't know you were back." I could hear Jamie trying to stifle a laugh.

"Yeah, we know," Anne grinned and winked at me.

As you were Ronnie and Jamie, as you were.

Doug and Brad returned in the wee hours. They'd bonded over the card tables. We were still chatting and sipping wine when they stepped through the door.

"How was the concert?" Doug asked. Anne and I looked at each other and then at the boys, "AMAZING!" I was shaking my head, "There are no other words, just wow! I loved it!" Brad laughed, encircling me with his arms and planted a kiss square on my lips. "That's great, Daisy."

"How was poker?" I asked.

"Well, I was up quite a bit and then down, so I'm about even. Doug had quite the night though, ended on a high."

Anne nodded, "That's great, handsome!" Doug wiggled over near Anne and gave her a squeeze and a wink, "Bedtime? Please!" Anne laughed, "Absolutely! Good night, you guys!"

Brad and I trundled along after them and made a hard left to our room, where we snuggled in tight together. I struggled to get through the story about Ronnie and Jamie's bed, I was trying so hard to stifle my laughter. Brad let loose and roared when I mentioned the squeaking and then the total annihilation of the bed.

It was dead for sure. They had killed it.

Brad looked into my eyes as he kissed me, "Feeling inspired?" I laughed, "Yup, bring it on, sexy! Mmm . . ."

The next day, Ronnie shared more of their adventures with Anne and me. "We started in the hotel room, just the two of us, playing and having fun. We figured 'When in Vegas!' so we ventured out to a sex club not far from here. We decided to hold nothing back." Ronnie was purring when she talked about the wild sex they'd shared.

"Almost immediately upon entering the club, we met a couple we were both interested in. They were totally into swapping with us. Things were getting good, escalating, and getting damn hot. The guy dove his cock into my pussy when all of a sudden, he jumped up, grabbed me by the throat and threw me against the wall. Initially it felt super-hot. He was holding me there by the throat. Then it got weird. I couldn't tell if I was turned on or scared as fuck. A strange mixture of hot and scary. His grip tightened. I couldn't breathe. I was scared. I needed help. I simultaneously hit the wall with my hand and forced out the biggest sound I could muster from my lips. It was squeaky and the sound was foreign to my ears. It was frightening."

"Jamie's head shot up, abandoning the man's wife that he had been dining on. He flew across the room and grabbed the guy's hand that was wrapped around my throat and threw him to the ground. Jamie caught me as I slid down the wall, in a state of shock, but fine. Jamie pointed to the door and yelled at the couple, 'Get the fuck out! Now! Both of you.' He asked me what I needed, how he could help. I shook my head, 'I need a better couple to swap with.'"

"Jamie laughed, 'Oh thank God you're ok.' He was kissing me gently, holding me close, examining me to make sure I was ok. Looking into his eyes, I said, 'I'm not kidding. I don't want that dick couple to be the last swap we have.' Jamie looked at me sideways, 'Really?' I said, 'Let's go find a better couple and report that asshole.' Jamie agreed. They booted the guy and his wife out of the club. Not acceptable."

"We found another couple and had a super-hot and sexy swap. Woohoo! We both had a blast. Aside from the wanker throat grabber, it was a great night. But I'll be damned if I'm going to let some jackass ruin MY night. Then we came back here, and Jamie was thoroughly devouring me, taking me good and hard, as you heard. Poor bed," Ronnie laughed.

The next night we walked to the T-Mobile Arena to enjoy the hockey game. It was a close one with the Calgary Flames trailing by one going into the third period. Ronnie was an Edmonton Oilers fan so couldn't possibly cheer for the Flames, so she cheered on the Las Vegas Golden Knights. Anne couldn't have cared less who won and I couldn't really tell who Jamie was cheering for. Doug, Brad, and I were hard-core Flames fans, so we went crazy when the

Flames scored only minutes into the third. The score remained tied until three minutes left when Gaudreau snuck the puck between Lehner's legs and scored. I was cheering and screaming at the top of my lungs when the buzzer went off. Woohoo!

We went straight from the game to Fremont Street. The mixed drinks on Fremont Street are deadly strong. *Beer for me, please.* That night I tried a new beer called Dead Horse Ale, made in Moab, Utah. I didn't know they could make beer in Utah, interesting. The slogan on it made me laugh, "You can't beat a dead horse." I giggled. Pointing at the slogan, I said to Brad, "Well, you can but to what end?!!" Brad grinned.

We hung out on Fremont Street enjoying some live cover bands, including my favorite, Spandex Nation, as they ripped out '80s rock. We were dancing, singing, jumping, chatting and having an excellent time listening to the tunes. Ronnie, Brad, Jamie and I even went for a ride on the superman zipline, a ridiculously fun zipline that goes down the entire length of Fremont Street. You're in superman position on your tummy, weeee! Anne and Doug declined to join us on the crazy ride. Instead, they made out and took pictures of us as we zipped.

Don't think we can't see you from up here!

When the bands took a break, we looked straight up and sang along with the light show on the overhanging video ceiling. A local band, Imagine Dragons was featured during this break in the live music. Very cool. Unfortunately, the night was winding down, the bands were finished their sets and it was time for bed, we had a morning flight home. We all agreed it had been an amazing get away and must soon be repeated.

49

house belly

AS BIG AS a house and as uncomfortable as having just had a nasty run in with a porcupine, Jen was in her final weeks of pregnancy. Chris was away on a business trip, having been assured by the doctor that the babe wasn't going to show up anytime soon.

Twila and I were keeping her company one Saturday afternoon, and abundant tales of her pregnancy were being spun. In addition to the swollen feet, lack of sleep, skin stretching beyond maximum stretchability, and peeing what seemed like every five minutes, she had many more stories. "What's with people thinking that because you're pregnant they can touch your belly?"

"I know, right?!" Twila laughed.

"I was in line at the drug store with only one till open and there was a big line behind me. I heard a familiar voice so turned to see who it was. The lady directly behind me gasped when my turn revealed my belly and the man behind her, well it looked like his eyes were going to bug right out of his head

"I can see how that could happen. You're carrying all up front. From behind you don't look pregnant at all," Twila smiled.

"I know! So funny though. The lady was super embarrassed after her gasp. She went several colors of red to the point of damn near purple. She apologized so many times. I just laughed and told her not to worry about it. Then a couple of dudes cut the line, walked up to me, and asked if they could feel my baby. 'Uh, sure,' but WTF?! They patted my belly and wished me luck and said congratulations."

"Who did the familiar voice belong to?" I asked.

"Oh, yeah, I forgot to tell that part, it was my neighbor, Judy. She was there with her grandson. I waited for them outside the store and the little guy asked if he could listen to the baby. He's a big brother so had done the same with his mom when his little sister was growing inside her. I smiled at him and said, 'Of course, Jimmy.' He snuggled in and put his ear to my tummy. I rustled his hair a bit. It was kinda sweet actually."

"Aww, that's cute," Twila giggled and then shook her head, "I've got a good one . . . before I was even showing, a bunch of us were hanging out. Some friend of a friend, a dude I didn't know all that well, started rubbing my tummy in circular motions, his other hand on my back, then he said, 'I'm rubbing the Buddha for good luck.' I jumped back and looked at the fucker like he had three heads. Uh... dude? Don't touch me. The Buddha? Good luck? Who are you? He just smiled and said, 'I'll never wash this hand again.'"

What the fuck?

"The weirdest experience I had was on my last week of work. I was about the same size as you, Jen and some lady on the elevator rubbed close to me, very invasively, her hand brushed against my belly several times. When I said, 'Excuse me?' She turned to look at me, 'What's your problem?' I cocked my head, 'Lady, you're touching me. I don't know you and I certainly didn't say you could touch me.' She was adamant, 'You're pregnant!' Uh, and?? I was stunned, speechless. Who did she think she was?"

Jen and Twila were shaking their heads. "The nerve of some people!" exclaimed Jen.

"Chris and I have been talking lots about our birth plan. After some discussion and thought, we've decided that we don't want our baby coming into this world high from all the meds they give you. We are going all natural, no meds, focusing on breathing, using a birthing ball, a shower, music, and a focal point. We've been practising breathing and Chris has been taking classes with me to learn how to focus past the pain."

Him or you?

"We discussed our plan with the doctor, but she totally irritated me. She said to keep an open mind. That sometimes these things change. I shook my head and said, 'No, we've decided, no pain meds. That's how it's going to go.' The doctor just nodded but I saw her smirk. Chris patted my hand reassuringly and gave me a hug after the doctor walked out of the room."

I smiled to myself. Adam and I had had a birth plan too. We'd talked about it through the entire pregnancy. Then in less than ten minutes, it went all to shit. A regular check up turned into an ultrasound which turned into a get to the hospital now, these babies are coming NOW.

Fuck!

"There's no urgency yet but you need to drive straight to the hospital. Your babies are ready to come out. I'll meet you in the operating room."

Turns out Ang had the umbilical cord wrapped around her neck, although not tightly, and Jess was taking over my womb, pushing Ang into the smallest corner.

Holy jeez! It felt like the horse I was riding on had just been kicked with spurs and slapped on the ass. Go, go, go!

Frig, a month and a half early.

The bloody hospital bag wasn't packed so Anne rushed over to our house to throw some stuff together and brought it to the hospital for us. The nurse gives you this overwhelming list of items to pack. We realized at the hospital that we needed exactly sweet fuck all from the hospital bag. The bloody thing went home unopened.

50

birth plan gone to shit

IT WAS two o'clock in the morning. My cell phone was ringing off the hook. I leapt out of bed and dove across the room, my elbow slamming against the bedside table, my toe stubbing hard into the corner of the dresser, as my hand slid across the top of the dresser to grab my phone, "Fuck!" Click. "Hello?"

"Daisy! My water just broke. I need to go to the hospital. Can you come get me?"

"Jen! Yes, throwing clothes on as we speak. I'll be there in ten minutes. Are you ok? How far apart are the contractions?"

Brad was now fully awake. He nodded at me, smiling and clearly under-standing what was going on. He gave me a quick hug as I pulled my jeans on and kissed my forehead, whispering, "I love you babe! Let me know how it goes."

"Fuuuuucccckkkkkkkkkkkk . . . owwwwwweeeeeee. Son of a bitch. Ah, ah, ah. Phew, that one's done."

"You ok? I'm getting my shoes on."

"Contractions about ten minutes apart. Quick, yet painful fuckers!"

"Don't I know it!"

"Ok, I'll see you soon."

"Want to stay on the line with me until I get there?"

"Nah, I gotta run a hot shower, my back is killing me. You'll be here for the next bastard contraction."

"Ok, sweetie, leave the door unlocked. See you in seven minutes."

When I opened Jen's front door, I heard the shower running. I removed my shoes and headed straight up the stairs. I knocked, opening the door, calling out, "Hey Jen! How're you feeling?" No answer. *Shit.* I peeked around the shower curtain and saw blood. *Fuck!* There was blood everywhere. I hoped the damn water was making it look worse than it was. *But fuck!* I looked for the source of the blood. I couldn't tell for sure, but it looked like she was bleeding from her vagina. *Fuck!* I was dialling 9-1-1 as I took in the rest of the scene. There was a giant gash on her temple. It was clear she'd hit her head.

"9-1-1 operator. What's your emergency?"

"Send an ambulance, quickly. 1234 Midlake Crescent SE." I shut the shower off, improving the look of the amount of blood.

"What's your emergency?"

"My friend Jen is nine months pregnant and is in labor. Her contractions were ten minutes apart about fifteen minutes ago. I just got to her house, she's bleeding, in the shower. She hit her head and is bleeding from her head. I can't tell for sure, but she may be bleeding from her vagina. Send someone quickly, please."

There's a police station and fire department about three minutes from Jen's house. The ambulance was there in two. The paramedics checked Jen's vitals. So far so good, I could see it in their eyes. They loaded her on the bed and got her into the ambulance. They installed an infant monitor as they were driving and put an oxygen mask on Jen's face.

Shit. Fuck. Shit. She'd better be ok.

I was kicking myself for not insisting we stay on the phone together.

Fuck. That was stupid, Daisy. Bad decision. Jen was still unconscious.

As we neared the South Calgary Health Campus, I hemmed and hawed about calling Chris. I wanted to wait until I had more information. But, if the tables were turned, I'd want Brad to know, I'd want to know if I were Brad. He wouldn't hear me over the sirens and I didn't want to alarm him. I texted Chris.

Hi, this is Daisy. I'm with Jen. She's in labor. She hit her head. She's being taken to the South Calgary Health Campus. I'll text you back when I have more information.

Ok, so I didn't tell him everything, but I didn't really know what to say, and I didn't want him freaking out, being hours away by plane.

I'll tell him more as it unfolds and becomes understood. Hmm, I don't like the looks the EMTs are exchanging. Now I'm getting scared.

We roared into the hospital. Doctors everywhere. Jen was whisked into one of the rooms. I was told, "Sit in the waiting room. Someone will update you when there's more information available." I nodded.

Well shit. Now what? Just sit here and wait. Patiently? Good luck with that.

I paced for a bit then tried to distract myself with work emails. I couldn't concentrate. The emails were just pissing me off. I paced some more. I sat down again and opened a book. I was reading every second line then went back read them again. It was taking me forever to read each page with all the back and forth. But at least I was calming down, focused on something other than Jen.

It was three-thirty now. Too early to text Brad and Anne. My cell phone dinged. It was Brad.

How's everything? How's Jen doing?

Oh crap, in all that mess, I hadn't thought to text Brad.

We're at the hospital.

That was quick.

No, I mean, yeah. Jen was unconscious in the shower when I got there. She hit her head. Sorry, I've been in the ambulance and pacing. Brad, I'm scared.

Shit, Daisy! I'm sure everything's going to be ok. Does Anne know?

No, it's too early to text her.

Daisy, Jen's in the hospital. Text her. I'm sure she'll be there in a quick minute.

Oh yeah, right. Shit. I'm not thinking clearly.

I can't imagine why not . . . frig. Pull your shit together, Daisy. Get your head out of your ass woman!

Do you want me to come?

Yes. But no, stay with the kids. I'm sure you're right. Anne will be right over.

I texted Anne: Jen's in the hospital.

Anne called me, "She's having her baby!?"

"Well, yes, but she also hit her head and was unconscious when I got to her place. I haven't seen her since the ambulance dropped us off. They won't tell me how she is. Or how the baby is," I started crying.

"Be there in fifteen minutes."

"Ohhhh kkaaayy," I blubbered.

"You going to be ok?"

"Yeah, it just all hit me. Boom! I'm fine. I'll see what I can find out."

I walked up to the nurses' station. "Hi, my friend Jen was brought here in an ambulance. She's nine months pregnant and was unconscious. Can someone please tell me how she is? How the baby is?"

The nurse nodded at me, "I'll have someone speak with you when we have something to update you with."

Hmm, that's not helpful. At all! I don't want to be a pain in the ass but holy hell, I want to know how my friend is. I feel so helpless, I have no control over anything that's going on here. This reminds me of Carson. I can't protect him from all the cruel humans out there. The transphobes. I hate feeling out of control, but sometimes there are things that are beyond me. Sometimes I just have to have faith in the experts, like Kyle and the nurses and doctors here. I must trust.

Anne had stopped to grab us coffees at Starbucks. She rushed in and embraced me. I shook my head, "No news. She said they'll update me when they have something to share."

The wait felt like forever. Finally, a nurse came out. "Your friend Jen and her baby girl are both healthy and doing well. We've put the baby in the nursery so Jen can get some rest. She had a c-section and needs to sleep. Her head needed stiches, too." She nodded at me, "It's a good thing you called 9-1-1 when you did. Her water had broken, and she was bleeding heavily. Have you reached her husband?"

I glanced down at my phone, "No, not yet."

She nodded, "Alright, thankfully it's a good news story. If you'd like to see her baby, I can point her out to you. I'm about to go off shift but I'd be happy to show her to you." We started walking over to the nursery, "Yes, please. Can we hold her?"

"For a minute or two, I suppose that'd be alright."

I picked her up and snuggled her into my chest. She was absolutely precious. Perfect. Anne took a picture to send to Chris and Jen's parents. "Would you like to hold her?"

I looked over at Anne and she had tears in her eyes, "Yes, just for a minute. You know, times like these remind me of that void, of that one regret with Kyle. I wish we'd had kids. Sometimes I feel like something is missing. I do love my life but sometimes I wonder what it would be like with kids. I always thought I'd have two or three kids. Oh my, she IS a gorgeous baby!"

I texted Chris the picture Anne had taken of "Baby Girl". He hadn't read any of my messages so far. He must've had his notifications turned off. The nurse took Jen and Chris's baby from Anne and put her back in the nursery.

All of a sudden, my phone started exploding with text messages. Clearly Chris had woken up. There were a bunch of panicked texts:

Daisy! What happened?

Is Jen ok?

And our baby?

Please, please, please, let Jen be ok.

I clicked on Chris's name to call and reassure him, "Jen's sleeping and recovering. Your baby girl is perfect. I let Jen's parents know as well."

"Oh Daisy, thank God! I'm going to rebook my flight and be home this afternoon. The doctor said we had time. Did we have twins?"

"No, just one baby girl. But who knows why she elected to come quickly, Chris? These things happen sometimes. The important thing is that everyone is healthy."

"Definitely! I'm so happy they're ok. You said she had a c-section? So much for our all-natural birth plan. Why does anyone even bother?!"

True to his word, Chris was back in the afternoon. A team of wild hyenas couldn't have kept him away. Rushing from the Uber, he ran through the hospital until he located room 215. Jen had "baby girl" swaddled in her arms. He rushed over and swept them both up in his arms. Kissing Jen on the lips and "baby girl" on the head, gently rubbing her forehead, then kissing them both again.

Jen and Chris were both crying tears of joy, while the baby slept, snoring sweetly. "I love you so much, Jen! I was so scared when I got Daisy's texts but I'm so relieved you and the baby are healthy. What name did you decide on?"

Glancing up at Chris, Jen took his hand, "I love you too, Chris. I didn't name her, honey. I wanted to wait until you got back. And I haven't been awake for all that long. That c-section knocked the bejeezus out of me." Chris stepped even closer, taking his wife and daughter deeper in his arms.

He had a tear in his eye, "Jen, I'm a dad. You're a mom. We're a family. We have a daughter!" Jen beamed, "I know honey! My heart is so full!"

"What should we name her? I feel a bit goofy calling our daughter 'baby girl'."

"She feels like a Lily to me. I know it wasn't on our list but maybe we could pick one of those names for her middle name. What do you think?"

Chris leaned in and gave Jen a kiss, "Lily Elizabeth. I like the sound of that. It's perfect, just like her."

"Yes, she sure is!"

51
beach holiday

WORK, school, and family life had been hectic, and we all needed a break. Brad and I bought tickets for the six of us to go to Costa Rica during Christmas break. To say it was painful to get Sara to sign off on Carson and Kris to go, is the understatement of the year. Instead of Sara just signing off on the travel consent letters, Brad had to go through his lawyer AGAIN. Finally, at the last minute, she relented and signed. For the life of me, I will never understand why a parent would want to block their child from going on a great trip with their other parent. If there was some perceived or real danger to the children being harmed or abducted, I understand that, of course. In our case, it was just plain selfish and manipulative, a power ploy.

We counted down the days, excited that we were going away, on December 27. My parents had agreed to watch our goofy dog while we were gone for ten days. The night before our vacation arrived and everyone was pumped. Kris seemed almost more excited than he'd been on Christmas Eve. He'd never been on a tropical beach vacation and his brother, and my girls, regaled him with stories of hanging out on the beach, making sandcastles, swimming in the ocean, relaxing by the pool and swimming up to the pool bar, feeling all grown up as they ordered their virgin cocktails. I was surprised my girls recalled so much, it had been at least six years since we had been on a beach holiday. It was with their dad, six months before he died. I sighed. That will never be easy. My heart still ached.

Vacation, yay! I couldn't wait! I needed a work detox. Drinks, sand, sun, and water were just what the doctor ordered. We got through check in and security quickly, due to the early hour. The kids were still half asleep. The plane was loaded early, squeezing Brad's hand as we waited to take off, I was getting more excited for this trip. No cell phones (we had agreed to lock them in the room safe) and just chill. Brad brough my hand to his lips, kissed it and then leaned over and kissed my cheek near my ear, and whispered, "I love you, Daisy! I'm so excited about this trip. One big happy family." I blushed as he whispered those words. *Yes. We are.* "I love you too, Brad, and our family." Brad squeezed my hand as the plane turned to jet down the runway, he exclaimed, "Here we go!" I glanced around at our kids and felt my heart's warmth spreading throughout my entire body.

The flight was great, and Kris was darn near squealing when we circled over the beach, ocean, and palm trees. We had an adjoining room with the kids. "Oh Brad, it's perfect. We have some privacy and it's great having the kids right next. The best of both worlds!"

Brad took me into his arms and kissed me on the forehead. "Yes, I thought it work well for us. Kids secure, check. Adult privacy time, check." He laughed and kissed me fully on the lips. "Oh my, is it bedtime for the kids yet?" I purred.

Princess Pussy jumped onto my shoulder and clapped her hands, "Indeed. Bedtime children!"

Brad laughed, "Not quite, sweetie. We promised the kids a walk around the pool and exploring the beach before suppertime."

I sighed, "Yes, of course, dear. I can't wait to explore it too." *Then I'll have you to myself.* Princess was drumming her fingers together in anticipation, while Bridget was shaking her head.

The beach was heavenly: water lapping, sailboats floating, kids playing, adults suntanning. Everything was magnificent. We stripped down to our swimsuits, laid out our towels and ran straight into the ocean. We played in the ocean and on the shore for an hour, then we relaxed on our towels, sipping pina coladas and virgin margaritas. Ang was reading the latest Women's Murder Club book, *21st Birthday* by James Patterson and Maxine Paetro. She was completely enthralled, paying no attention to the world around her. Kris was playing in the sand, making a sandcastle, his first of many for week. Jess and Carson were listening to music and sunbathing, while Brad and I chatted, sipping our drinks.

We had booked an early morning sunrise sailing adventure for the next day. The kids grumbled a bit, but we figured it would be easier to get them up earlier sooner in the vacation, before we'd all grown accustomed to sleeping in.

The sun was just coming up as we rounded the bend, adjacent to the beach, sailing on the catamaran we'd hired. It was the full sailing experience where we were trained as crew members, taking turns relaxing and helping pilot the boat. Kris was completely into it. The girls and Carson were still asleep, I think. Although I did catch a few grins here and there from them as they were preparing to "come about" under the watchful guidance of our captain. Once the sun was high in the sky, we anchored in shallow water for some snorkeling and swimming, followed by a lovely brunch on the boat.

The kids were squealing, Brad may have let out a squeak or two as well, as they saw the many colors of tropical fish below us. A rather large lemon shark graced us with its presence as well. I'd be lying if I said my heart didn't stop immediately upon seeing that large shark's fin. *JAWS! AHHHHHH!* I'd say the shark was about ten feet long, plenty long enough to make me clamor toward the boat. Our captain assured us we had nothing to fear from the lemon shark. I'm not so sure about that, "not thought to be a large threat to humans" is not the same as it's safe to frolic in the ocean with them. *Eeek!*

Once my heart began beating again, I dove down deep with my snorkel and fins. I was underneath the kids. It was amazing to look up at them and to look at the fish between us and then glance down at the fish even deeper in the ocean. The sand was a gorgeous light brown colour, creating a beautiful back-drop with the greenery. I snapped a couple pictures with my underwater camera, knowing that it wouldn't do the fish justice, but still wanting to try to capture the beauty. After we felt quite waterlogged, we climbed back aboard the sailboat and enjoyed a feast they had prepared for us. It was midafternoon now, so more lupper than brunch. There were cuts of meat, cheese, veggies, and buns, along with a vast array of drinks, both virgin and alcoholic for us to enjoy. I giggled inside, thinking of a time long ago, when I was the presentation of the charcuterie. My mind wandered for a moment, then I brought myself back to the present, and my family. As I looked around, I surmised that life just couldn't get better than this.

. . .

Our children disappeared after supper, to a special activity for older kids. After enjoying a drink together, Brad took my hand and led me down to the beach. The lighting and scene were similar to the dream that I had on my girls' trip, except there was no lion and I was not afraid. I felt full, and happy, blissful really. Continuing down the beach, Brad took me in his arms, and we began to slowly dance to the music that was pumped from the speakers in the palm trees. He took my face in his hands and kissed me deeply. As we were kissing, his hands encircled me, and he pulled me even closer.

He then stepped back, holding onto my hands then let one go as he fell to one knee. My breath caught. He gazed up at me, as he reached into his pocket with his free hand saying, "Daisy, I love you with my whole heart. I can't imagine a world without you and our kids in my life. Will you marry me?" Tears were streaming down my face. Tears of joy. "Yes, Brad, I will marry you. A million times, yes. I love you so much."

Cheers erupted from the nearest palm tree. "Yahoo! Woohoo! Hooray! Ya, Dad! We love you both! Finally!" Our kids jumped out from behind the tree and hugged us both.

So much for their "special activity".

Somewhere in all that excitement, Brad slipped an engagement ring on my finger. It was a family ring with six gems, birth stones: one for each member of our family. It was perfect.

Carson

I breathed a sigh of relief. A giant weight was lifted off my shoulders. My old mother, Sara, was dead to me. Just like my dead name. And now, it's official with their engagement, I have a new mother. A wonderfully, supportive mother. Daisy. A lady who took me under her wing and became a ferocious, yet kind, caring, loving, and sweet, mama bear to me, and Kris. There is nothing she won't do for us.

Daisy was there for me through my darkest days; focused on how to support me, how to help me find light and happier times, how to get through the crap. There were times I was miserable, a dark cloud hanging over me, where I felt there was no hope, and she remained a shining light through it all. My dad is great and has supported me as best as he could, but I know even he became frustrated and lost in his own thoughts and feelings. I could feel him pull away sometimes and go internal to deal with everything that was happening. It's only natural. I can't imagine what it would be like to be a parent, feeling helpless, but I know how dark it was for me. But Daisy, she didn't waiver, not one iota. She kept fighting for me, my beacon of hope, resolute and strong for me and my dad. She is one amazing woman. We're so lucky to have her in our lives. She loves us deeply. We feel the same.

Brad

Thank the stars she said yes. She is my home, my love, the woman of my dreams. Her strength complements my own. She remained strong through everything we've been through with Carson. When I couldn't handle it, she was there, a solid pillar holding me up, helping me up when I fell, and rebuilding my own strength stores. What an amazing woman.

Carson is in a good place. The darkest dark is behind us now. The change in him has been incredible. The tightrope has all but disappeared. I won't fall, not with Daisy by my side. By my side, forever. A lifelong team. My love for this woman brims over on a daily basis. Words cannot describe how special she is to me. How important she has become in my life, in my kids' lives. And her daughters, who could ask for more amazing girls. It's not surprising with a fantastic mom like that.

I truly feel like the six of us are a family. A cohesive family unit. I've never felt like this before. Sara, the boys, and I were not like this. We didn't have that bond. I thought it was pretty good but now that I've felt greatness, I know how bad it was. Thank you, sweet Daisy, for coming into our lives. I can't believe I almost screwed it all up the first time we met. Let's face it, I did screw it up. Daisy's just such a great person that she gave me another chance.

I'm excited for the future and what that will bring. The adventures we'll have. To watch our four children continue to grow and mature. Our wedding.

What an amazing day that will be. My beautiful bride coming down the aisle, putting our love on paper, sealing the deal.

Daisy

Family. I feel whole again. My heart is full. My soul is on fire with excitement. Brad is such a wonderful man, so great with his kids and mine. An excellent lover and loving partner. We're so connected. I love him with all my heart.

Our families have merged into one love-filled supporting and caring family over the past months. Carson is doing wonderfully. I know the worst is behind him. He's flourishing and becoming more and more confident in who he is. My girls are blossoming into beautiful young ladies, both inside and out. I couldn't be prouder of them. And Kris, my sweet little guy.

Our family of six, poised for whatever life throws at us: adventures, struggles, lots of high points to come as the kids continue to grow and change. As I'm standing here, I'm beaming thinking about all of the experiences ahead. We've learned so much about each other in the past year and that will just continue, getting closer and closer to one another.

When Brad got on his knee and asked me to marry him, my heart swelled a number of sizes. It reminded me of that scene in the *How the Grinch Stole Christmas* when he realizes what Christmas is all about. Mine swelled because I feel complete. That line from *Jerry Maguire*, "You complete me." I would apply that to my entire family: Brad, Jess, Ang, Carson and Kris. Yes, they complete me.

The future . . . what more can I say . . . I'm pumped!